THE HURLYBURLY'S HUSBAND

Jean Teulé lives in the Marais with his companion, the French film actress Miou-Miou. An illustrator, film maker and television presenter, he is also the prize-winning author of more than ten books including *The Suicide Shop*.

Alison Anderson has translated many books into English including *The Elegance of the Hedgehog* and is herself a published novelist. She lives near Lausanne, Switzerland.

Praise for *The Hurlyburly's Husband*

'Teulé recreates with gusto the bizarre social mores of the nobility at that time: appalling, dirty and wicked . . . the author explores the hidden corners of history with the ease of a seasoned veteran.' *l'Express*

'A magnificent novel' *Paris Match*

'An unrestrained, nightmarish, hilarious, and moving portrait of the underbelly of the Grand Siècle, wading through its baseness, its excrement and its entrails.' *Elle*

'Jean Teulé reveals the very particular skills of a nobleman who sets out on a quest to contest the legitimacy of the divine right of kings long before the Revolution . . . An exhilarating novel.' *Figaro Littéraire*

'The husband of Louis XIV's favourite never came to terms with being deceived by the king. Jean Teulé has restored the name of this magnificent cuckold.' *Figaro Littéraire*

THE HURLYBURLY'S HUSBAND

GALLIC

THE HURLYBURLY'S HUSBAND

A NOVEL BY
JEAN TEULÉ

Translated from the French by Alison Anderson

GALLIC BOOKS
London

This book is supported by the Institut français du Royaume-Uni
as part of the Burgess programme.
www.frenchbooknews.com

A Gallic Book

First published in France as *Le Montespan* by Éditions Julliard, Paris
Copyright © Éditions Julliard Paris, 2008

First published in Great Britain as *Monsieur Montespan* in 2010 by
Gallic Books, 59 Ebury Street, London SW1W 0NZ

A CIP record for this book is available from the British Library
ISBN 978-1-906040-65-9

Typeset in Fournier by Gallic Books
Printed and bound by
CPI Group (UK) Ltd, Croydon, CR0 4YY
2 4 6 8 10 9 7 5 3

The King's been beating the drum
The King's been beating the drum
To see all the ladies
And the first that e'er he saw
Did steal his heart away

Tell me, Marquis, do you know her?
Tell me, Marquis, do you know her?
Who is this lady fair?
And the marquis to the King did say
'Sire, my own wife is she . . .'

Chanson du
Saintonge,
seventeenth century

I.

On Saturday, 20 January 1663, at eleven o'clock in the evening, two young men burst out of the Palais-Royal where Monsieur, the King's brother, was hosting a great ball. Six others immediately followed. They began to heap insults upon one another, in a blaze of feathers and lace.

'Son of a priest!'

'Mewling vassal!'

A tall fellow in a flamboyant diamond-encrusted outfit, his lips stretched over his gums, shoved a short potbellied man in a black wig, who seemed to be standing on stilts so very high were his heels. In his many rings and bracelets, he staggered on his shoes and choked, 'Vassal? La Frette, how dare you compare me to a slave – me, the Prince of Chalais?'

'Prince of inverts, you mean – sodomite! Like Monsieur,

you prefer a young squire to a chatty wench. And I have an aversion to that kind of vice. Let them indulge such things in Naples!'

'Oh!'

During this altercation, the door to the well-lit ballroom, filled with music, fumes and the movements of the dancers, closed again, and the eight fine fellows found themselves in the icy darkness of the street.

A hunchback crouching against a column, holding a pole with a large lantern on the end of it, stood up, went over to them and called out, 'A lantern-bearer to accompany you to your homes, Messieurs?'

He was limping and swaying, having one leg shorter than the other. His hair lay flat against his skull, tied at the nape of his neck like a well rope, and he circled around them, casting the light of his lantern.

Little Chalais slapped La Frette; his shaken head exuded a cloud of periwig powder. Humiliated, the tall fellow snapped his mouth shut over his teeth, which he had adorned in the Dutch style, plugging the cavities in his incisors and canines with butter. He had been stretching his mouth wide over his lips to keep his dairy plaster fresh and prevent it from melting but now, in his rage, he pursed his lips, puffing his cheeks out. He was burning with resentment. When he opened his mouth again, his teeth were oozing. 'Did you see, Saint-Aignan? He slap—'

'Did you smack my brother, vassal?'

A cruel-looking chevalier of nineteen years of age, with a hat decorated with very long feathers, and one eye ravaged by smallpox, planted himself before Chalais. The lantern-bearer scurried to offer his itinerant lighting services to them both, explaining, 'At night, gentlemen, there are rascals, purse-snatchers and rapscallions who lie in wait for passers-by out late and hurrying to their homes . . .'

Divided into two groups, the eight bewigged youths cursed, scowled at each other and tore at the silks and ribbons of each other's garments. The lantern-bearer raised his luminous bladder. One of the youths, who had just been referred to as 'Flamarens, you filthy whore', was pale of face. With a paintbrush he had traced false lines of blue, the colour of nobility and purity of blood. The lantern-bearer lowered his beam onto the shining shoes and cobblestones. The oil of his lamp was smoking.

'Five *sols* to take you thither! What are five *sols* to gentlemen who wear the red heels of aristocrats, like your good selves!'

Chalais's friend Noirmoutier unsheathed a dagger; it flashed treacherously and left a wound upon a surprised face. The wounded gent's hand reached for his sword: he would stick Noirmoutier like a pig. The one Noirmoutier called d'Antin – 'D'Antin, don't meddle!' – intervened all the same in the fast-degenerating quarrel: 'Zounds, be reasonable!'

The lantern-bearer concurred wholeheartedly: 'Aye, be

reasonable . . . The darkest, most deserted forest in the realm is a place of safety compared to Paris . . .'

La Frette spat the rancid butter from his rotten stumps into Chalais's face.

'Fat harlot of a tripemonger, I will see you on the field of honour, tomorrow morning!'

D'Antin looked dumbfounded. 'The field? Are you mad? The edicts—'

But the offended party, tall La Frette, standing next to Saint-Aignan, ordered, 'Arnelieu, Amilly, we're going now.'

Four of them left in the direction of the lighted windows of the Tuileries, and the other four headed the opposite way. As for the lantern-bearer, he shuffled and swayed along Rue Saint-Honoré. The light of his bladder cast a hunchbacked dancing shadow onto the walls, whilst he memorised the names: 'La Frette, Saint-Aignan, Amilly, Arnelieu . . . and Chalais, Flamarens, d'Antin, Noirmou . . .'

At first light of the silent dawn, through the thick fog shrouding the field, d'Antin heard the silver-buckled shoes of the Chevalier de Saint-Aignan crunching over the frozen puddles. He turned to his neighbour Noirmoutier for his flask of Schaffhausen water, excellent for treating apoplexy.

The cockerel had not yet crowed, and there was not a

4

sound in all of Paris. Standing in a row against a hedge of frozen hazel trees, the supporters of the offending party, Chalais, discerned the pale misty figures of La Frette's clique emerging from a vast hay barn. They, too, moved forward in a row, straight towards their adversaries.

Soon they would be a breath away, for the rectangular field was narrow. To the right were sleeping mansions. To the left, the charterhouse of Boulevard Saint-Germain, with its cloisters and cells, and the monks whom they must not alert by shouting pointless invectives.

In any event, there was no more to be said. They had moved beyond words; this was a duel to the death, and d'Antin, beneath his heavy curled wig, was not feeling well. Yet, he struck a fine pose in his scarlet cloak, which was thrown over one shoulder, and his black hat, its brim turned up in the Catalan style, placing one foot forward, his hand on his hip. But his fingers were trembling. As soon as the duel had been called, his eyelids had started to swell and an erysipelatous rash had broken out on his forehead. His ears oozed, a fearsome scab had appeared on his neck, and beneath his chin and armpits he itched with scurf.

Chance had paired off the golden youths. La Frette would confront Chalais, Amilly would face Flamarens. Noirmoutier would take on Arnelieu, and d'Antin saw the Chevalier de Saint-Aignan striding towards him.

He was like a human bird with his mane of Greek curls and his splendid plumage, despite the eye lost to contamination by the whores in the brothels. He looked his adversary up and down, never slowing his pace through the fog, and his confident face betrayed no fear. He was most impressive as, sword in hand, he prepared to avenge his brother's honour. He took long strides, thumbing the blade of his weapon. D'Antin wondered when he would stop and stand on guard, but the other fellow continued on his way as if he intended to go through the hedge of hazel trees. *Thwack!* D'Antin felt the bone of his forehead burst under the tip of the sword as it passed over his entire head. It dragged his wig behind his skull, and he tried to catch it – how stupid . . . How stupid to die like this in the frosty dawn, falling flat on his back in his pearl-grey breeches and pink silk stockings fastened with garters, when all around there was nothing but carnage. To his right, his three partners were moaning in the grass. Their adversaries departed.

Little Chalais got to his feet, twisting his ankles because of his thick soles. Bleeding profusely, he slapped a hand to his belly. Flamarens dragged a bloody leg behind him and hobbled towards the pale outline of a carriage. Noirmoutier, with a torn shoulder, ran in the opposite direction, to his horse.

'Where will you go?' asked the other two.

'Portugal.'

The cockerel crowed. Cartwrights, blacksmiths, carters, weavers and saddlers opened the shutters of their little workshops. The fog lifted. The sun rose above the roofs of the mansions, to reveal a body lying on the ground . . .

At noon, the vertical shadows were sharp, and fell in triangles on the crowd from the roofs all around Place de Grève. The silence was impressive; windows had been rented at auction. Guards stood neatly in order around a platform.

'That makes six!'

The hooded executioner's axe fell so swiftly and cleanly that Saint-Aignan's head remained poised on the block. For a moment the executioner believed he had missed and would have to strike a second time, but then the head collapsed onto the other five scattered on the floor of the platform, like a pile of cabbages. It looked as if, reconciled at last, they were kissing one another – on the forehead, the ears, the lips (and that is what they should have done in the first place, in their lifetime). The executioner wiped his forehead and turned to speak to someone just below the platform.

'Monsieur de La Reynie, six in a row, that's too much! I am not the *Machine du monde*, after all . . .'

'Don't complain. There should have been eight,' sniggered the lieutenant of the Paris police, the prosecutor in cases of duelling, as he walked away towards the Châtelet.

*

'Monsieur le marquis, there is no greater violation, no greater sacrilege of the laws of heaven than the frenzied rage of a duel. Do they not teach you that in your native land of Guyenne?!'

The young Gascon thus roundly admonished in the courtroom at the Châtelet gazed through the window at the late-afternoon sun . . . The only person seated in one of the courtroom's chairs, he sighed, 'You may say that to me, yet I am not involved, for I am not of a quarrelsome nature. Nor was my brother, for that matter—'

'And yet he took part in a duel!' La Reynie interrupted, brutally. 'The nobility must cease, absolutely, from drawing their swords at the slightest provocation! These duels are decimating the French aristocracy, and since 1651 a royal edict has outlawed this bloody manner of avenging one's honour. Duels are, first of all, in defiance of His Majesty's authority, for his authority alone can decide who must die, and how we must live!'

Solemn and erect, La Reynie had reached this point in his sermon when, at the back of the room, behind the young marquis's back, a door creaked, and he heard footsteps on the tiles. The disheartened Gascon looked down at his red-heeled shoes and caught a glimpse of a rustling cloak and petticoats as they sat down to his right.

'Forgive me for being late, Monsieur de La Reynie,' she said; 'I but lately heard the news.'

Her voice was soft and even. The prosecutor declared,

'Mademoiselle, if your future husband, Louis-Alexandre de La Trémoille, Marquis de Noirmoutier, returns to France, he shall be beheaded.'

The Gascon heard his neighbour unclasp her cloak and lower her hood onto her shoulders, then he looked up at La Reynie and saw he was speechless, his mouth agape; on either side of his aquiline nose, his eyes were transfixed. Who could she be, this young woman able to so discomfit such a prosecutor? Was she a Medusa who transformed men into stone? But La Reynie gathered his wits about him and came to stand opposite the Gascon, who was wiping his damp palms against his white satin breeches.

'Monsieur,' declared the prosecutor, 'His Majesty's investigation will be merciless, and will go so far as to rule *in absentia* against the memory of your brother, the late lord of Antin.'

The marquis replied docilely, 'With all due respect and all imaginable zeal, I am the very humble, very obedient and most indebted servant of His Serene Highness . . .'

His neighbour enquired of the prosecutor, 'How were you informed of the duel?'

'The lantern-bearers who wait outside the spectacles and balls are our best informers,' smiled the chief of police.

The crestfallen marquis sadly lifted his plumed hat from the chair to his left, stood up and turned at last to face his neighbour, who had also stood up. Zounds! It was all he could do not to sit down again. She was not merely beauteous, she was beauty personified. The twenty-two-year-old Gascon's breath was taken away. He had always had a preference for plump blondes, and he was utterly captivated by this voluptuous marvel, who must have been his own age. A milky complexion, the green eyes of the Southern Seas, blond hair curled in the peasant style . . . Her gown was cut low in a deep décolletage from her shoulders, the sleeves stopping at the elbows in a cascade of lace. She was wearing gloves. The marquis could barely contain himself. He set his white hat on top of his enormous wig shaped like a horse's mane (which weighed more than two pounds and was terribly hot), only to find that he had put it on backwards: the ostrich feather now hung in front of his face. In his effort to swivel his headpiece he dislodged his wig, which now covered one eye. The girl had a charming laugh, of the sort to rouse tenderness deep in any heart. He bid farewell to La Reynie and then – 'Goodbye, Madame! Oh . . .' – he excused himself as the amused young lady strode and bounced to keep pace with his gangling figure loping, knock-kneed, towards the far end of the hall. He tried to open the door for her but only just managed not to thump her, decided to let her go out first, then went ahead himself. She was immediately charmed by such gauche thoughtfulness – not to mention the adoring gazes he bestowed upon her.

'Where are you going?' she asked, with a smile.

'That way, um, this way, and you?'

'Straight ahead.'

On leaving the Palais de Justice at the Châtelet, they were immediately caught up in the noise, mud and stench, the extraordinary bustle, the permanent commotion of the city. Open sewers, mounds of excrement and pigs foraging in the rubbish meant that the perfumed gloves or bouquets of violets placed beneath one's nose were indispensable as a remedy for nausea. But the marquis was oblivious to all that.

'I have no more brothers. The eldest, Roger, succumbed during the siege of Mardyck. Just de Pardaillan died in the army, and now the Marquis d'Antin has been killed in a duel . . .'

'And I have no more future husband,' echoed the fair lady. The air she breathed out was purer than the air she breathed in. 'Noirmoutier clearly cares more about his own skin than about me.' Her profile was proud and noble. Rebellious blond strands escaped from beneath the hood of her cloak. Her nostrils quivered like the wings of a bird. Her laughing mouth, not a little scheming, had a delightful effect on the marquis, as the sun dipped behind the trees . . .

Their double loss had brought them together. While they made their way past song merchants – selling drinking songs, dining songs, songs for dancing or hailing the news – the two young people spoke of the deceased man and the exiled fiancé, finding ways to compliment, to

11

please, to console. A group of Savoyard street minstrels proclaimed 'Bring me back my sparrow, fair redhead' and 'Ah, how vast is the world'.

''Tis all the more exasperating,' nodded the lovely blond head, 'that when they brought the news to me, on Rue Saint-Honoré, I was trying on my wedding gown, for next Sunday. I do not know what I shall do with it.'

''Twould be a great pity, were it to go to ruin . . .'

A street performer took a swallow of water and spat it back out in a spray of various colours and scents.

'What I mean, that is,' stammered the marquis, 'it is because of the moths. 'Tis true, sometimes one puts away new garments in a chest and then later, when one unfolds them again, they are ruined, consumed by grubs and full of holes . . . And then one regrets one did not wear them . . .'

The demoiselle in her pointed high-heeled slippers contemplated the fumbling Gascon. He amused her, and was not without charm. 'Might you be implying that you . . . ?'

'Well, one doesn't fall in love only once in a lifetime.'

A *pâtissier* stood in his doorway, proudly adjusting his appearance: a ribbon for a cravat, a beret with a large knot, and a sprig of flowers to attract the ladies. The abandoned fiancée placed her head on the marquis's shoulder in an intimate gesture. And the marquis, an assiduous devotee of the lansquenet circles and reversi tables in the *hôtels particuliers* of the Marais, now thought he was playing the finest game on earth. Astonished and adrift, on a square teeming with horse carts and ecclesiastics, he scratched his periwig.

'Is it not paradise here?'

'Ah, no, Monsieur, in paradise there wouldn't be so many bishops!'

They burst out laughing. For his part, the marquis was certain that an angel had blessed him, and he raised his eyes to heaven.

The vaults of the church of Saint-Sulpice, forming a lofty sky of stone, resounded with laughter. After the reading of the Gospel, the blonde in the red pearl-embroidered dress had knelt before the altar alongside the marquis in lavender grey, then exploded with laughter, murmuring in his ear, 'You know what we're kneeling on, you know how we forgot the embroidered silk cushions and had them sent for from Rue des Rosiers, at the Hôtel Mortemart . . .'

'Yes?' asked the young Gascon.

'The servant made a mistake. She brought the dogs' cushions.'

'No!'

They laughed and dusted off the dog hairs like mischievous little children dressed up in garments of embroidered silk. Their guests were seated behind them at the heart of the vast church, which was still under construction. The Gascon, in a fine light-coloured horsehair wig, radiated happiness. His bride, graceful and glowing in the gentle brilliance of her twenty-two years, was still full of the candour of childhood.

Near the entrance to the church, sitting on a prie-dieu, a chubby-cheeked duc with protuberant green eyes and a small, full-lipped mouth exclaimed ecstatically to his neighbour, 'My daughter is extremely amusing! One is never bored when she is present. Do you see that obese boy in the first row? That is my eldest, Vivonne. The other day, when I was reproaching my daughter for not taking enough exercise, she replied, "How can you say that? Not a day goes by that I do not walk four times round my brother!"'

The man to whom he was speaking, an elderly man with a great hooked nose that seemed to take up his entire face, enquired, 'Is that your wife next to your son? She seems most exceedingly pious . . .'

'Oh, indeed,' said the husband, 'where adultery is concerned, I believe I am safe before mankind, but before God, I surely wear my horns!'

'Look at my wife, then: she prefers to live away from me, the great Chrestienne de Zamet there on the right – she's the same,' grumbled the man with the hooked nose. 'She knows perfectly how to season a mother's tenderness with that of a bride of Jesus Christ! Ha-ha-ha!'

The two fathers of the wedded couple guffawed; they were witty and cheerfully debauched. Someone in front of them turned round with a frown, then whispered to his neighbour, 'Those two have found perfect company in each other . . .'

And the young couple had found perfect company, too, now married only eight days after meeting. They pledged their troth on a wintry Sunday before the priest and four trusty witnesses. The cleric inscribed the date – 28 January 1663 – in the parish register, then the names of the turtledoves, proclaiming them out loud: 'Françoise de Rochechouart de Mortemart, also known as Mademoiselle de Tonnay-Charente, and . . .'

The voluptuous blonde Françoise took up the goose quill as it was handed to her and, as the priest pronounced the name of her spouse – 'Louis-Henri de Pardaillan de Gondrin, Marquis de . . .' – for the first time she signed her new name:

2.

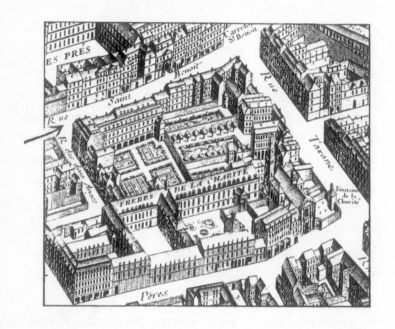

An apple-green gilded carriage arrived at Rue Saint-Benoît, its doors adorned with the coat of arms of the Marquis de Montespan. The vehicle rattled along the rutted street, its body supported by thick leather straps on a four-wheel axle.

Dustmen, collecting the city's waste that would be tipped from their carts into the Seine, blocked the vehicle's progress. Through their windows, Françoise and Louis-Henri contemplated the world outside. The *quartier* teemed with life, full of craftsmen with their displays and workshops and noise. The dustmen's rags were hardly different from those of the beggars they passed. Françoise told Louis-Henri, 'When I was a little girl, one holy-day my mother wanted me to wash the feet of the poor outside a church. I went up to the first pauper and could not bring myself to bend down. I stepped back, in tears. Poverty was there before me, inescapable, and it filled the child I was with revulsion. I did not wash the feet of the poor.'

Suddenly the way was clear, the carriage moved on and turned into Rue Taranne, stopping almost immediately on the left beneath a wooden sign depicting a wig. Louis-Henri climbed down from the carriage, saying, 'The misfortunes of the people are the will of God, and do not warrant that we should waste our feelings upon them.'

He went round the vehicle to open the door for Françoise. 'All my feelings are for you.'

He gazed on her admiringly and bit his lip.

'I do feel I love you more than anyone on earth is wont to love, but I only know how to tell you so in the way that everyone on earth would tell you. I despair that all declarations of love so resemble one another.'

The marquise, lovely in her flowered hat, stepped down, reaching for the hand he was holding out to her.

'That's sweet . . .' But then she began to poke fun,

mincing and simpering in exaggerated fashion. 'It is the greatest honour to be shown such admiration! Oh, I do love such heady stuff; I do love to be loved!'

Louis-Henri adored the way she used jest to hide emotion. While the carriage was manoeuvring – the coachman gripping the mare's bit – to pull in beneath the roof of the stables beyond the well in the courtyard, Françoise went through the wigmaker's door and exclaimed, 'Monsieur Joseph Abraham, our *de*-lightful landlord! We have mislaid our key yet again. May we come through the shop?'

'Ten o'clock in the morning and 'tis only now that you two are coming home? Did you spend the night in the Marais again, playing bassette and bagatelle! I hope you won a few *écus* withal, this time.'

'Nay, we lost everything!'

Louis-Henri came into the shop. It was a clean place, all of beige and ochre, where long bunches of hair hung from the ceiling, almost touching the floor. A 'red-heel', his shaved crown covered with lard to avoid irritation and parasites, stood waiting for the periwig that an employee had nearly finished curling. An ecclesiastic stepped back to admire his platinum-blond tonsured wig in a mirror he was holding. Next to him, jovial and good-natured, Joseph Abraham saw his wife turn to Françoise and say, 'But 'tis open, my dear! The cook, Madame Larivière, has been waiting with your new servant to serve dinner since yesterday evening. I do believe she prepared a squab bisque and minced capon.'

'Ah, I know she did, but one card game led to another . . . We thought we might win back our losses, but . . .We'll go through the door at the back of the shop, shall we, Madame Abraham? Farewell, gentlemen! We're off to bed!'

Six apprentices on the wigmaker's mezzanine, leaning over the railing, admired the departure of Françoise's deep décolletage from above. They were rooted to the spot. The wigmaker clapped his hands: 'Now then!'

Françoise's bodice gaped open, possibly accidentally, then she entered the dark stairwell. Louis-Henri smiled. 'As lovely as the day, with a devilish-fine spirit!'

Her proud rounded breasts gave off the only true perfume: her very own scent. Louis-Henri extended a hand towards the radiant bosom.

'Oh, my! Take heed, Monsieur!' The marquise pretended to be offended. 'Do not forget it is scarcely two years since I left the convent.'

'And so?'

'Let me see, first of all, what your face is like: your chin is too long, your nose is too big, your eyelids droop, you have freckles. Taken separately, all of that is hardly handsome, but all together rather pleasing. All right. You may go up . . .'

Her moiré skirt flowed like a tide over the first steps of the stairway. Louis-Henri, standing by the copper ball of the newel post, played the sulking husband.

'I'm not sure now . . . With a wife who is from the *noblesse de robe*, I don't know . . . I could have found many others who would have better suited my position, in the matter of the dowry, for I am from the old nobility! Montespan . . . my noble family goes back to the Crusades, to the battles between the Comtes de Bigorre and the Comtes de Foix, or against Simon de Monfort! Whereas a Mortemart . . . a mistress made for moonlight, a woman of secret trysts and borrowed beds . . . Yes, really I hesitate . . .'

'You're right,' laughed Françoise. 'To marry for love means to marry disadvantageously, carried away by a blind passion. Let us speak of it no more,' she concluded, climbing a few more steps with an exaggerated sway of her hips.

The marquis's pupils dilated at the thought of the beauty of her body beneath the silk of her deep-pleated dress. Like a horse, he began to breathe through his nose whilst the fair woman began a recital of her attractions.

'Do you know that I am wearing three petticoats? Observe the first one, this pale-blue thing, it is known as the *modesty*,' she said, lightly lifting the back of her dress to reveal a skirt that she then raised in turn. 'The second, dark blue, is called the *saucy* . . .'

Louis-Henri would have liked to seize his wife round the waist but she slipped through his fingers. Her flexibility, her agility, were admirable. The newlyweds' apartments had been divided up vertically over three storeys – a nonsensical distribution due to the narrow plots allotted in Paris, which obliged the inhabitants to build upwards. Such comings and goings in the stairway! The firewood stored in the cellar had to be carried up, as had the water, in buckets drawn from the well in the courtyard. The marquis was suddenly lustful, and ogled his wife, roaring comically and rolling his eyes.

'I have done all I can not to offend God and not to succumb to my passion,' he explained, climbing a few steps. 'But I am forced to confess that it has become stronger than my reason. I can no longer resist its violence, and I do not even feel inclined to do so . . . Raah!'

'Help!' Madame de Montespan fled up the stairs, pursued by her husband who galloped after her traitorous petticoats, which she raised too high, offering the tempting vision of the fruit. All her petticoats were very light indeed and lifted at the slightest breeze, wafting a perfume of tuberose and waxed wood inside the dark stairwell.

On the first floor, to the left, a door opened onto a salon modestly furnished with folding seats made of webbing and heavy canvas, a mirror from Venice and a gaming table with several drawers. On a green-painted wall hung a framed tapestry from Rouen, mere cotton threads now, but representing the story of Moses. Louis-Henri chased after Françoise in a clattering of steps. There was a bulge in the front of his grey satin breeches. The marquise turned round, saw it and cried, 'Dear Lord!'

On the second floor was the kitchen with a brick oven,

cast-iron spits and frying pans, pitchers, pots and stoneware terrines. Food was stored inside boxes covered in wire netting to protect it from mice and flies. Salt meat hung from the ceiling above Madame Larivière and the new servant. Sitting side by side on a little bench, they were eating soup from earthenware bowls on their laps using wooden spoons. They watched as their masters scurried by, but their masters did not notice them, so intent were they on their celebration of the senses.

'As for the third petticoat,' said Françoise with a peal of laughter, 'it is the *secret*. Mine is sea blue!'

Her dress and petticoats were now over her head revealing that, like all the women of her era, she wore no undergarments. Louis-Henri hurried behind her naked rump, bathed in the light from the window in the stairway as it turned right towards the servants' garret beneath the roof, but then the naked rump veered to the left, into a room boasting an enormous bed. Its four twisting columns supported loosely tied curtains of green and red serge. The two bodies flung themselves on top of one another on the mattress, jostling the frame, whilst the curtains swayed open beneath the canopy then closed again, a barrier against the cold but also a shield for their conjugal intimacy.

'What is this finger that has no nail?'

That was what was heard by the new servant, a girl of eight, for the Montespans had not closed the door to their room. In the kitchen, standing by Madame Larivière, she looked at the ceiling as she heard the legs of a bed creaking, which annoyed the cook: 'Ah, the marquise is a flame all too easy to ignite. I like to call her "the Cascade", for she has a voracious appetite for pleasure. She knows how to make love and burn the besom.'

For 'twas true that above their heads the masters were all a-tangle. Françoise breathed happiness from a time of fairy-tales, into her husband's mouth, indulging the ever-delightful little gestures that titillated, the hundred thousand little moves that preceded the conclusion. Words and discourse complemented her actions.

'Ah . . . Mmm . . . Oh!'

On the floor below, Madame Larivière — frizzy black hair, olive complexion and spindly legs, not exactly kin with Venus — emptied the ashes from the stove into a jug she handed to the servant child.

'Here, Dorothée, rather than listen to them at their game of tousing and mousing, go and sell this ash to the launderer at the end of the street. You may keep the money for yourself, and save it to buy yourself a blanket, for the servants' rooms are never heated. And then, so as not to come back empty-handed, take this bucket and fill it at the well in the courtyard. The water fountain is nearly empty,' she said, tapping her nails against a hollow-sounding copper basin with a lid and a spigot.

Dorothée, to her distress, discovered on the steps the

large chestnut wig that the marquis had torn from his head. It lay there, a mass of curls, like a dead animal.

The lodgings, which were always dark, were not in fact a very pleasant place to live, but up there, under the sheets, the exquisite line of Françoise's back undulated and, in the shadow of the curtains, their breathing rose, rhythmic and light. The marquise's senses sought, everywhere, endlessly, the bliss of knowing her husband's lip, his hand, all of him. How divine, too, Louis-Henri's pleasure as he pushed aside his wife's shift, and her honour. To elicit a saucy shiver, she extended her neck in a vaguely unseemly manner. And then there was a prolonged kiss. What would happen next? Gad! All reason and morality would take flight. Now for nuptials without restraint, a merriment of vice and cruelty.

3.

'Ah, the young must do as the young will do . . .'

On a starry June night the Montespans' carriage rattled to a halt at the top of a hill in the gently rolling countryside around the chateau of Saint-Germain-en-Laye. The coachman sitting on the outside seat resigned himself philosophically to the shaking: 'I don't know where they find the energy.'

He was jostled and shaken, by the jostling and shaking inside the carriage. The marquis was taking the marquise doggy style (*more canino*). Kneeling the length of the seat, with her cheek flat against the window in the door, Françoise could watch the avenues lit with countless torches and the slow meandering of gondolas on tranquil waters that were part of the royal celebration taking place far in the distance below them. A troupe of musicians lent graceful strains to the charm of the summer night. At each meeting of the pathways, there were symphonies and banquets offered by servants disguised as fauns, satyrs and sylvan gods. An orchestra was playing Lully's most recent composition, whilst nymphs rose from the fountains to recite poetry. Lions, tigers and elephants were promenaded on leads.

'How lovely . . .'

'Ah, indeed, how lovely. Françoise, your bottom shames the very stars.'

It was true that the marquise's posterior was very lovely, and all that was lacking in its gaiety was speech. It was there that Louis-Henri found the most exquisite pleasure, and now he melted into her like snow in fire: 'Charming miracle, divine paradise for the eyes, unique masterwork of the gods!'

She turned all the way round. Now he loved her mouth and the gracious play of her lips and teeth, which sometimes nibbled his tongue and sometimes did something even better that was almost as good as being inside her. This woman, dear God, made him lose his head, whilst the rest of him luxuriated in fucking; zounds, his blood was on fire. The happy man exploded with pleasure on every side.

After that was done, and each of them had known that little death – and such a death! – Françoise was reborn amidst a new tumult, only to die again more loudly and splendidly. Sprawling on the leather horsehair seat, her curves, her *you know what*, all said to the marquis, 'Come!'

And the heat rose. 'Stay!' And he stayed in her voracious body (the god of love required good lungs). Legs in the air and breasts bared — 'Breasts that loved to be on display, worthy of a god,' noted her husband — Françoise naughtily wriggled her bewitching calves.

'Here we go again!' sighed the coachman, once again swaying and slipping on his seat.

Her head thrown back, this time the marquise was able to contemplate the distant celebration with its six hundred guests . . . upside down. Louis-Henri apologised that he could not take her there.

'We Montespans are not welcome at court. Some time ago, the Pardaillan de Gondrins rebelled against the King . . . And he is still holding it against us.'

Personae not too gratae at Saint-Germain-en-Laye, due to the disgrace of an uncle who had rebelled against the Bourbons; that was why Louis-Henri had not been invited. So it was from their carriage that the Montespans attended the festivities.

There were entertainments, spectacles, games, lottos and ballets. Tapestries from La Savonnerie were spread among the trees in the large garden, and in the groves marzipan was served. There was a golden weeping willow whose branches sprayed a hundred jets of water and petals of anemone and jasmine from Spain. And now the King was coming out of the chateau and the courtiers gathered round him. In the darkness, he was incomparably dazzling.

'I've heard he wears twelve million *livres*' worth of diamonds on his person,' said Louis-Henri, sitting up above Françoise whose legs were still spread wide.

'Those who wish to ask a favour are advised to behold him first from afar before they draw near, for fear of being struck dumb at the sight of him. He often plays the role of Jupiter on stage,' continued the marquise.

She began to roll her hips again. Suddenly, bright lights transformed the great fountain into a sea of fire beneath cascades of fireworks. Statues became naked dancers, painted grey. Even the trees with their long shadows seemed to uproot themselves to follow the King's progress. In that uncertain world, glittering with illusion, he was the focal point around which all the universe turned. Everything seemed subjected to his will. Battalions of under-gardeners leapt from one fountain to the next, struggling to open the taps, their hands soaked, their breath short, since when the King went for a walk, water and music had to accompany him. Although it was summer, there were pyramids of ice everywhere. Their presence suggested a miracle, and Louis adored anything that proved his power over nature (like eating chilled food in summer). Fruit and wine were served in bowls of frozen water.

''Tis said the King need only walk abroad for the rain to stop.'

Then, suddenly, fragrances of ambergris and rosewater, mingled with the emanations of gunpowder, wafted to the

Montespans' carriage on the hill. In the sky a spray of fireworks described two giant arabesques, interlaced with two 'L's.

'Why is there a second "L"?' asked Françoise.

''Tis the initial of Louise de La Vallière, the favourite,' replied her husband.

'He dares to honour his mistress before the Queen, and in public?' said Françoise, astonished.

'What can His Majesty not do?' asked Louis-Henri.

The vast royal domain was now a whirl of flying rockets, twisting curls, firecrackers, flame blowers, girandoles. Suddenly there was an immense final explosion, and the entire sky was light blue.

'He can even restore daylight to darkest night . . .' said the marquise in awe, sitting up and pulling the translucent folds of her underskirts back over her thighs.

The coloured silk skirts were usually worn over a simple black dress, but Françoise, to most pleasing effect, wore them next to her skin – they were garments that were easily removed in private, allowing rapid access to her body. Françoise's raiment was deliciously daring.

'I'm hungry. Louis-Henri, what do you think of the name Athénaïs?'

'Why?' smiled her husband, pulling up his grey satin breeches.

'To bow to the fashion of Antiquity – all the rage at the moment – I would like to take the name Athénaïs . . .'

'Athénaïs or Françoise, it's all the same to me, provided it is you . . .'

''Tis from the name of the Greek goddess of virginity. A rebellious virgin, Athena rejected all her mortal suitors.'

'Is that so?'

Saint-Germain-en-Laye was three hours by carriage from Paris. Françoise, her appetite aroused by their lovemaking on the seat, suggested they stop halfway to sup at L'Écu de France.

'As it pleases you,' replied her husband, 'for you know that you alone provide all sustenance for me. Which reminds me; there is something I would like to tell you, Athénaïs . . .'

In the renowned coaching inn – a red house of several storeys (all tile and brick), overlooking a lawn edged with camomile – the atmosphere was subdued and intimate; the windowpanes were small.

As the dining hall was filled with patrons, bewigged like Louis-Henri, who had just readjusted his own wig above his shoulders, a table was brought and laid for the Montespans next to a cold fireplace (it was June) and a stairway gleaming with beeswax. Françoise sat down, eager to eat.

'I will order only those dishes that were not allowed when I was at the convent, those of a lust-inducing sort:

oysters, so-called "Aphroditic" red beans, and asparagus, all forbidden to young ladies.'

She laughed, a peal of pearls spilling onto marble steps. The patrons in the hall turned to look at her. Her fair hands, her arms fashioned as if by a master potter, her teeth so perfect and white – a rarity in those times: the noblemen and burghers in the establishment, with their *soupe à la bière*, felt their jaws dropping in amazement.

'Who is she?'

'The fairest lady of our time . . .'

'A triumphant beauty to display to ambassadors!'

Her firm chin, straight nose, fine wrists, waist and neck; her thick and plentiful blond locks. She had invented a style of coiffure and baptised it the *hurluberlu*. Her hair had been pulled back from the forehead and was held in place by a hoop on top of her head, leaving her hair to fall on either side in a cascade of curls that framed her face.

'I can see that becoming a fashion,' predicted a patron, in response to his sour-tempered wife's frown.

As for Louis-Henri, he admired his wife's flamboyance; her brilliant red lips, whence nothing emerged that was not a word he loved, were a nest of delight. But he lowered his eyes to his plate.

'Athénaïs, we play cards all the time, we lose, debts are piling up like clouds. I owe money everywhere – to my tailor, my gunsmith, my friends. Financially, we have no support, and we are embarking upon a perilous life.'

A *valet de table* brought Athénaïs a plate of oysters, 'all alive', and some cabbage with bacon for Louis-Henri. The molluscs' muscles had already been snipped in the kitchen, so the fair blonde needed only to raise them up, tilt the shell and let the flesh slide between her lips. As in the time of Ancient Rome, she preferred her oysters milky, so before swallowing them, she bit the pouch. The milk ran to the edge of her lips: a few ducs looked on, and the temperature rose. They tugged at their collars whilst the Marquis de Montespan continued, 'In five months, we have already exhausted the fifteen thousand *livres* of annual pension my parents send me, and the interest on the dowry paid by your parents, who do not have vast means either. And everything is dear in Paris, and two servants in the house! Everything costs double or triple here. One hundred *livres* the rent for the apartments, maintenance of the carriage and the coachman costs twelve *livres* a day. So I have taken a decision . . .'

'Are we going to live in the foothills of the Pyrenees in your Château de Montespan?' smiled the marquise dreamily, swallowing another oyster, just as the asparagus and red beans were brought to their table.

'Nay, for 'twould not be good enough for you. Ennobled by Louis XIII as a reward for services rendered by an ancestor, the land of the two villages – Antin and Montespan – was established as a marquisate. The family settled first in the chateau at Antin, but because it was about to collapse, they removed to the one at Montespan. Until that chateau, too, was in dire condition. And so they went to live at Bonnefont, where I was born. Alas, it is not a fine chateau. With its broken stones, covered in brambles, surrounded by the stagnant water of the moat, it is not worthy of you . . .'

'What, then, is your idea to set things aright, my fine husband?' she asked Louis-Henri, giving him as always an amused smile.

She picked up an asparagus shoot and raised it to her lips as if she were playing a flute. She turned her gaze towards the comtes in the room, who lifted a corner of the tablecloth to wipe their brows, whilst Louis-Henri continued with what he had to say.

'I will go to serve in the army, pay the blood tribute, and become captain of a company of pikemen.'

Athénaïs continued to look at the dining hall, at the velvet curtains in the windows, the bouquets of flowers on the tables.

'Monsieur, I forbid you to put a single one of your charming feet upon a battlefield.' Then she looked Louis-Henri straight in the eye. 'Your three brothers have already gone to their deaths in combat, and you are made for peace. Do not do it for me. We shall—'

But Montespan interrupted her. 'It is the only way out, for aristocrats do not have the right to work, and business and trade are forbidden to us. A military exploit would also be the most glorious way to obtain amnesty from His Majesty for my family's sins. I have been considering it for a long time, waiting for a war. Fortunately, a city in Lorraine has just rebelled against the King's power, and he has decided to besiege it. This is my long-awaited opportunity. I will go further into debt to equip my troops but I dream only of a battle to rescue me from obscurity.'

'You are not eating?' asked the marquise, astonished, pecking at a piece of bacon from her husband's plate. 'Will it be dangerous? What is the problem with that city? Is it not the one that defends Metz, Lunéville and Nancy?'

'Last year, Charles IV, Duc de Lorraine, agreed by treaty to give the city of Marsal to the King of France. But he has reneged on his promise, on the deceitful pretext that the treaty was signed only by his nephew. The King has announced his intention to send an expeditionary corps to persuade the duc to honour his commitment. And I have volunteered, enthusiastically.'

'But what if you should die there!' exclaimed Athénaïs, her eyes suddenly misting over.

'Then the name of Marsal,' smiled Louis-Henri, 'would for ever make you think of me. But nothing shall befall me. This campaign will bring us a host of advantages . . . And since to please God it is not necessary to cry or to starve, let us laugh, my dear, and eat our fill! May I have this oyster?'

Beneath the stars as they returned to Paris, the Montespans' carriage clattered along the road, and the coachman knew only too well that the shaking was not solely the result of the ruts along the King's highway. Inside the vehicle, Françoise-Athénaïs straddled her husband frenetically (oysters, asparagus, 'Aphroditic' beans?). They faced one another, their mouths clamped together. The marquise squeezed her thighs to prevent the virile member from escaping as they jolted along. Louis-Henri clung to her with all his strength: 'Hold tight to me, lest I come undone.'

4.

A company of pikemen marched at sixty paces a minute to the rhythm of drums, oboes, fifes and trumpets playing military music. Their mounted captain was none other than the Marquis de Montespan.

He observed his infantry soldiers as they advanced across a wide plain surrounded by a circular plateau, wooded in places. Marsal, the fortified city they were to take by storm, sat in the hollow of a natural basin.

These men under Louis-Henri's command, marching doggedly, were clumsy farm boys that a recruiting sergeant had found in the region of Chartres.

'Several of them are bound to be killed,' Athénaïs had sighed.

'Whether they die stirring the earth in front of an enemy town or stirring it in a field in Beauce, it is still in the service of the King,' her husband had said dismissively.

The pikemen carried a pike two *toises* in length to confront the enemy cavalry. When the gates in the walled city were opened and the charge was given, they would have to ram their weapons deep into the horses' guts; there would be fountains of blood splattering cloth, clothes would be torn, and all of it would cost him . . . the marquis added up his expenses.

War was a ruinous undertaking. The aristocrat who bought a military commission also had to finance his company: provide for horses, carts, mules, household and camp utensils, tents, beds, dishes. A gentleman's soldiers were not allowed to have their 'king's bread' and their uniforms had to be bought for them. Louis-Henri watched as his Beaucerons advanced.

Every item of the entire iron-grey outfit – jacket, breeches, boots, cravat, helmet – must have cost upwards of . . . but he could not shout out to them, 'Mind your clothing!' And then, they ate vast quantities, these soldiers who were about to face a horse: two pounds of bread, a pound of meat and a pint of wine, in addition to the five *sols* of pay each day. So much to disburse! Particularly as the marquis had also bought himself three rows of fusiliers – one row to shoot, one preparing to shoot, and one reloading their muskets, the lot of them moving forward, in turn, behind the pikemen. Louis-Henri, on a white horse, commanded them to remain calm and quiet so that they could hear the orders, and reminded them that they were to fight in silence and that each man had always to have a bullet in his mouth, to reload all the more quickly.

Montespan, in the vanguard, was not afraid, this 2 September 1663. And although this was his first battle, the Gascon was suddenly fired up, gripping his taffeta standard and dreaming of nothing but ripping open the enemy. He knew that this was his opportunity to prove his bravery and – if he was not slain – to hope for some financial largesse – at last – on the part of a grateful sovereign.

He was not afraid when he came across sappers digging blast holes for explosives at the foot of the walls, nor to know that when they collapsed the moment would have come for hand-to-hand fighting, and he would have to go at it, steel against flesh! He knew why he was there, above all for whom he was there. The thought of his wife and the comfort he would bestow upon her carried him forward. The pikemen encouraged one another, shouting, 'Kill! Kill!' The fusiliers cried, 'Forward fearlessly!' Louis-Henri closed his eyes, bit his lower lip and thought, for Athénaïs! Clumps of earth flew up beneath his horse's hooves, and the pikemen running at his side stirred up the dust. The clatter of firearms continued behind him.

Now he would have to show his mettle. Already, in the hedges they passed, the crushed blackberries bled like wounds. The hills all around were covered in flowers. The air was still. They prepared themselves for the end of the world. Louis-Henri's banner, with his coat of arms, fluttered in the landscape. A bird flew overhead with fruit from the hedge in its beak; its reflection in the stream lingered after its passage. Montespan's mind roved and wandered aimlessly, in quest of shadows and a charming labour. He was filled with bloodlust. For his wife – his soul mate, his precious care – he had made this leap into the silent abyss, and he brandished yellow and black taffeta against the sky. Marsal's fortifications seemed to loom higher and higher when suddenly there came music from inside the city.

'What is that?' wondered the marquis, pulling on his horse's reins.

'The chamade,' replied a pikeman standing near.

'The what?'

'The call of trumpets from the besieged, signalling that they surrender.'

'What? Oh, no, it cannot be! Why are they surrendering? They have no right! I've borrowed twelve thousand *livres tournois* – twelve thousand! – to pay for this war! So they must defend themselves, and pour boiling oil upon us, and shoot at us, and launch the cavalry . . . and give me my chance to act the hero!'

But white flags were waving above the towers of Marsal. The Marquis de Montespan, utterly disconcerted, turned about. And what did he discover, far behind him – blazons flapping in the wind, an immense army filling the entire horizon on the cliff above the plateau. So many cannons, and kettledrums, and flags, and standards! Montespan stuttered at the sight, 'But-but-but who are all those people?'

'His Majesty with his personal army.'

'The monarch has come? But I did not know. I did think, three companies of squires like myself do not amount to much to attack a city . . .'

An envoy from the King galloped to the city gates, took a message and sped back the other way to confirm the news: 'The Duc de Lorraine agrees to honour his promise!'

Montespan's fusiliers fired into the sky to show their joy. Only Louis-Henri was sulking. He could have wept. All it took was for the King to show his strength on the horizon and the rebels surrendered their arms without firing a single musket. And now Montespan would have to go home without a shred of fame, more in debt than ever. What an unfortunate end to what had been a very strange war. Sometimes fate dealt one an unexpected hand.

As they returned to the capital, Louis-Henri rode for a spell alongside Maréchal Luxembourg, nicknamed the 'Tapestry-maker of Notre-Dame' for the great number of flags he had collected from the enemy and which he sent to decorate the cathedral. Under his arm he was carrying the flag of the Duc de Lorraine . . .

All the way to Paris, in every town they went through, the monarch ordered street performances — ballets, plays

– which his courtiers also applauded. All the splendour of the kings of Persia could not compare with the pomp that followed Louis XIV. The streets were filled with plumes and gilded garments, raiments adorned with lace and feathers, mules with superb harnesses, and parade horses wearing caparisons woven with golden thread.

It was impossible for Louis-Henri to catch a glimpse of His Majesty, for he was surrounded by a multitude of guards, courtiers, and artists in a frenzy of genuflection. A man of forty years or so – Jean de La Fontaine – was reciting a poem that he had just composed, 'Sonnet on the Capture of Marsal'.

> *'Rever'd monarch, greatest on earth*
> *Your illustrious name is feared by all;*
> *Ambition's power, in your thrall*
> *Crumbles to less than glass or dirt.'*

The fabulist seemed overcome, and spoke in a little voice, quavering and trembling with emotion. The courtiers exploded with exclamations of 'Jesus and Mary, how beautiful, how true, how well put! Please continue, Master, we beg you!' The poet, who drew a pension from His Majesty, needed no further urging:

> *'Marsal did boast of taking you to war*
> *But from the first bedazzling bolt of thunder*

It lowered its bold brow as you drew near
And now surrenders ere you raise your fist.'

They all applauded frenetically with the tips of their powdered fingers. The inspired native of Château-Thierry continued:

'Had its rebellious pride inspir'd your wrath
Had it found glory in extraordinary combat
How sweet 'twould then have been to sing its
    praises . . .
But e'en now my muse begins to dread
Too rarely might your victory banner be raised
For lack of enemies who dare resist you.'

Ah . . . All were on the verge of swooning with ecstasy over a short person whom Montespan could not see, other than the top of a black wig bobbing with satisfaction. It must have been the monarch himself, whom Louis-Henri had imagined to be much taller, as on his paintings. At that very instant, the artist Charles Le Brun went up to the King: 'Sire, allow me to submit to you this cartoon for a tapestry celebrating the surrender of Marsal. You see, you are portrayed here on horseback, your head in profile, at the top of the wooded plateau overlooking the plain. The Duc de Lorraine is at your feet and begs you to accept the keys to the city of Marsal, which you can see in the distance.'

Behind the picture, cautious courtiers awaited His Majesty's remarks, to determine whether they were to continue sighing in rapture. And when the King's calm voice, level with their shoulders, declared, 'Monsieur, have the Gobelins weave it,' the ducs and princes and marquis shouted themselves hoarse. 'Ah, how lovely, how well designed!' Louis-Henri heard the monarch calling his playwrights, musicians and sculptors to him: 'I entrust you with the most important thing on earth: my fame.'

Once back in Paris, his horse's tail between its hind legs, the poor disappointed Marquis de Montespan arrived at Rue Taranne. His staff (Madame Larivière and Dorothée) were waiting on the pavement to greet their master. Françoise rushed to embrace him.

'Louis-Henri, you are alive!'

She led him back to their home with its massive, cumbersome old furnishings. The marquis told the tale of his expedition – a bottomless pit – and said, 'And it all stopped there. 'Twas enough for the King to show his face. So here I am again, with nothing else to tell you, nothing to show you, no medal or title, more penniless than ever. Twelve thousand *livres* further in debt, lent me by my father, who in turn was forced to borrow. And did I not promise you, "Athénaïs, when I return, our finances shall be on the mend . . ."?'

In the dark salon, in front of the tapestry depicting Moses, Dorothée was spraying perfume using a pair of bellows, filling the room with scent, whilst Françoise sought to console her husband.

'Louis-Henri, put your hands here.'

He placed them on her belly. His eyes opened wide. 'Athénaïs!'

'I went to consult a soothsayer.'

'You believe in such folk?'

'And you do not?'

'I believe in you alone.'

'It will be a boy!'

5.

'Marie-Christine, don't lean towards your mother like that! You'll fall out of your cradle and injure yourself.'

In the salon on the first floor, sitting face to face across a gaming table, the destitute young Montespans were playing reversi as they dined. Between each course Athénaïs dealt the cards with dexterity whilst Louis-Henri put his dried beans in as stakes and watched over their baby beside them.

'She looks at you the way I gaze at you.'

'It is true that she has your eyes, your rather big nose, and your lovely mouth. She's the picture of her father . . .'

'She's always reaching out for you. Perhaps she would like you to nurse her.'

The marquise slipped a comforter shaped like a fleur-de-lis between her daughter's lips; the baby immediately spat it out, and Athénaïs called out towards the stairwell,

'Madame Larivière! Chew up some porridge for Marie-Christine – she's hungry!'

Her husband was astonished. 'She no longer feeds at the breast? You want to wean her so young? Is she not too small? She is not yet—'

'It all depends on the child,' said la Montespan, looking at her playing cards. 'They are all different. The King, for example, nibbled his ladies heartily from infancy, for he was born, most exceptionally, with a full set of teeth. The first women he caused to suffer were his wet nurses, bruising their breasts and wounding their nipples – he had the appetite of a lion cub.'

'How do you know that?' asked Louis-Henri, raising his wager by three pretend *écus* (three dried beans).

Wedged into a candlestick on the table, a mutton-suet candle began to smoke. The flame flickered over Athénaïs's face, glowing on her hands as she reached out to lay down her cards. 'Lost again. Your *écu*-beans are for me.'

The cook, Madame Larivière, came into the dark salon. She was wearing a bonnet with flaps and holding a bowl into which she spat what she had chewed up. She rolled tiny nuggets between her thumb and index finger and slipped them between the infant's lips, whilst the marquise told a story.

'One day, whilst you were in Lorraine, my father and brother Vivonne and I went to see the construction of the new palace at Versailles. At the ministry of war, which has

46

already been built, my fat brother bought a military commission for the campaign against the Barbary corsairs. They will embark from Marseilles on 13 July 1664. It will be the King's first maritime war, but he won't go. His cousin Beaufort will be in command.'

The dinner the loving Montespans were taking on the gaming table was a charming concoction of ground meat and stew of the sort even God did not enjoy. The wine had no name, but they were not proud. Should they not drink it, since it had been opened? Louis-Henri tilted the flat-bottomed bottle with its wicker covering. The cork had been left by the cards, a piece of wood wrapped with a weave of hemp and dipped in suet. The wine flowed into Athénaïs's glass and she pretended that she was not eager to drink.

'Tsk-tsk, husband! Women are advised not to drink wine, because it might inflame and excite them and cause them to lose their honour!'

Madame Larivière raised her eyes to the ceiling as she left the room, whilst Dorothée came in to rock sleepy little Marie-Christine in her cradle. From the bottom of the stairs came a sudden sharp rapping. The cook, who was accustomed to this, stopped on the landing.

'Oh, these creditors, they come every day and now in the evening . . .' grumbled Louis-Henri in a hushed voice.

The Montespans heard Joseph Abraham – wigmaker and sympathetic landlord – out in the street, declaring (probably hand on heart), 'But I swear to you that they are not home and I do not know when they will return. What? No, that cannot be a light you see in the window on the first floor. It must be the reflection of the moon against the glass.'

Athénaïs blew out the candle. In the silence and darkness, there was an unpleasant smell of mutton-suet smoke. Fine candles of pure beeswax were rare and very costly.

'In Versailles, they burn only wax,' murmured the marquise.

Her husband whispered, 'I, too, will set sail, like your brother, on board one of His Majesty's vessels. And if the King is absent, the expedition against the pirates will not be as easy as in Marsal. Athénaïs, our fortune may lie on the other side of the ocean, in the region of Algiers . . . The most difficult part will be to find the eighteen thousand *livres* required for the equipage.'

'I forbid you, Louis-Henri!' said his wife angrily, in a low voice. 'Do you hear me? I forbid you to go off and risk your life again. I'd rather die than be three months without seeing you.'

The marquis placed his lips against hers. 'All you need to do is go with your father to Versailles for some amusement . . .'

They could hear the sound of the wheels from the creditors' carriage growing fainter down Rue Taranne, and so Marie-Christine's mother relit the candle with an ember.

'I met Louise de La Vallière at the new palace. You know, the King's favourite . . . She found me very pretty, and has invited me to come and dance before the court in a ballet by Benserade: *Hercules in Love*. The performances will be held this autumn. And since he will not be in Algeria, perhaps the King will attend . . .'

She stood up and led her husband in a dance around the cradle. Dorothée went back up to the kitchen. The marquise whispered to her husband's mouth, ''Tis in the dance that one appears as one truly is. In the eyes of the spectators, all your steps, all your gestures are telling, and display the good and bad with which art and nature have favoured or disgraced your person . . .'

But her tall marquis with his heavy wig was clumsy. He stepped on her toes, could not keep the rhythm she tried to impose. She laughed and flung her arms about him. Caressed him with her hands. Her fingers fluttered over his brow. He received caresses beyond those prescribed by conjugal duty, and received them also in the daytime, not a usual hour for husbands.

She had entwined her legs around the Gascon's hips and, once he had pulled up Marie-Christine's blanket, he carried his wife back to the landing, then upstairs to their bedroom. And the moon, in the little window of the stairway, could attest without lying that they loved each other. The marquis found his bounty in her pleas for more. Athénaïs was charming with her lover, probably her last, one supposed.

On their bed, they abandoned modesty and succumbed to their nature with delight. Over his wife's body, whilst undressing her, he justified the war he had to wage.

'His Majesty has decided to do battle with those Barbary corsairs. He's planning a brilliant campaign. Apparently, insolent Turkish pirates, protected by the Ottoman Empire, are plying the Algerian coast, pillaging and sowing terror throughout the Mediterranean, which the King now claims to control. They attack the merchant ships, steal their cargos, reduce the Christians on board to slavery, and take the women for their harems.'

'For their harems?! Aaah . . . So they become whores in the sun?'

The blonde voluptuous marquise, her hair loose, was now totally naked. Louis-Henri was surprised by an odd sphere dangling from a chain around her neck.

'What is this?'

'A cat's eye worn against the chest improves vision.'

'You believe overmuch in witchcraft.'

Her husband licked the tip of her breast, only to withdraw immediately, making a face. Athénaïs laughed at his surprise.

'I have anointed my nipples with an extract of pulp of bitter-apple to force Marie-Christine to prefer another source of food.'

Le Montespan caressed *la* Montespan's breasts. Her proud globes filled his hands.

'His Majesty's armies must capture and fortify a little Kabyle port: Gigeri. It looks just like your belly. Behind, like your breasts, the arid peaks of the Montagne Sèche descend gently in terraces to the sea.'

Beneath his fair lady's breastbone he drew with his thumb the round outline of her floating ribs.

'Gigeri is at the entrance to a small but deep gulf, the Anse aux Galères.'

Louis-Henri slipped between his wife's legs then, starting with his head between her knees, moved up along her thighs.

'We shall arrive through here. A fleet consisting of fifteen war vessels and ten transport ships carrying six thousand soldiers.'

'Of whom many will die . . .'

'If the life of a man lasted a thousand years, there would be cause for regret. But as it is so short, it matters little whether they lose it twenty years earlier or later.'

The marquis's lips brushed against a blond curly fleece.

'The aim will be to establish and fortify a permanent military base in this strategic region and to overcome the formidable enemies who covet it. I read all of this in last week's *Gazette*.'

The marquise felt her husband's warm breath, so close to her. He had stopped moving. She closed her eyes.

''Tis said that France has no more navy, or, at least, that it is in a most pitiful state.'

'The departure will not take place before two months have passed, and by that time the ships shall be made seaworthy. We must trust His Majesty.'

The husband, with a jerk of his neck, gathered momentum to plant a deep kiss within his wife's sex, but she stopped his brow with her palms and warned him that she had her menses: 'The cardinal is in residence.'

6.

His face was covered in blood and splattered with fragments of brain; it was a rout. On the beach of this legendary city and pirate stronghold which smelt of spices, Officer Montespan was kneeling in the sand beneath the stars. Nearby, swirls of light bounced off the corners of a building. As he encouraged his men in their regalia, he felt punch-drunk. A first line moved ahead fearlessly, fired and withdrew. A second line took its place, and so on. The sound of cannons added to the shooting, but the enemy were legion. Bullets and cannonballs were fired blindly and Louis-Henri's men fell, the ranks growing thinner. Bombardments and exchanges of musket fire doubled in intensity. A burst of flames signalled the explosion, under heavy fire, of one of their defences. Their blackened chests now exposed, the marquis's soldiers, once held close by fair demoiselles, fell together on the sand in a hideous parody of the act of love. And all around the thunder howled. The fire was fierce; nature unleashed death. The vaguely indecent strangeness of it all would haunt his dreams. The enemy slavered at the walls. They climbed and swarmed. All the disastrous sounds arced through the air over the glow of the battlefield: this was hell. The fire was everywhere, city walls were attacked, weapons were fired. Since eleven o'clock in the morning the situation had been untenable. After three months occupying the city of Gigeri, His Majesty's army was suddenly pushed back to the sea, this evening of All Saints' Day, 1664.

Two days earlier, Montespan had attended the deliberations of the council of war, where he had stood off to one side. There had been much discussion about how to finish the wall built from west to east, from the sea at the foot of the Montagne Sèche to the Pointe du Marabout, forming a broken semicircle. Clerville, who was in charge of the fortifications, had called out plaintively to Gadagne, the commander of the troops on the ground: 'It has suddenly become impossible to obtain the supplies of wood and limestone we need to manufacture lime! Why is this? Furthermore, you promised me that the natives would supply the materials to me. Where are they?'

The commander of the ground troops, in his armour, did not know how to reply, so Beaufort had ordered, 'If we need stones, take them from the cemetery; the wall must go through there.'

Montespan, leaning against a wall, had ventured to voice his doubts out loud: 'Are you sure? The Kabyles have already vehemently insisted that we stop the work before we reach the rocky headland at the end of the beach. The place is sacred to them; it is home to the mausoleum of a marabout and the graves of Muslim dignitaries. Sidi Mohamed, who hitherto supported our efforts to fight against the pirates, will proclaim a holy war . . .'

'Who is this captain who dares to interfere!' said the King's cousin, head of the expedition, much irritated. 'Monsieur, the presence of men such as yourself in the navy, men with poorly defined powers, is not to everyone's liking. Know that His Majesty's true warriors despise such opportunistic captains and mock them as "curly-haired marquis", or, worse yet, "petticoat bastards"!'

Montespan, contrite, fell silent and did not intervene again. He had not gone deep into debt yet again and come here just to have the monarch's cousin turn against him. He had only been trying to . . . But almost all the officers – La Châtre, Martel, Charuel, Lestancourt, etc. – had sniggered servilely as they stood round Beaufort. Only the Chevalier de Saint-Germain had observed the marquis attentively. Fat Vivonne had also doubled up with laughter (seeming to forget that he himself had bought a naval commission without hitherto ever having set his red heels on board even a riverboat). The King's cousin, very sure of himself, then said derisively, as he smoothed his perfumed moustache, 'Is the world's greatest power to fear a band of goatherds wearing cloaks? Come now, even the army's launderesses could hold the forts at Gigeri and the redoubts in the jebel of El-Korn. Go and take what you need from the cemetery.'

The soldiers had then hastened away to remove the stones from the mausoleums to finish building their wall. The following night, in the desert, a voice had chanted in Arabic, 'The dead who have been deprived of their tombs have obtained permission from heaven to take their revenge. The Prophet has appeared before them, and has promised to make the Frenchmen's cannonballs melt like wax!'

Montespan had looked worriedly upon the fires the Kabyles had lit on the hills, calling upon the faraway Turkish gunners and encampments to attack the Christian position. Which is precisely what they had done.

*

'Twas the rebellion of the Koran, driven by the sirocco! Stars pierced the walls. Everywhere the fortifications were embellished with blazing flowers and, in the sky, science forged haphazard moments of magic. Stores of powder and ammunition exploded, reducing a thousand Frenchmen all around to a smoking heap. The order to evacuate this spicy country had been given. The first boats fled, drifting with the fogbanks. Standing next to the golden drums and red cannons abandoned on the sand, Montespan, the last captain still on land, tried with his musketeers to slow the enemy's progress just long enough to allow the boats to reach the ships waiting off shore. But the Turkish army was formidable; it roared with strength, howled like a dog and crashed like the sea, with lances and iron pikes, drums and market vendors' cries. Montespan's eyes rolled in their sockets. Over his left shoulder, slung both to the front and behind, was a double saddlebag, of the type used on the back of a horse. The open leather pouches were overflowing with jewels, bars of gold, fistfuls of diamonds, fine porcelain and pearls, that he in turn had pillaged, hurriedly, from the pirates' den. He had not wanted to leave behind all the riches stolen by the Barbary corsairs, which filled the port. This would serve to compensate him for the disastrous expedition, pay all his debts and cover Athénaïs in jewels. Even at that moment, in the blinding light of cannon fire, he was thinking of *her*. His vision faltered. She was everything to him, and thanks be! Then he ran to the sea, but the soldiers were trying in vain to free a grounded launch where a hundred or more wounded lay. So, with Saint-Germain and three of his men, he returned to the beach. Saint-Germain had been wounded in the thigh, and collapsed in the water. Followed by his three companions, Louis-Henri hurled himself in fury at the first Kabyles and killed two of them with his sword (without even knowing how he did it), breaking the enemy's momentum. When he saw that at last the launch was moving away from the shore, he fell back and threw himself into the water with the last remaining soldiers. The Turks were now lined up on the beach and used the bobbing figures in the shallows for target practice. Two men were killed, but the third was saved from drowning. Saint-Germain was wounded twice more. His strength was failing. In a final burst he managed to reach up to the outstretched arms on the launch. Louis-Henri, already on board, clutched his hand and hoisted him slowly out of the sea. Saint-Germain, streaming with water, promised, 'I am very close to the King and will convey your perspicacity and heroism to him. His Majesty shall reward . . .'

Just at this moment a cannonball caught him right in the head. The chevalier's torso fell into Montespan's outstretched arms.

The waves rose and fell in the starless night amid the

muted sounds and creaking of the vessel – *La Lune* –
where the Gascon had found a berth. The ship, overloaded
with the wounded, was the last to weigh anchor. The other
transport ships – *L'Hercule* and *La Reine* – (in better
condition) carried the high command to the open sea whilst
Louis-Henri was on board his leaky, sluggish tub. It had
been poorly refitted by Rodolphe, a carpenter in Toulon.
Planks were giving way on deck, where the badly burned
survivors had left their shirts of skin. Winds drifted over
human detritus where the marquis was seated. The stumps
in that military laundry, that public bathhouse, were
wrapped in blue and white cloth; to those of a sensitive
nature, these men were more terrifying than monsters.
Over there were the sweating shapes of hundreds of
Christ-like faces with dark, gentle eyes. Not far from
Louis-Henri a man lay humming, his guts spilling out. His
mouth gaped open and his sleeves gestured in the air,
making mad signs that no one responded to. He sang,

> *'Beaufort, you're a clever one*
> *And we're right to fear ye*
> *But the way ye're reasoning*
> *We'd take ye for a gosling.'*

Long oars reached out and lapped the rhythm across the
surface of the water. In the morning, near the peninsula of
Giens, a terrible cracking sound ripped through *La Lune*:

it split in two and sank in a second, like a block of marble. One thousand two hundred wounded men from the regiments of Picardy and Normandy were lost. A few survived miraculously, clinging to a rowing boat. Montespan was pulled deep into the roiling waves. He struggled to make it back to the surface, burdened by his saddlebag, which had not left his side. The gold was weighing him down. He had to get rid of it. In the rush of swirling water as the ship touched bottom, sand rose and scratched his face; he groped blindly in his treasure and filled the pockets of his military greatcoat. He let go of the saddlebag and rose breathless to the surface, his lungs bursting. The rowing boat was far away and he had no strength left to shout. He tried to calm himself and swam among the mutilated bodies. He clung to one of them to recover his breath and, at water level, contemplated the disaster of this failed expedition against the Barbary corsairs. He was astonished to find himself thinking, 'Where is La Fontaine? Could the fabulist not pen a lovely sonnet? And Le Brun – these floating stumps, would they not inspire a pretty tapestry?' Slowly he set off, swimming across a Mediterranean in mourning, but he was truly too exhausted and, on either side, the heavy pockets of his greatcoat pulled him towards the bottom. He plunged his head underwater and tore at the seams of his coat. He watched wearily as the heavy bracelets sank straight down, with sets of diamonds and necklaces of precious stones gliding away like snakes. Broken strands of pearls hovered, and their little white globes escaped from the string. They scattered, shone and disappeared into the black water.

Finally he saw a meadow in the distance, where the last buttercups, the last daisies begged the day for mercy. He washed up on the beach, like a jellyfish. With one cheek in the sand, his lips blew bubbles, a rosary of love: 'Athénaïs . . .'

He returned to France: the war had brought no glory to his name. Once again, Montespan had come back covered not in honour but in shame and debt. His head wound in rags, he arrived on foot, and only in his shirt, at Rue Taranne. He climbed the steps, and opened the door to the kitchen. Athénaïs was sitting in a tub, taking a bath. She stood up, clutching a towel to her, then, on recognising her husband, she dropped the towel in the water. Louis-Henri looked at her round belly and gaped.

7.

'A girl, and now a boy: 'tis what is called "the King's choice"!'

Constance Abraham, the wigmaker's wife on Rue Taranne, waxed ecstatic as she gazed at the sleeping infant before picking him up. 'Ah, praise be to God, is he not lovely, this little Louis-Antoine with his fair white skin. He is the image of his mother!'

But Athénaïs, standing next to her in the shop, was wringing her hands whilst Marie-Christine, now two years of age, tugged at her mother's skirt. Athénaïs pushed her away: 'Leave me alone.'

Louis-Henri de Pardaillan was sitting in a tall armchair being shaved. He looked at his wife.

'Are you all right, Athénaïs?'

The marquise was not all right. She felt oppressed, had

difficulty breathing, and had sudden violent urges to weep. The kindly, plump wigmaker's wife thought she understood her malaise.

'Don't worry, my dear, this must be a *post partum* reaction; 'tis quite frequent. I had the same, did I not, after my son's birth. Do you recall, Joseph?'

'I do!' exclaimed the wigmaker, trying a new wig on Montespan's scalp. 'Dear me, you became so sensitive that the slightest vexation, sometimes even a compliment, brought on a fit of tears or anger. You lost your appetite, you couldn't sleep, and you were so distracted I wondered if you were not thinking about someone else.'

'Boo-hoo!'

The fair marquise burst into tears. Her husband lifted the towel from his lap to wipe the shaving cream from his face. He pushed the copper basin in front of him away and got to his feet.

'Athénaïs!'

He embraced his wife whilst their little girl clung to her, saying, 'Maman, Maman.'

'Do stop pulling on my skirt, you'll tear it! Oh!'

Athénaïs wept profusely, knelt down and immediately apologised to the little girl. 'Forgive me, Marie-Christine. I am not a proper sort of mother. I have no maternal instinct . . .'

'But you do!' protested Constance Abraham loudly, waking the infant still in her arms, who began to cry. 'Have no fear, my sweet, a *post partum* depression never lasts very long. In the space of a few hours or a few days you will once again feel like the happiest of mothers. And you will want many more children.'

'Particularly as you are fearsome fertile; your powder ignites easily,' said the wigmaker. 'Whenever your husband returns from the army, he finds you with child.'

Constance rocked Louis-Antoine, who continued to wail.

'The only question one must ask is, after the first child who so resembles her father, and the second child who so resembles his mother, who will the third child resemble?'

'Boo-hoo!'

The marquise stood up, shaken by violent spasms; she was in an extraordinary state of sadness and anxiety. Leaning over the railing of the mezzanine, the apprentices – holding curling irons, curlpapers, and sticky pomade made from cherry-tree sap for hardening the curls – were able to ogle Athénaïs's breasts from directly above. As she sobbed, her breasts bounced, and they were bigger than ever, for they were about to produce milk, and several buttons on her bodice popped open. The apprentices leant further. Athénaïs's skirt of watered silk swept over the tiles of the shop as she fled. Her hips swayed as she headed for the door at the rear and the stairway leading to their apartments. She called out in apology, 'Forgive me – I am ridiculous!'

The apprentices were breathless at the sight of the shuddering curves of her bottom. Joseph Abraham, raising his head, discovered that more than one of them was fondling himself. 'You up there, do you want me to come up and give you a hand?'

Montespan was distraught. He was sitting with traces of shaving cream on his chin, whilst wearing a wig that was still under construction, from which there dangled strands of hemp to tie the hair, and little wire teeth to untangle and restrain it.

Madame Abraham, calmly seeking to soothe the infant's cries, slipped a fleur-de-lis comforter into his mouth. Louis-Antoine instantly sucked avidly, and silence fell.

'Go upstairs and see to your wife,' the wigmaker's spouse advised the husband, 'and find something to distract her. Don't worry about the children, I can keep them until the morrow if you wish . . .'

'By then I shall have finished your wig,' added Joseph. 'Give it me that I may curl it.'

Louis-Henri de Pardaillan, his hair disarrayed from trying on the wig, thanked his landlords. He gently stroked little Louis-Antoine's cheek with the back of his index finger, and went over to his daughter, who worshipped Athénaïs as much as he himself did. Marie-Christine had been leaning against the wall beneath the bunches of fresh hair from Normandy that hung from the ceiling; now she lifted the blond strands on either side of her ears. She twirled her fingers and tried to make ringlets to imitate the hairstyle her mother had invented.

8.

When Louis-Henri entered the salon, he found his wife slumped in a chair.

'Do you feel better, Athénaïs?'

She did not reply. The marquis, standing by the window, looked out on the roofs of the city and the falling twilight. A foretaste of boredom loomed on the horizon. The marquise was chewing the inside of her cheek, making faces. Finally she announced like one of the oracles, 'Tomorrow will be worse, and the day after worse still.'

Montespan sat down at the gaming table and opened an ivory snuffbox. He handed a pinch scented with bergamot to his wife, who pursed her lips and looked away. He lit a long white pipe with a little bowl, drawing the tobacco smoke up the bone stem.

'Why do you say that?'

She adjusted her hoop, rubbed her handwarmer and stared at her husband. Then she lowered her eyes, playing with her fan, mumbled two incomplete and incomprehensible words and, leaving time suspended, lapsed into a long, unhappy silence.

'I say that because I should like to be protected from the parade of misery and creditors that my husband offers me every day! I should like to stop doing the rounds of notaries and moneylenders, and stop pledging our good name and our insignia of nobility. I should like to stop seeing you hiding on payment days!'

Louis-Henri shrugged and picked up the snuffbox.

'Ah, yes, I know I am a man of little consideration, and my credit is that of a dog at the butcher's. I am poorer than ever, but I have the curve of your neck, your nimble and frivolous arms, and the caresses, day and night, of your words. I have the wealth of your eyes. I live in your essence alone. I am rich in your countless kisses, the only thing I am rich in. What do I care if the hours seem dark if there is sunlight between us?'

'There is no sunlight in me.'

'Then I will take my chances on another war. I am told that France and Spain will fight in Flanders. I will bring you cloth from Ghent, and laurels of glory, and jewels from Antwerp, and bars of gold . . .'

'Oh, do not speak to me of gold – I would do anything for gold! I am no longer in a mood to live in poverty.'

'While I was away fighting the Barbary corsairs, might you have been corrupted by luxury when you went to dance at Versailles?'

'Naturally! I love luxury. I can scarcely sleep for love of luxury – the clothes and meals and dances and interiors and everything that goes with it!'

She spluttered, 'I will have money, and pots of it! And I need it right away, lest a catastrophe befall us.'

Louis-Henri murmured, 'For me, the worst would be to say one day, "She is no longer here."'

Madame Larivière came into the salon and placed the Montespans' dinner on the gaming table: fresh eggs and two artichoke hearts, and a pitcher of water. Athénaïs burst into tears. Louis-Henri stood up.

'Let us go to a salon in the Marais, and dine, and play hoca and piquet and quadrille. That is where one finds the best amusement. And we shall drink wines from Champagne!'

Outside, the long green flame of a poplar tree stretched towards the sky in astonishment. Its leaves shimmered against the windowpanes as if in sympathy with the marquise's shuddering sobs as she looked up through her fingers. Her husband knelt before her. He kissed her hands which were like holy relics or religious statuary made of precious metal.

'This morning, I arranged to lease our carriage horses for one year to the launderer in our street. I needed the money to repay a moneylender. Never mind, the Jew shall wait!' concluded Louis-Henri, brusquely seizing Athénaïs by the waist and sweeping up her petticoats – *modest, saucy, secret* – all at once.

Embarrassed, Madame Larivière asked, 'So what shall I do with the dinner then? Should Dorothée go up with the warming pan and heat your bed?'

The husband grabbed his wife as if she were a soldier's wench, the fair lady's thighs laid bare, her calves above his shoulders. The armchair collapsed in a volley of caresses and playful blows. Madame Larivière left the room and on meeting the servant said, 'Don't you go in there.'

And Athénaïs's little feet once again touched the floor; a flurry of kisses and good spirits abounded, and the light from the fireplace flickering on the waxed furniture danced once again. Montespan said, 'Your laughter lights my heart like a lantern in a cellar.'

'Dearest, I shall put on my last remaining jewels, my emerald necklace.'

On his head Louis-Henri wore a worn-out double wig that was no longer very fashionable. In Rue Taranne, they hailed two sedan chairs. Athénaïs entered the first chair, calling, 'To the Hôtel de Montausier!'

The bearers of the second chair, where Louis-Henri had taken his seat, did their best to keep up.

9.

In the Marais salon, Louis-Henri scarcely recognised his wife. That afternoon she had been so desperate, yet now she was in her element. She wandered amongst the gaming tables. A good number of people had come up to Paris from court and they immediately fixed their gaze upon her, went up to her and paid her compliments. 'What a marvellous gown, and you wear it with such grace! Was it not woven in secret by fairies; no living soul could have produced such a thing!' Athénaïs's conversation sparkled with charming words more naïve than they were shrewd, although they were shrewd all the same. She was offered some chocolate from a silver platter and pretended to take herself in hand. 'I shan't have too many . . . The Marquise de Coëtlogon told me that it was not her position as a slave-trader but rather her overfondness for chocolates as a child that caused her to give birth to a little boy as black as the devil!'

All around her there was laughter, and clouds of bean powder fell from rocking wigs. Athénaïs walked by the billiard table, where there was talk of a duc from Auvergne who had recently been appointed a maréchal of the realm, and she remarked, 'A maréchal who swoons away at the mere sight of young wild boar.' Her ferocious humour enchanted as it hit the bull's eye. 'He's neither man, nor woman, nor little; he's a little woman.'

'Oh!'

The courtiers guffawed. They drew back their lips to reveal broken, rotten teeth, but they sucked on cinnamon and cloves to sweeten their breath. One aristocrat counselled another: 'Cavities are due to dental worms that one must kill with poultices of stag's-horn powder mixed with honey.' And they raised their glasses of fennel spirits in a toast and asked Montespan, 'What do you think?' Beneath the gilded ceiling, Louis-Henri, in his worn lace cravat, threadbare jerkin and misshapen organ-pipe hose, turned his dirty jacket and did not answer. He did not feel at ease among these people with whom one always had to have one's mouth open in order to laugh or speak. Just ahead of him he recognised Athénaïs's characteristic hairstyle, hair drawn back and kept in place by a hoop, then falling on either side of her neck. He seized her by the waist from behind, leant towards her ear. She turned round. It was not Athénaïs but a stranger with the same hairstyle. He apologised: 'Please forgive me, I thought that . . .' and he noticed that many of the women at the gathering that evening had adopted his wife's *hurluberlu*. A duc (Lauzun), of ordinary height, sniggered at the way the women presented themselves. 'If women already were what they become through artifice, their faces as lit up and leaden with the rouge they wear, they would be inconsolable.'

Three little dogs from Boulogne were at his side. When Lauzun farted, he accused them of the misdeed. Montespan moved away. An orchestra of violins was playing a mixture of *branles* and *courants*. Candied fruit was served by a cohort of lackeys. At one of the hoca tables, Louis-Henri made a small wager and played cards. He encountered mocking whispers and felt gazes upon him, but he only had eyes for his own blonde.

Stretched out on a divan and much in demand, she resembled a magnificent voluptuous toy. The sparkling scene beneath the stucco ceiling, embellished with flowers, fruit and pastoral scenes, pleased her. She delighted in the volatile nature of words.

'Madame de Ludres has been left by her lover and no longer talks of a retreat among the Carmelites; 'twas enough to have spoken of it. Her chambermaid fell at her feet to prevent her; how can one resist such a thing?'

The frills and flounces on everyone's clothing came alive,

whilst Athénaïs continued her story. 'She is fatter by a foot since her misfortune befell her. Most astonishing. Every whale I meet reminds me of her. The other day, when she climbed out of her carriage, I caught a glimpse of one of her legs, almost as fat as my chest. But to be fair, I must say that I have lost a great deal of weight!'

'Aaaah!'

Women stood up and pissed beneath their gowns; servants appeared with mops. Montespan was filled with tenderness as he watched Athénaïs in her endeavours to shine forth, amidst the laughter she provoked, like a child playing at being a princess. No doubt because Louis-Henri's armed exploits had all come to a sudden end, and he had been unable to find glory on the battlefield and ensure the monarch's favour, his wife had determined to succeed, with the means at her disposal. When speaking of Madame de Guiche, who had been disgraced at the palace, Athénaïs dealt the death blow. 'She is asymmetrical down to her very eyes. They are two different colours, and as our eyes are the mirror of our soul, such a departure from nature must serve as a warning to those who go near her not to set great store by her friendship.'

Athénaïs professed the most murderous truths quite absently in a naïve tone of voice.

'Madame de Guiche curls her hair, powders her nose and eats all at once, the same fingers in turn holding a powder puff and the bread. She eats her powder and butters her hair. Which all makes for a delicious luncheon and a charming hairstyle!'

In this egotistical, frivolous company in the Marais, infinitely uncharitable by nature and where the struggle for favour could take a most savage turn, Athénaïs excelled.

'The King's confessor? That Father La Chaise is a veritable commode. He has a mistress, Madame de Bretonvilliers, whom I refer to as "the Cathedral".'

La Montespan had a mocking word for everyone: 'Mademoiselle Thingamajig? Lovely from head to toe but no more wit than a kitten.' 'Madame Whatsit: her grace and beauty have turned to dust.' 'The Duc de What's-his-name is so fond of entertaining that his tablecloth is nailed down. He has a fake diamond that may dazzle the dull-witted but cannot deceive those who think.' 'Mademoiselle Thingy is equally self-important and unimportant.' 'Monsieur is the silliest woman in the world and his wife, Madame, the silliest man ever seen. Her husband gives her children with the help of a rosary that he winds around his staff, thereby causing prolific clicking beneath the conjugal sheets.'

'Ooooh!'

Laughter splattered from the stinking toothless gums of idiotic powdered courtiers . . . What could have been more magnificent than the clothing of all these people! As for Louis-Henri, he felt gauche in his old rags, beneath his enormous, heavy, poorly mended wig. Amidst the elegantly casual attire and coloured mantillas, the earrings and the necklaces, he felt ashamed, cumbersome, encumbered. Athénaïs, bowing her head to acclaim, now looked up and noticed her husband standing alone on the other side of the room. She got up and went over to him.

'Are you not bored, Louis-Henri? Would you prefer we went home? Are you all right?'

'I'm well enough. To see you so glad to be here makes me very happy.'

'You are kind . . .'

'When you enter the room, the other women become invisible. When you speak, you strike them dumb. You are so amusing, so lovely . . .'

'Marquise, your husband is right,' exclaimed their hostess, the Duchesse de Montausier, coming up to the Montespans; in her arms she was holding a cat wearing necklaces and earrings. 'In France there is no woman wittier than you are, and very few who are your equal. To come within your sight is to expose oneself to your wicked tongue!'

'Aye,' said Athénaïs with a smile, 'I do have a talent for saying pleasant and singular things, always fresh, which no one, not even I myself, expects.'

'Ah!'

Le Montespan chuckled, as did the Duchesse de Montausier. Her husband joined them and laughed as well, saying, 'As for your beauty, Marquise, one autumn day you came to dance at Versailles and I said to His Majesty,

"Look, Sire, there is a most beautiful statue; when I saw it, I wondered whether it was not created by the chisel of Girardon, and I was most surprised when I was told it was alive." The King replied, "A statue if you like but, God be praised, 'tis a beautiful creature.'"

Louis-Henri was astounded. 'Do you hear, Athénaïs, the greatest monarch on earth finds you to his liking!'

La Montespan blushed. The Duchesse de Montausier – sixty years of age, with thinning frizzy white hair – was followed by a black slave. Attired in richly coloured garments, with a turban on his head, he carried a parasol (in her apartments!). He was like one of those little domestic animals that were all the rage, and the colour of his skin caused the whiteness of the hostess's to stand out all the more as she took Athénaïs by the arm and led her into another salon.

'Precisely, my dear, I was thinking . . . Queen Marie-Thérèse, fearful that she might be providing a harem for the King, has decided to dismiss all her ladies-in-waiting and replace them with respectable spouses.'

'His Majesty had a tendency to come and pick the lovely flowers in the Queen's "garden",' the Duc de Montausier explained to Montespan, who nodded his head knowingly.

'The King will select six ladies before the end of December,' continued the hostess. 'The places will be limited to two princesses, two duchesses, two marquises or comtesses. Almost all the women at court aspire to such a position, and each has her own cabal.'

'Let us hope that this time none of them will become his mistress,' remarked the duc, behind Athénaïs, who turned round and said, 'God save me from such a fate, and if I should become one, I should be most shamed in the eyes of the Queen.' Louis-Henri approved her words with a nod of his head.

'The princesses of Elboeuf and Baden, the duchesses of Armagnac and Créqui, and the Marquise d'Humière all seem to be in a good position to be chosen,' predicted their hostess. 'There was also the Comtesse de Guiche, but, as you so amusingly related just now, she is in disgrace, therefore . . . Do you see what I mean, Monsieur?' asked the duchesse beneath her parasol, turning to Montespan, who stood there with his mouth agape. 'I might make enquiries of the monarch, if you would allow me, regarding the appointment of your wife as lady-in-waiting to the Queen.'

'Oh, that would be splendid for Athénaïs!' exclaimed Louis-Henri.

His wife looked at him with eyes wide open; she could not believe what she had heard. 'Lady-in-waiting . . . at Versailles! Do you think that might be possible, Madame de Montausier?'

'You have all the qualities required: so many charms, so much appeal, such allure! In a word: a real arsenal!'

'As for yourself, speaking of arsenals . . .' whispered the duc to Montespan, 'Marsal and Gigeri have left you greatly in debt and brought you nothing, so I've heard. Bear in mind that ladies-in-waiting have a handsome pension!' he added, to convince Louis-Henri, who had no need of convincing. 'Naturally, the position does not include the husband.'

'Naturally.'

In one corner, by a red curtain, players screamed, pulled out their hair and wept uncontrollably. The Marquis de Beaumont had just lost his entire fortune in one game. He remained imperturbably calm. Everyone knew that in a short while, when he went home, he would blow his brains out. Athénaïs said, 'Let us go. My head is spinning.'

After their goodbyes and thanks and promises to return soon, the Montespans took their leave. On Place Royale, a squatting hunchback got to his feet and came out from under an arcade. He was holding a large lantern at the end of a pole.

'Five *sols* to guide you! What are five *sols* to a gentleman who wears red heels, like your good self, Monsieur?'

The marquis gave his address and the coin with it.

'You are sensible,' said the lantern-bearer appreciatively. 'The darkest, most deserted forest in the realm is a place of safety compared to Paris . . .'

His luminous balloon bobbed and swayed. Shadows fell and stretched across walls. The lovers of Rue Taranne walked arm in arm as they followed the hunchback. Athénaïs laid her head on her tall husband's shoulder.

'If I were to obtain the position, we could buy back the hire of our coach horses.'

She took a cat's eye from her purse and kissed it. On Rue Saint-Benoît, Louis-Henri said, 'I did not know that the King had seen you . . .'

'And I saw him as well.'

'Indeed, and how is he? Once, in a crowd, I was able to see the top of his wig, nothing more.'

'He is short. He has dark eyes with an exotic charm.'

Outside the door of the Montespans' modest dwelling, the lame lantern-bearer turned round to wait for them. He seemed able to read the clouds of condensation that rose from their lips on that chill early December night. Then, like a winged insect, he scurried to the Châtelet, mumbling, 'Exotic charm . . .'

10.

'Grrrr . . . Oh, oh, oh! . . . Frrrr . . .'

Athénaïs growled, pulled back her ringlets and pointed them skywards like the devil's horns. She made a dreadful face, rolling her eyes. 'Beware, I'm a demon . . .'

Her three-year-old daughter – thin, pale Marie-Christine – ran away across the wigmaker's tiled floor, shrieking with terror and happiness, whilst her mother chased her towards the stairway leading to the Montespans' apartments.

'Grrr . . . Oh, oh, oh!'

'Your wife is feeling better, it would seem, after the repercussions of her child-bearing,' remarked Joseph Abraham in the shop, placing a new wig on Louis-Henri's scalp. 'Not at all like she was yesterday. Might it be your night upon the town which did her so much good?'

'She learnt that the King has noticed her and, this morning, she was informed that he wishes to meet her this very day.'

'The King! But to what end?'

'One cannot say until it has been confirmed. Athénaïs claims that it is bad luck to announce something before 'tis due. Is that not true, my dearest?' he called to the mirror placed in front of him so that he might admire his wig, and where he could see the reflection of the young marquise in the guise of Beelzebub as she pursued Marie-Christine.

'Grrr . . . Oh, oh, oh! . . . Frrr . . .'

The child hid between her father's legs; he was sitting in an armchair whose arms were reinforced with tacked padded leather patches. While his wig was being powdered with starch, he caressed his daughter's fine hair; she was crimson, her heart racing. Madame Abraham was holding the infant in her arms and she smiled.

'Your children were charming yesterday, Athénaïs. Louis-Antoine suckled his wet nurse and slept through the night. And the little girl, when she sees you again and you play with her, she seems so happy . . . It's as if she's come back to life.'

'Grrr . . . Oh, oh, oh! . . . Frrr . . .'

The child ran out from between her father's legs. Once again mother and daughter galloped round the room, whilst Montespan and the wigmaker began to talk of politics.

'What do you think of the new war that is in the offing, against Spain this time?' Monsieur Abraham asked the marquis, shaving him all the while.

'His Majesty is quite right! Philip IV tried to make his daughter Marie-Thérèse renounce the succession to Spain once she had married Louis, and in compensation agreed to award her a dowry of five hundred thousand *écus* in gold, to be paid in three instalments . . . If the dowry was not paid, the renunciation became invalid. That is a fact, set down in writing. Spain has never had the means to settle the promised amount – considerable, to be sure. In consequence, now that Philip has died, Louis is demanding, on behalf of his wife, her share in the succession. In the name of the right of devolution, France is laying claim to Spanish Flanders. Philip IV's widow has just rejected a written ultimatum. She will yield nothing, not even one hamlet in the Netherlands. Her response does not take into account the reality of the situation. The King of France clearly has might on his side. However, there are bound to be uprisings along the border in the Pyrenees . . .'

'Will you take part in this war, too?'

'I should like to . . .' sighed tall Louis-Henri, getting to his feet and squirting himself with his perfume: liquorice and orange-flower water. 'I should like to . . . All the more so as I understand His Majesty. As a husband, he is opposed to such usurpation. And rightfully so! There are limits to what one can accept. Certain things simply are not done.'

Athénaïs came up behind Louis-Henri and sniffed his neck, then lowered her eyes. 'You smell good,' she said. 'I would recognise that smell anywhere. Even when I am very old and blind and you have abandoned me in a hospice, if you came into the room, I would know you.'

He turned round and she kissed him.

'Don't go to war. If all goes as I hope, I assure you that through my good offices I will make His Majesty forget your uncle's indiscretions and you, too, shall have your place at court. Let me act, this time.'

'No, Athénaïs, the King must notice me on the battlefield! If he does not see me, I quite simply do not exist. When he declares in speaking of someone, "I do not know him, he is a man I never see," it means that he is nothing. The monarch's smile is life, his silence is death . . . But when one spends one's time robbing Peter to pay Paul, where is one to find money enough for a company of eighty-four well-mounted soldiers, in addition to the equipage of valets, and thirty horses and mules?'

Around her neck the marquise was wearing an emerald necklace, which she now unfastened. 'Sell my necklace. A pawnbroker on Rue des Anglais told me it was worth fifteen hundred *livres*. This will enable you to outfit a few soldiers.'

'But – and you? You are going to Saint-Germain-en-Laye . . .'

'And so? I will go bare-necked.'

'Ah, true love . . .' Constance Abraham said with a sigh.

Marie-Christine put her arms round her mother's knees. The child pulled on the back of the pale-pink dress, accentuating the curve of the marquise's bottom, the narrowness of her waist, the shape of her thighs . . . it was as if she were naked. The apprentices leaning over the railing in the mezzanine stood open-mouthed. They watched from above as she called out, 'Farewell, gentlemen! I shan't be back for several days. The Duchesse de Montausier will accommodate me in her chateau and lend me some gowns. I must fly! I would not want to miss the coach for Saint-Germain! Monsieur de Montespan, I entrust you with our children. As for you, my little girl . . . Grrr . . . oh, oh, oh! . . . Frrr . . .'

Marie-Christine ran off. Her mother turned round and lifted her arms high in the air. Her breasts, on rising, spilt over the top of her bodice, revealing her nipples. It was too much. The apprentices, in pairs, grabbed each other from behind in a frenzy as they stood by the railing. They stuck out their tongues like madmen. Joseph Abraham, who had noticed, took a rod and climbed up to the mezzanine, banging on the steps as he went.

'Stop it, you're like rutting dogs!'

11.

The Montespans' servant Dorothée, who was now eleven years of age, and already rather stooped and timid, was pouring water flavoured with eucalyptus leaf onto Louis-Henri's fingers. The marquis wiped his hands on the tablecloth of the gaming table, then lifted a pewter spoon to his lips. Madame Larivière stood next to him, hands on hips, and enquired, 'What do you think of the soup? Can you taste the lemon – I mixed the juice with some egg yolks and verjuice.'

'Yes, it's very good.'

'Next you shall have a salad of hop sprouts, and for dessert, "vilaines d'Anjou" pears. And I've filled a jug with Cahors wine.'

'Thank you, Madame Larivière.'

Montespan, whilst eating, was reading the foreign

affairs page in the *Mercure Galant*, which lay next to his plate, when the door to the salon opened. A beam of light entered. He raised his eyes and his face lit up.

'Hogs' swill! Where have you been these ten days?'

'Have you heard how he speaks to me, a lady-in-waiting to Her Majesty the Queen of France?'

'You're not!' The marquis bounded out of his chair and opened his arms to receive his wife's urgent embrace. Their daughter, sitting by the fireplace, ran to her mother's legs. The collision of the three bodies gave off a cloud of golden dust in the sunbeam coming through the window, and a shower of stars slowly drifted onto the cradle where Louis-Antoine was sleeping.

'I am so happy for you!' cried the loving husband, then planted his mouth full on his wife's own.

Madame Larivière looked away. Louis-Henri's big hands grabbed Athénaïs's buttocks. The cook, with a jerk of her chin, motioned to the servant to leave the room, then she asked, 'Will Madame be having lunch as well?'

'And that is not all!' declared the marquise to her husband. 'The King is also offering me the succession to all the butcher shops in Paris!'

'The what?' asked Louis-Henri, astounded.

'The tax which the butchers pay when they pass on their produce. Before, the aristocrat who owned this privilege received an *aboivrement* from the butchers – a feast and a cake made with eggs – but now it's gold coins.'

'And the King has made you such a gift? What a curious idea.'

'It is to help us.'

'But why should he do so?'

'I believe His Majesty appreciates me. I cheer him by imitating the expressions and simpering ways of the girls who seek to capture his royal heart. Ever since I arrived at Versailles, Louis has been attending the Queen's going-to-bed ceremony. He comes to hear me chronicle the day's events: no one escapes the gibes of my wit. He has deserted his mistress La Vallière to come and listen to me. The Queen is most pleased with me and has heaped her thanks upon me.'

'This is wonderful!' said Montespan, sitting down at the table, whilst the cook served the marquise and she joined him.

'What do you make of—'

'Have you inadvertently dropped a lemon in the soup? How different from the delicacies prepared by the master chefs at Versailles,' remarked Athénaïs, putting her spoon down and pushing her dish away in front of Madame Larivière, who registered the affront.

'For this evening I had planned some cauliflower steamed in a nutmeg bouillon. But perhaps Madame would prefer a sole – the partridge of the sea – or some woodcocks with buttered toast.'

'I won't be dining here. I merely came to fetch some

gowns before returning to court. Tell the servant to prepare them for me.'

'You're leaving already?' asked her husband.

His spouse, her elbows on the table, interlaced her fingers and rested her chin on them. 'You know that His Majesty also appreciates you, Louis-Henri.'

'Me?'

'Yes, you, and with regard to your company of light cavalry and miquelets, for which you are lacking funds, the King has ordered the State to pay the difference.'

'You jest! He never does anything of the like for anyone, so for . . .'

'This message from Louvois is addressed to you,' Athénaïs said with a smile, taking a letter from beneath her bodice.

'The Secretary of State for War would write to me?'

The Gascon could not get over what he had just learnt, and he read the letter out loud.

'Monsieur de Montespan,

Notwithstanding His Majesty's resolution to abstain from lending any support to cavalry companies, he did nevertheless order me to inform you that he is willing to support your company considering the expense you have incurred in order to equip it.

'Well, I never . . .

> *'I am presently informing the Duc de Noailles of His Majesty's decision in your favour, in order that he may expedite your company to a district of Roussillon, where there will be greater opportunity to serve the King—*

'On the Spanish border? I would have preferred to follow him to Flanders, but . . .

> *'—so that you shall thereby be worthy of a regiment at the first opportunity that arises.*

'What? A regiment, for me?

> *'I am most pleased for your sake about the consideration His Majesty has shown you, and assure you that I shall always facilitate further such consideration as may come your way.*

> *François Michel Le Tellier*
> *Marquis de Louvois*

'Further consideration? But why?'

Athénaïs avoided raising her eyes from the edge of the table.

'I don't know . . .'

Madame Larivière watched her for a moment, then picked up the dishes, which no one seemed to be interested in. She left the salon and on the landing she called out, 'Dorothée!' Louis-Henri was touched to see the way Marie-Christine, standing by the chair, wrapped her arms around one of her mother's as she sat with her palms face down on her lap.

The little girl rubbed her cheek against her mother's elbow. Eyes closed, she seemed to be breathing again, as if all the time that this maternal warmth had been in Versailles she had been living in a state of breathlessness. Her father understood. He, too, loved to caress Athénaïs. She was so gracious, the most beautiful woman in all of France – as perfect as the idealised stone statues seen only in the royal parks. And this creature was his wife! He could have wept for happiness. The perfect oval of Athénaïs's face; her high blond eyebrows; her mouth that puckered comically whenever she was astonished or thoughtful; all this belonged to him.

Her mind no doubt still full of gondola processions along the Grand Canal, her bored gaze now lingered on her shabby home in Rue Taranne. She despaired of the peeling grey-green walls; the broken skirting boards the colour of crushed raspberry saddened her; the worn leather strap chairs seemed to bind her hand and foot; the threadbare Moses tapestry dispirited her and the sight of the black tannin of the old-fashioned furniture was like a long-forgotten nightmare. Her daughter bored her, clinging to her like that. She pushed her away: 'Stop it now!' then declared to her husband, 'We must find a solution. You will be at the Spanish border and I will be at court; I shan't be able to look after two children.'

'Would you like me to take Marie-Christine to Bonnefont on my way to Roussillon? My mother can look after her.'

Athénaïs did not reply. She felt, stirring within her, aspirations towards another existence; she was already impatient to be going from fête to fête in His Majesty's wake. She murmured, 'One day there were gusts of rain and the Sun King removed his hat and placed it on my head before the astonished courtiers and led me back to the Palais.'

'What spell have you cast on the monarch?'

Louis-Henri watched as his blonde became paler than the pearls around her neck.

'Are you wearing a new necklace? Is it also the King who . . .'

Happy, he struck the table with his two large paws.

'Such consideration! A title as lady-in-waiting, a Parisian succession, a helping hat in a shower, a string of pearls . . . And presently I shall have my colonel's brevet! At last His Majesty has given up his hostility towards my family and has restored it to its former favour.'

He stood up; a ray of sun left a broad swathe of light on

the uneven grey tiles. He went and opened the window, and in the beam of light he exalted the diurnal star. His wife watched as he called out, '*Vive le roi!*'

12.

Athénaïs found herself staying for longer and longer periods in Saint-Germain-en-Laye, at the Château de Marly, or at Versailles, returning later and later to her marital home. Her husband did not take offence. He sat patiently through the succession of grey days in the little apartment, now virtually deserted by his spouse. He was waiting for the War of Devolution against Spain and philosophically whiled away his ennui without his wife: she was off in an orbit circling ever nearer to the Sun King. One evening when she returned displaying a dizzying décolletage, Madame Larivière was watching from the landing and, as Athénaïs went by in the stairway, she grumbled to Dorothée, 'Making such a display of her breast merely broadcasts the fact that the creature is for hire.'

Louis-Henri was in the salon standing over the maps of the Pyrenees he had unrolled on the gaming table, holding a glass of water. Just as he was lifting the glass to his lips, his wife entered the room. He saw her eyes were lowered. She had not changed colour, but he who knew her well found her discomfited all the same.

'Louis-Henri, I have a favour to request of you, but you must grant it me. Should you fail to, I confess I should be most vexed.'

Athénaïs wanted to leave the court behind, and she asked her husband to take her away to Bonnefont. 'It is all too much – being lady-in-waiting, and receiving gold from the butchers' shops, and the King's contribution to your company – it is all too much, living at court. Let us go and live with your mother and our children in Guyenne.'

Montespan refused to consider it. 'In an uncomfortable old chateau in the wilderness of the far reaches of the realm, surrounded by country bumpkins? You will be bored.'

She begged Louis-Henri to forgo his military aspirations and take her away. He laughed at her distress and made fun of her when she insisted.

'Versailles is a dreadful place,' she lamented; 'there is not a single person whose head is not turned by it. The court changes even the best of souls.'

'It shall not change you. I have greater trust in you than you have yourself.'

*

Then one day Athénaïs arrived red and embarrassed, with a new pearl necklace. She hid her face on her husband's chest, with his scent of liquorice and orange-flower water. 'There is still time to leave.'

Louis-Henri, in his Indian dressing gown, smiled and spoke to her quite formally. 'Pray explain yourself, Madame!'

'Explain myself? Then you should know that this fête everyone is talking about, entitled "Disguised Love", where I shall figure as the water nymph and His Majesty as Neptune brandishing a trident in gilded wood – the King is giving this fête in my honour.'

'Well, are you not lovely enough to deserve a fête in your honour?'

'Louis-Henri, since I must spell it out, the King is in love with me.'

'Well then! A King's love is no insult.'

'Louis-Henri, I am afraid.'

'What can you be afraid of?'

'Last night, at Versailles, I had a dream. In the dream, I was climbing a mountain. When I reached the peak, I was dazzled by a brilliant cloud, before plunging into a darkness so deep that my fear awoke me.'

13.

'Louis-Henri, do you think I am the devil?'

'Of course not, why do you say such a thing? Do you think I am Marie-Christine? Are you going to growl at me? Grrr . . . oh, oh, oh ! . . . Frrr.'

On a clear night, in their bed of twisted columns in Rue Taranne, the marquise had raised her husband's lids and roused him from sleep. An infinitely pale glow of moonlight hovered and shimmered over her face. Her eyes were two large holes. She told her husband a story she had never told him before.

'During my childhood in Lussac, I often shivered with fear listening to my nurse at night, when she would tell me the family legend about an ancestor in the sixteenth century. Renée Taveau, the daughter of the Baron de Mortemart, had married my great-grandfather, François de Rochechouart. But the young bride quickly fell ill and was dying. She was no longer breathing, had no pulse, and they buried her, not yet twenty years of age, with her flawless diamond ring. This gem is too brilliant to be left in the obscurity of a tomb, thought a covetous valet. He waited until nightfall to raid the burial place and steal the jewel. But it was impossible to slide the ring from her stiff, bent finger. So he decided to cut it off by biting the joint. When he dug his teeth into the icy flesh, the "dead" woman suddenly awoke with a scream. Naturally, the word spread quickly that Renée was a diabolical creature with supernatural powers. However, the husband was so glad to be with his wife again that he gave her a child – my grandfather.'

The naked Montespans found warmth under a woven blanket from Holland, mingling their souls. As the walnut bed creaked, Athénaïs declared to her husband, 'I am the resurrection of a dead body . . .'

'Do you mean a miracle? That I knew, that you are a miracle.'

'Do you think that I am a demon?'

Louis-Henri paused above his blonde: her sex was voracious, man-eating, avid for the milk of his flesh. As for other women — fie upon them! He never thought of them. *She* was here, supple and refreshing; the dreams she offered him were boundless. He became a saint, it seemed. A prayer was chanted in a voice so hushed it could have been mistaken for a flight of angels. Then . . . Hush your murmuring, Morality, you could not control their intimate bond.

14.

'In my father's garden the lilacs are in bloom
In my father's garden the lilacs are in bloom
And all the birds in all the world come here to make
    their nest

> My little blonde lassie
> Let me sleep beside you now
> My little blonde lassie
> Sleep beside me now

All the birds in all the world come here to make their nest
All the birds in all the world come here to make their nest
Quails and turtledoves and pretty partridges too'

On the great royal highway leading to Bordeaux, a uniformed miquelet, on foot at the head of the column, was singing at the top of his lungs, bellowing the couplets of a song that the other soldiers would soon drum out with their heels behind him, as they picked up the refrain:

> *'My little blonde lassie*
> *Let me sleep beside you now*
> *My little blonde lassie*
> *Sleep beside me now'*

This miquelet, a Sergeant Cartet by name, was a thick brutish fellow, fond of his blade. He wore his moustache as if it were the hilt of a dagger, curled back with a curling iron, and he sang, his mouth open wide on his black, crumbling teeth;

> *'Quails and turtledoves and pretty partridges too*
> *Quails and turtledoves and pretty partridges too*
> *And my lovely dove who sings both day and night*
> *My little blonde lassie*
> *Let me sleep beside you now*
> *My little blonde lassie*
> *Sleep beside me now'*

They sang the refrain in a chorus, and all the accents of France were to be heard, for the enlisted men came from many parts of the realm. They followed Cartet, who was marching them to Catalonia, and they listened as he belted out:

> *'And my pretty dove who sings both day and night*
> *And my pretty dove who sings both day and night*
> *Who sings for all the girls who have not found a mate*
> *My little blonde lassie*
> *Let me sleep beside beside you now*
> *My little blonde lassie*
> *Sleep beside me now*
> *Who sings for all the girls who have not found a mate*
> *Who sings for all the girls who have not found a mate*
> *She does not sing for me, for I've a lovely one'*

Montespan, on horseback, smiled when he came upon the sergeant with the fearsome moustache singing of a lovely mate.

> *'My little blonde lassie*
> *Let me sleep beside you now*
> *My little blonde lassie*
> *Sleep beside me now*
> *She does not sing for me, for I've a lovely one*
> *She does not sing for me, for I've a lovely one*
> *Tell us then, my lovely, where's your husband dear?'*

Louis-Henri looked away and thought of Athénaïs: before he had left Paris, he had signed a 'general power of attorney granting the right to govern all their common property during his absence', for he trusted her wholly and entirely.

'My little blonde lassie
Let me sleep beside you now
My little blonde lassie
Sleep beside me now
Tell us then, my lovely, where's your husband dear?
Tell us then, my lovely, where's your husband dear?
He's gone off to Holland, the Dutch have kept him there'

The marquis found himself humming along.

'My little blonde lassie
Let me sleep beside you now
My little blonde lassie
Sleep beside me now'

The loving husband rode alongside the convoy, a pale, handsome cavalryman beneath the banner of the Duc de Noailles. In his saddle holsters he had slipped his fair lady's stockings. Sometimes he lifted them out to sniff them.

The road climbed up the first hills. They went past meadows into a silent village, where not a cockerel or an anvil was to be heard; the inhabitants had bolted themselves indoors. Not a cloud, not a breath of air, nothing was stirring. Wasps flew here and there, black and yellow.

The journey was long and so was their marching song – fortunately, for it passed the time. They had left at the end of January and would not reach their destination until the beginning of March, to combat the Spanish Angelets. Away on the horizon there were peasants in the fields, who moved away when they noticed the soldiers.

'He's gone off to Holland, the Dutch have kept him there.
He's gone off to Holland, the Dutch have kept him there.
What would you give, fair lady, your husband for to see?'

Following the troops was a baggage train, burdened with trunks and pulled by mules. Montespan, in his blue coat, the plumes of his hat rising into the sky, pulled on the reins and let the miquelets march ahead of him, in their outfits of red broadcloth; many of them would be killed. 'To die, to sleep,' says Shakespeare. If 'tis but that . . . thought the marquis dismissively. He pulled up next to a cart covered in a tarpaulin and lifted up the grey canvas.

'My little blonde lassie
Let me sleep beside you now
My little blonde lassie
Sleep beside me now

What would you give, fair lady, your husband for to see?
What would you give, fair lady, your husband for to see?
I'd give all Versailles, Paris and Saint-Denis'

Beneath the tarpaulin, sheltered from the light, little Marie-Christine slept stretched out on sacks of gunpowder, dried meat and salt, among bushels of candles and jugs of vinegar. Louis-Henri would make a detour through Bonnefont and leave his daughter with Chrestienne de Zamet.

'My little blonde lassie
Let me sleep beside you now
My little blonde lassie
Sleep beside me now
I'd give all Versailles, Paris and Saint-Denis
I'd give all Versailles, Paris and Saint-Denis
The towers of Notre-Dame and my own church bells'

Perhaps the child was dreaming of her mother as she moved her lips. Sometimes it seemed she, too, was murmuring:

'My little blonde lassie
Let me sleep beside you now
My little blonde lassie
Sleep beside me now'

15.

The air smelt strongly of battle here. By Puigcerdá, red bursts of grapeshot whistled through the blue sky. Wounds ruptured flesh. The air was lethal, a ghastly storm of treacherous laughter.

Sergeant Cartet was crawling forward on his stomach and elbows to join Montespan where he sheltered behind a rock, near his horse.

'Captain, a military postilion has just brought news. The King's campaign in Flanders is like a stroll in the fresh air. Turenne is nimbly seizing the entire region from the regent of Spain. Theirs is a triumphal journey. Entire cities are crumbling like houses of cards. Whenever he takes a city, His Majesty gives a masked ball. The fair Flemish ladies come and visit the court that conquers with singing and dancing.'

'Well, confounded vassal, 'tis not the same here in the Pyrenees!'

All around Louis-Henri lyrical scenes were accompanied by fife and drum, on steep land hot with the sun and red with blood. Cannonballs flew in a crash of colours. A cruel lead missile shone as it whistled and clove through the air. Cartet ducked his head and said, 'His Majesty is having a rousing good time, capturing Flanders from his royal coach. He sits opposite the Queen, with his favourite, Louise de La Vallière, on his right, and on his left your wife.'

'Oh, is my wife there? I did not know. Excellent, Sergeant! Let us not take root here on this mountainside!'

The marquis, with his musket in his hand, jumped on his mount and rode off, bare-headed. Boldness, despair, such pathetic grandeur . . . He was wounded ten or twelve times in his arms, shoulders and legs. And still he resisted, but his wounded animal died beneath him. On his feet again, without a horse and greatly weakened by the loss of blood from his wounds, he thought of this war on the border of the Pyrenees – a pitiful tale that had lasted for nearly six months now.

The region of Catalonia, given to the Crown of France by the treaty of the Pyrenees in 1659, had to pay more taxes now than when it had been Spanish, including the gabelle salt tax, and this had greatly incensed the populace. There had been uprisings. The peasants had summoned the

Angelets to the sound of the tocsin; they were financed by Spain and there was no fighting by the rules. The French soldiers, poorly prepared for guerrilla warfare, for ambushes in the heart of hostile, extreme wilderness, had been decimated. The marquis had lost many of his light cavalry. The others had been forced to flee and Montespan, covered in blood, was delirious. He saw his wife everywhere. There she was, behind the rose bushes. With its captain injured, the company sounded the retreat. The marquis felt the weight of a terrible solitude overcome him. He was on the ground, injured, among all those whose backs were burning, but Cartet, on his knees and laughing, put his large arms around him: 'Captain, Captain, stay alive! Spain and France are to sign a peace treaty in Aix-la-Chapelle. Louis has revoked the gabelle in Roussillon . . .'

Louis-Henri stared at the sergeant's face, confusing it with his wife's.

'What strange teeth you show me when you smile, Athénaïs! Those that are whole are scarcely white, and the others are mere black fragments. They hardly hold to your gums. If you cough you might find them loose and bloody at your feet. Ah, do not indulge any thoughts of laughing for a livelihood, my fair one,' he said to an astonished Cartet. 'Hide those stumps, dearest, and frequent funeral processions instead; make yourself a mourner.'

The sergeant also informed him that the military

postilion had brought a letter from Louvois. Cartet read the missive: '"Monsieur de Montespan, having considered that your presence in the service of His Majesty is no longer required in the place where you are, I am writing this letter to inform you that the King now finds it meet that you should make your way hence and go wherever your own affairs might lead you",' but Louis-Henri did not hear, for he had fainted away.

Rough Cartet, with his dagger-hilt moustache, and his hands more deadly than a machine and stronger than an ox (he who had sung during the journey in his thick voice that he had a lovely mate), delicately lifted Athénaïs's husband.

'As we head north, I will leave him at his chateau in Bonnefont.'

16.

'Ah, you have a limp now, Monsieur le marquis?' asked Madame Larivière, astonished, as she emerged from the kitchen on the second floor in Rue Taranne.

On the landing, she wiped her hands on her apron whilst Montespan began to climb the dark stairs, clinging to the banister.

'And your shoulders, your arms, have the strangest shape, there . . .' said the cook worriedly, coming down a few steps.

'I've been to war, Madame Larivière . . . These lumps in my sleeves are bits of shredded linen placed on my wounds, and they make my clothes misshapen.'

'Did your company win the battle this time?'

'Is my wife not here?' asked the husband, limping

into the salon on the first floor.

'I thought it was her when I heard the door open downstairs. She sent word that she would stop by quickly this morning.'

By the fireplace, the servant Dorothée, who had been putting logs on the fire, for it was November, turned round and seemed to be looking for someone other than the marquis.

'You haven't brought Marie-Christine back with you?'

'No, I left her in Bonnefont with my mother and the sergeant of my company, whom I've hired as a steward. He will have his work cut out, for the chateau is in a pitiful—'

Suddenly there came the sound of a key opening a downstairs door and a voice boomed, 'Cook, servant! Are my things ready? Come, bring them down from my bedroom! A royal carriage is waiting to take me back to Saint-Germain-en-Laye. Make haste, quickly!'

They heard Athénaïs clap her hands to hurry everyone along as she climbed the stairs rapidly, her stylish shoes clicking on the steps. She came into the salon, removing her coat.

Thus her astonished husband found her in a very original gown of ample and flowing green silk muslin that he had never seen before.

'Madame invented this robe and has called it "The Innocent" . . . 'Tis the latest fashion in the Marais and also at court, so it seems,' mocked the cook, as the marquise frowned at her.

The loving husband walked round his fair lady in her new-style 'innocent' gown: it hung loosely like a large man's shirt, ballooning below the waist, and it hid the belly where Montespan now placed his palms. Her belly was rounded.

'Oh, dear Lord, Athénaïs, are you again . . .'

Louis-Henri quickly did some calculations. He had left for the Pyrenees eleven months previously: this advanced pregnancy therefore had nothing to do with a husband's labours.

'How is this possible?'

''Tis the hand of God, the work of the Holy Ghost,' sniggered the cook, as the marquis asked his wife, 'Who is the father?'

'Louis-Henri, I told you not to leave me near the King . . . one can refuse His Majesty nothing.'

Dorothée squeezed the bellows whilst Montespan felt unsteady on his feet.

'In Bonnefont I received an anonymous letter informing me that the King had left his favourite to become your lover. I dared not believe it.'

'Husbands are the last to open their eyes to the reality of their misfortune,' explained the cook from under her bonnet.

'I said to myself, this country is full of gossips and braggarts only too eager to sully the most honest of wives, and I am not about to confer the glory of History upon such boudoir tittle-tattle . . .'

'The brilliant manner in which she deceived the Queen shows that she has a pretty gift for treachery,' Madame Larivière said boldly, looking right at Athénaïs, who replied, 'Do you know who I am?'

'Aye, I believe so, Madame. Are you not the woman who bought Mademoiselle de La Vallière's commission?'

'Leave this salon!'

The cook motioned to Dorothée, then leant towards her mistress's ear. She told her that she was a liar, a rascally wench, a strumpet and a dog's harlot.

'Leave this house!' exclaimed La Montespan.

The two servants closed the door behind them. Tears came to the marquis's eyes which spoke far more eloquently than any words he could have said.

'My God, how your belly weighs upon me! And you are not the only one it oppresses,' he sighed, contemplating the pregnant lady-in-waiting ('wounded in service').

'One does not abandon one's spouse to fêtes and the dangers of the court, Louis-Henri; it is impossible to extricate oneself from the King's pressing advances,' murmured Athénaïs.

'He can only obtain that which you consent to give him.'

'No one can hide from the King's desires. And from women he demands immediate submission. To refuse would have irrevocable consequences for me, for you, and for the children. Both our families, all of us, would have been banished from France.'

Horns sprouted on the marquis's head. Mourning of all mournings, misfortune of all misfortunes, all this triumph buried, sheer madness.

'I have never felt a pain more piercing than that which I feel today, my dear.'

He suffered so greatly that he would fain have poisoned himself with the quicksilver in the mirror.

'And I would do anything on earth to take my revenge.'

'What shall you do, Louis-Henri?'

His reply was that of an oracle, of the sort that men are wont to make when first they love. 'I will love you all my life.'

He went over to the fair woman and placed his palms on the green silk muslin of her shoulders, but she pushed his arms away.

'I do not have the right to belong to another man, even my own husband! And you must dismiss the cook! Her arrogance and ill humour towards me are unbearable, and the very sight of her is unpleasant. She has a face like a rear end. She is quite deformed, and her head wobbles incessantly from the moment she sees me. You see the trouble the old hag causes. She—'

The marquis slapped his wife's left cheek with the flat of his hand so violently that she would bear the mark on her white skin for at least three months.

17.

At the Montausiers' *hôtel particulier*, all the women had adopted the *hurluberlu*. In addition to wearing 'innocent' gowns they bore, on their left cheek, a five-fingered mauve and blue mark like a star on their skin. Louis-Henri was dumbfounded. On seeing the loose muslin floating over the bellies of all these ladies of rank, he wondered whether the King had not impregnated them as well.

For weeks Louis-Henri had spent sleepless nights, and he had lost all semblance of a man who was happy in his marriage. His face was like that of a skinned cat, with bloodshot eyes. His periwig sat askew when he bolted like a fury into the first-floor gaming circle, spewing insults and outrage. He shouted that the King was a second David, a vile seducer and a thief. He raged and spouted every insolence imaginable against His Majesty. From the billiards to the trou-madame table, the courtiers were terrorised and, fearful of seeing their position at court compromised should they chance to hear the marquis's imprecations, they fled.

There had been joy and abundance. They had been eating well and wagering high ('twas rolling in money there) – and then suddenly Montespan came and spoilt it all. He provoked a dreadful row. He condemned and castigated the attitude of a monarch who, for his own good pleasure, trampled all principles of family and of love! His tirades were tiresome and embarrassing; and when people were not yawning, they scoffed at this husband who had the poor taste to complain that the King had seduced his wife.

'The conceited man doth protest, whilst the fool laments and tears his hair. The honourable man the King betrays goes hence; to speak he does not dare.'

But Montespan continued his vehement criticism, unwisely showering a thousand biblical curses upon the sovereign's august head. One lady said to him, 'You are mad, you must not continue with all your fairy tales.' Blinded by rage, Montespan paid no attention to her warning. His eyes darted everywhere, he was looking for someone, and at last he saw the old duchesse Julie de Montausier.

Poised on a chair pierced with a hole above a pewter basin, the duchesse was defecating in public, whilst the nobles around her held a wind-passing contest they found wildly entertaining. The duchesse herself let out a few farts. Montespan swooped down upon her.

'Give my Françoise back to me!'

'Who is Françoise?'

'My wife, whom I will never again call by any other name than that with which she was baptised. Athénaïs – 'tis too . . .Versailles. You took my wife from me to hand her to the King. Give her back! I love her.'

La Montausier was most astonished.

'You were joined in holy matrimony four years ago and you still love your wife? If I may be so bold, your fishmonger feels the same penchant for his wife. But you, Monsieur, are a marquis. Do you believe that my husband loves me? Monsieur le duc,' she asked, turning her head to the right, 'do you love me?'

'Of course not,' replied her husband.

Montespan was flabbergasted.

'And yet,' he said to the duc, 'were you not the finest wit of the time, did you not write *La Guirlande de Julie*? That unique collection of madrigals, composed for her name-day, a more delicate and enduring bouquet than any real flowers could make?'

''Tis true . . . each poem compared Julie to a different flower: a rose, a tulip . . . but above all it was the dowry of Mademoiselle de Rambouillet that I coveted.'

And she had gone on to become his wife; now she was not in the least offended, unlike Louis-Henri, who continued, 'But when I saw the two of you, I thought that—'

'If you judge by appearances in this place, Monsieur de Montespan, you will often be led astray. What appears to be is almost never what is *chez nous*.'

The Gascon stood there open-mouthed.

'As for the King,' continued the white-haired old woman, 'if he deems it his duty to take your wife as his mistress – the most beautiful woman in France, the most desirable in the kingdom – and to flaunt her like a treasure, there is no cause for anger and for coming to bore us with some petty quarrel of the kind a German might make. You would do better to invoke Saint Leonard, the patron saint of childbirth, for the successful arrival of the bastard!'

Montespan could not believe his ears. He had been a captain of the light cavalry and had become so forgetful of good form that he addressed the duchesse in the language of the barracks. She would have another flower that she could add to her *Guirlande de Julie*.

'You are nothing but a flower of priggish pedantry and vileness, perfumed with lucre and servility, cultivated in a soil of hypocrisy!'

'Oooooh!'

'Rag-bag, harpy, hog's tripe, old maggot-pie! Dislodge your buttocks from there and go and fetch me my wife or I'll blow your backside to kingdom come!'

'Oooooh!'

The duchesse began to tremble beneath the parasol held by the black slave. So shocked by the Gascon's cruel words was the Princesse d'Harcourt that she defecated in her gown. Thick-lipped, with white hair, she often had an urge to shit and was prompt to find relief when on her feet, which drove all those she visited to despair. She moved off into the glow of the flames from the grand fireplace, where they flickered against the golden interior; she dirtied the parquet floor with a ghastly smear. Lauzun went up to Montespan, chuckled and told him, 'One time, a count put a firecracker under her seat in a salon where she was playing piquet. Just as he was about to light it, being a charitable soul I advised him that the firecracker would maim her, and thereby I stayed his hand. Then there was an evening at Saint-Germain-en-Laye when the courtiers introduced twenty or more Swiss guards with drums into her chambers and roused her from her sleep. They assailed her with snowballs. She sat up, her hair all dishevelled, shouting at the top of her lungs and wriggling like an eel, not knowing where to hide. The nymph was afloat, and with water pouring from her bed, the room was awash. Enough to finish her off!'

Louis-Henri took his leave. In the street, a singer was bellowing a fashionable refrain.

> *'Tis said that fair Montespan*
> *Hey nelly nelly, hey nelly*
> *'Tis said that fair Montespan*
> *Hides a round belly.'*

On Rue des Rosiers, at the Hôtel Mortemart, the Gascon was greeted by Françoise's moon-faced father. The marquis immediately asked his father-in-law what he thought of the disaster.

'God be praised, good fortune has entered our house!' he responded.

The son-in-law failed to understand. 'What do you mean?'

The Duc de Mortemart with his big green protruding eyes and jovial little mouth explained.

'I was three hundred thousand *livres* in debt, and the King paid them for me, simply because I am the father of his new mistress . . . He also offered me the title of governor of Paris and Île-de-France. And to compensate him for having appropriated his sister's virtue, His Majesty appointed my son Vivonne (that imbecile) general of the galleys and vice-admiral of the Levant! Therefore you, the husband, can well imagine the glories you may hope for!'

'I hope only for Françoise . . .'

'Louis-Henri, you are a fool. Every favour, every honour is about to rain upon you, if you will only hold your tongue and close your eyes. But there you go, shouting out loud, even when you know you stand to suffer cruelly from what is arbitrary. That is why many will not forgive you. You disturb them by daring as you do to put a great king in a regrettable position.'

'I place him in a regrettable position?'

'You ought to be shut away in the Petites-Maisons like a madman. Cast off that grey hat. His Majesty despises grey hats and one must never displease His Majesty.'

Montespan was finding that the air here, too, was rotten. His father-in-law was getting carried away, flapping his lace. 'Ah, why can you not be like the others! You would have made your existence a fine one, and died a marshal of France and governor of a good province, instead of trailing a pack of creditors in your wake.'

'I am in love with your daughter . . .'

'The Prince de Soubise was certainly more elegant than you are and yet he, too, in the beginning, baulked when Louis laid eyes upon his wife. He even attempted to make His Majesty believe that she was scrofulous: "She's a fine apple, sire, but she is rotten within." "Indeed?" replied the King. "I will see for myself by venturing therein." Then the husband bowed his head and had the tact to stay out of sight for the duration of the liaison. In compensation he received a considerable sum of money and one of the finest houses in Paris. He transformed his horns of shame into horns of plenty.'

Gabriel de Rochechouart, Duc de Mortemart, poured himself a little cherry liqueur, and offered some to his son-in-law, who declined with a wave of his hand and a sigh.

'Thus, there is only my uncle left – Henri Gondrin, the Archbishop of Sens – who might take my side . . . He shall condemn the King's adultery from his very pulpit.'

'His Majesty will soften him with a cardinal's hat. Louis-Henri, to be a king's cuckold is the chance of a lifetime. Do not let it go by, it will not come your way again.'

'How can anyone think I shall remain silent and accept this?'

'You are mad.'

'Mad about Françoise.'

'Ah, there he goes again! Such a fuss because the King likes to play the libertine with my daughter!'

Montespan restrained himself from doing violence to his father-in-law.

'Louis-Henri, accept this state of affairs, else everyone will find you in poor taste. The King is vexed by the noisy, repeated demonstrations of a subject who is insolent enough to dare lay claim to his wife. You have become a figure of fun in Paris. 'Tis said Molière is writing a play about you.'

'Oh, really?'

18.

AMPHITRION

Amphitryon arrived on stage in front of his domain in
Thebes, and stood next to a servant (Sosie) played by the

author of the play; he was angry with Jupiter because he had just heard an unlikely story. He had discovered that whilst he had been away at war, the god (who rode astride an eagle, up there on his cloud) had cuckolded him by taking on his physical appearance in order to spend the night with his wife (Alcmene); from this union a child would be born:

JUPITER: *To you a son shall be born who, under the name of Hercules . . .*

A married man rarely appreciates another man announcing to him that his wife is with child and that the name has been chosen without consulting him. It might have amused the spectators at the Théâtre du Palais-Royal but it clearly did not amuse Amphitryon, or Montespan, in the theatre.

Louis-Henri, standing among the crowd in the stalls, had paid fifteen *sols* for his ticket. The seats costing six *livres* were in the dress circle, the boxes, and on either side of the stage where the King, accompanied by Françoise, was attending the performance that 16 January 1668. The husband could not make out his rival's features so grand were the King's plumes, but from time to time he could just perceive, behind His Majesty, and depending on whether she leant forward or back on the seat, the blond curls on his wife's neck, or sometimes her profile. Often the actors turned deferentially to the monarch. At other times, they shouted abuse at Montespan in the audience.

'He may now console himself, for strokes from the wand of a god confer honour on him who has to submit to them.'

'Upon my word, Monsieur God, I am your servant; I could have done without your attentions . . .'

All around the marquis the crowd were laughing. The aristocrats shoved him with their shoulders or their hips. And bit by bit they propelled him to the centre of the hall, directly under the enormous candelabra on the ceiling. This was the first time Louis-Henri had been to the theatre. He did not know that he was standing in the very spot one absolutely had to avoid in the stalls: beneath the light with its many candles that dripped profusely by the end of the performance. After a prologue and two acts, this was the third and final act. The wax was overflowing its little bowls, raining upon the marquis's thick periwig, but he did not notice, so absorbed was he by the spectacle. He listened to the pleasing consolation to the betrayed husband on stage.

JUPITER: *Sharing something with Jupiter has nothing that in the least dishonours, for doubtless, it can be but glorious to find one's self the rival of the sovereign of the gods.*

Montespan grasped the transparent allusions to his own

situation in an era where the pleasure of the mighty was the only law. What did he think of the play? That it was a toadying sort of play, a courtier's play. Molière was clearly on the King's side (quite rightly had he kept the role of valet for himself!). And Jupiter tried to convince Amphitryon that he should not remain bitter, but consider himself, rather, as the happiest of men, for he would gain much thereby.

> JUPITER: *A glorious future crowned with a thousand blessings shall let everyone see I am your support; I will make your fate the envy of the whole world.*

These words were not of a nature to appease Amphitryon, who acted vexed and droll. In the myth of the birth of Hercules, Molière had found an opportunity to ridicule Montespan and amuse the audience. It was a play full of machinery, with many traps and pulleys and a winch, and to the delight of the spectators it was most spectacular, as Jupiter rose into the air on his cloud to the sound of thunder. Hurling thunderbolts, he disappeared into the heavens, shrouded in smoke, whilst the audience applauded. Wax rained upon the marquis's wig, it dribbled through the curls, stiffened them and turned them white. It brought to mind a hot snowdrift, gradually hardening and making the wig most heavy, whilst Molière, in the role of Sosie, seemed to be addressing the

Gascon directly as he reminded him that his tribulations were in the order of things, but that:

'*The Seigneur Jupiter knows how to gild the pill.*'

On one side of the stage, behind the row of candles whose light no longer sufficed, the lackey playwright concluded the play.

SOSIE: *Nothing could be better than this. But, nevertheless, let us cut short our speeches, and each one retire quietly to his own house. In such affairs as these, it is always best not to say anything.*

In these final words Louis-Henri heard an order addressed to ordinary mortals: do not presume to judge Jupiter! Keep your thoughts to yourself! 'In such affairs as these,' Sosie had concluded, 'it is always best not to say anything.' The injunction applied not only to the importunate husband but also to gossips. No more mumbling: 'Let us cut short our speeches,' Molière had said, 'and each one retire quietly to his own house.' Madame de Sceaux and Madame de La Trémoille, after an orgy of curry at noon, were now overcome with a pressing urge in their box. They relieved themselves into their cupped hands then tossed their mess down into the stalls in the direction of Louis-Henri. The marquis's shoulders now stank of shit and curry. He looked on astonished as the ladies' waste seeped into the sleeves of his jerkin. He raised his eyes to the ceiling and on his face received a downpour of burning wax. Everyone had stepped back in a circle around him. He was like a mushroom in the middle of a forest clearing. White stalactites hung on either side of his face from his periwig. He had truly been an easy target both in the theatre and on stage. And the one time he had actually gone to the theatre! This was not about to make him want to come again. There was a smell of something burning. Behind his back someone had set fire to his clothing. An emergency door was open, directly ahead of him. Louis-Henri rushed forward, he had to find a gutter quickly, with some water. Flames were rising from his back. He moved through a sea of laughter pouring from loose and rotten teeth, he smelt the rancid butter and mouldy honey in their cavities. People put out their feet to trip him and stall his progress. He feared he would be burnt alive, when an ecclesiastic's cape descended upon him and crushed him close to extinguish the fire.

'Uncle!'

It was Henri Gondrin, Archbishop of Sens, the brother of Montespan's father: a man of vision and a lofty soul, with a clean reputation where women were concerned, something rare among prelates. Louis-Henri, who had fallen to the ground, was ashamed that his uncle had seen him humiliated in public in this way, but the man was already striding over to the King, who had left the stage.

'Sire, your adultery is blasphemous, a sacrilege physically incarnate in a holy body!'

The Gascon was on the ground, tapping his shoulders, his sleeves, to put out the last little flames as bitter whiffs of smoke rose from his person, and had his back turned to the King. His fingers were full of ash and shit from his clothing, there was sticky wax all over his knuckles, and he did not see the monarch, but he could hear the dressing-down he gave his uncle.

'Keep your preaching to your diocese, or I will condemn you to exile and imprison you on your estate until further notice!'

Louis-Henri, sitting on the tiles, turned his head. Near him stood Lully in his pink silk stockings, laughing hysterically at the sight of the crestfallen marquis. The musician struck the marble sharply several times with the iron tip of his walking stick, nearly crushing the marquis's fingers, but Louis-Henri, sitting just under the Italian's legs, only had eyes for Françoise where she stood by her royal lover. The Archbishop of Sens planted himself in front of her and said solemnly, 'This is on behalf of your husband,' and with all his might he slapped her on the right cheek.

19.

The next morning, as he staggered back to the Hôtel Montausier, Montespan discovered that all the ladies now sported a slap mark on both cheeks. He sniggered. 'If someday the monarch has a fistula on his anus, they shall all have an operation on their arsehole, claiming a harquebus wound, and that varlet Lully shall compose a *Te Deum* about it – God save the King! – and bang his walking stick on the floor. And ere long it shall become a hymn . . . In any event, I hope the Italian shall crush his own foot and die of it!'

Lauzun came up to him, took a good look and smiled. 'Who is speaking of His Majesty's posterior?' The courtier waxed lyrical as he evoked the colour of His Majesty's excrement. 'The other day, he evacuated eight times before dinner, twice during his Council and, a final flourish, one hour after he'd gone to bed.'

Lauzun leant over to the Gascon's ear.

'There are some who pay up to one hundred and eighty thousand *livres* a year to see the King shit.'

Louis-Henri felt like a sparrow in an oven.

'I see no sign of that old baggage Montausier. I've come to give her an earful. Where is she? Well? In her apartments at Saint-Germain-en-Laye? I had ordered her to bring my wife back to me.'

'You disappoint your wife,' interrupted a princess. 'Athénaïs told me that she was ashamed to see her husband entertaining the populace like a parrot, spouting such vulgar gibberish.'

'That is not true. You are lying! She would never have said that. We loved one another! You cannot even begin to imagine how much two people can love one another! Versailles is hell. Get my wife out of there. She is too fragile. She believes in all sorts of strange things . . .'

Montespan burst into tears.

'A broken glass, a spilt saltcellar – both are signs of bad luck to her . . . She said that during childbirth a mother will give birth more quickly if she wears the father's shoes and stockings. She believes that after you cut the umbilical cord, you must place it against the baby's head to ensure long life. She did so for our daughter! And for the boy, she buried the cord under a rosebush to give the child clear skin.'

His face streaming with tears, he continued, 'Françoise

was certain that if the wedding was held on a Thursday, the husband would be cuck—'

The aristocrats around him delighted in seeing how he dared not utter the word.

'There's a manual of demonology she often reads: *The Witches' Hammer*. She thinks that if a woman wants to be loved, she must use a potion made of holy water, wine and the powder from a dead man's bone taken from a recent grave. Often, before leaving for court, she went to obtain some from the soothsayers and witches in their secret shops in the poorer quarters of the capital, above all from La Voisin, on Rue Beauregard . . .'

'Who did you say? Where? La Voisin?'

The women moved away, asking each other, 'Do you know where Rue Beauregard is?' The Princess of Monaco, reputed to be generous with her favours, knew where the street was to be found, and spoke gaily of the King of France's genitalia. She said that, unlike King Charles of England, his power was great but his sceptre was quite small, and it was for that reason that in the palace sodomy, in particular, had triumphed. Her neighbour, a comtesse, thought for a moment and was forced to concede, ''Tis true, in Versailles there is a fair amount of buggery . . .'

Montespan, dismayed, watched as they returned to the gaming tables. Then, from the emanations of fennel spirits in which the man had indulged to excess all night, Louis-Henri became aware of Lauzun's presence.

'I often find you near me.'

'That is because, as captain of the royal guards, it is also my duty to keep an eye on you.'

Lauzun was a little man, with dull blond hair and no attractive features. Ill-humoured, solitary, prickly, and shifty by nature, one sensed that he might on occasion have made a good friend, although it must have been rare. The tip of his nose was red and pointed, his hair was lifeless, but there floated about him something like a scent of secret sensuality. The Gascon sighed. 'My wife has succumbed to a bad dream. Can you help me bring her back to reality?'

'For as long as the King wants her, he shall not give her back to you, but how long will that last? In general, the *maîtresse-en-titre* introduces him to the new one. Madame Henriette introduced La Vallière. La Vallière brought your wife to dance before the King. La Montespan will introduce her successor to His Majesty. For you the pill is hard to swallow but if it's gilded, no doubt it will go down more easily.'

'What can she see in those people, what does she do there?'

'In the evening, when . . . "Jupiter" goes back to sleep with his wife, the favourite fashions little filigree coaches for the child she will bear, and she harnesses six mice to the coaches and lets them bite her pretty fingers without a single cry.'

20.

Montespan was strolling along the Seine, where barges laden with fodder, grain and sand sailed to and fro. The river was polluted by faecal matter and rubbish of all sorts. Like a sickly old snake, the Seine slithered slowly through Paris, conveying towards its harbours all manner of shipments of timber and corpses.

Little boys in short trousers ran after rusty barrel hoops. Girls dressed in homespun petticoats gathered at the waist went barefoot amidst the filth and shards of glass. Beggars and fishwives hurled abuse upon honest folk, vile slander that Louis-Henri did not hear. What was the slander of men to him now, this squire whom nobility had abandoned and now shunned? He had just sold his fine fob watch at the Pont-au-Change. What did he care now for the hour or the year? Time was of no importance to him. At the age of twenty-seven, his life was finished. A vendor of rat poison declaimed,

> *'A soldier who in combat*
> *Made all the world to tremble*
> *His wretchedness cannot dissemble*
> *And cries, "Death to the rat!"'*

The vagabond wandered along, carrying his box of poison by his side. His doublet was full of holes, he had a wooden leg and an old-fashioned ruff; he was ridiculous and grotesque. Over his shoulder he carried a long pole decorated with trophies: his dead rats. The marquis saw himself in the cripple. Montespan, who heretofore had never heeded the life of the street, now observed everything: vinegar vendors shouting, 'Good fine vinegar! We have mustard vinegar!', musicians wearing wooden clogs blowing into flageolets and banging tambourines. Here you could buy combs from Limoges, ice cream, powder containers, lancets forged in Toulouse. Over there a woman sold tight bundles of matches from a wicker basket – twigs of reed impregnated with inflammable material. Three craftsmen under an awning were sewing footwear on a workbench covered with hides and tools. They wore leather aprons and used their knees as a vice. Louis-Henri wandered through this place where all these humble folk had come with their goods, their wits and a will to live that he had lost. The marquis turned around and headed into a foul-smelling maze of alleyways where miscreants ruled day and night.

The absence of any foundations caused the earth to move; the tall narrow houses leant and buckled, their façades cracked. The twisting little streets – often mere dirt paths – were full of recesses and daylight rarely entered the lodgings. Here, too, one was shoved about, life was intense, there were altercations among the vendors, oaths, blows, theft, rubbish tossed from windows, bottlenecks and coachmen's shouts, mules and carts pulled by hand. There was a smallpox epidemic; to protect themselves many people breathed only through a sponge soaked in sage and juniper, but Montespan strode ahead, his hands in his pockets. Why should he care about smallpox? It started to rain. The streets immediately became a cesspool of mud. A thin harlot, wearied by her libertine errands, sheltered beneath a doorway by the window of a cabaret-brothel. Louis-Henri stared at her in the downpour and she gave him a strange, furtive glance.

A curious idea occurred to the marquis. In the end, why not go and have a laugh with this shrimp, this strumpet, with her long, drawling entreaty of 'Follow me, Gentleman Sir'. He went up to her. She walked around him, laughing from her toothless mouth.

'What's this jerkin all burnt up in the back? Some dragon making love to you from behind? And what's that white stuff sticking to your wig? Did he come all over your scalp? And the smell . . . Ah, he shat on your shoulders!'

The prostitute, who knew her clients, could guess from the Gascon's manner what was wrong. 'Oh, d'ye have a broken heart?'

'Give me syphilis or the pox, then I'll go and rape my wife so she can infect the King in turn.'

Another whore, standing next to them, asked, 'What did he say?'

'Nothin', he's drunk.'

The door to the brothel opened with a gust reeking of dead sperm and dried menses.

21.

The bawdy house had a bad reputation. Its wines came from vineyards steeped in mud and sewage from the city. Louis-Henri imbibed nectars redolent of fish glue and pigeon shit, and the trollops were unclean. That was what he liked.

The whores – doll-like creatures with ragged features – were riddled with venereal disease, and Montespan wallowed in it. He licked their pimples and pustules, their oozing sores, anything that seeped in intimate places, and he asked for more.

'Give me warts on my willie, a good case of the clap and *le mal français*! Give me magnificent mutilating contagion, for I know someone whom I would like to see infected, impregnated and ravaged o'erall! Has no one the plague here? Or rabies?'

The Gascon stayed for days and nights on end. From one full moon to the next, he did not leave the establishment. One of the girls was astonished.

'But don't you have a wife, and children?'

'My wife . . . My son is with my landlord. Come here, you.'

With the money from his watch he paid as he went along for his women and his adulterated wine, served by the glass. Twenty-nine days and nights spent inside different women. One lumpy, heavy redhead with an insipid manner said hardly a word to him, and that one word was something to do with a little present. There was another as shrivelled as a prune, who croaked incessantly in her garlicky accent. Still another one had lately been a singer in the port of Dieppe, and she imitated the sailors' waddle and bawled at him. Then there was one who was as good as gold, flat-chested, with light-brown hair: she sucked him and sometimes she prayed to God: the devil take her satanic signs of the cross! Louis-Henri wanted yet more, worse still. All the rotten harlots in the neighbourhood, whom even the butchers refused – although they were not known to be very fussy (but still, let's not exaggerate) – the marquis wanted them all. One morning, he offered a very tall, fat, one-eyed Flemish whore the rest of the money from his watch, and said, 'Will you sell me your dress?'

22.

With his face concealed behind an open fan and wearing the Flemish whore's dress, Montespan arrived at the chateau of Saint-Germain-en-Laye to rape Françoise.

He had thrown away his soiled periwig and covered his shoulders with a cape, the hood pulled low over his forehead; his legs were naked and hairy under the dress, and the heels of his huge feet hung over the backs of the ladies' mules he was wearing. Disguised as a woman, he eluded the watchmen, and hugged the walls, walking with a stoop. He followed a maid carrying a tray full of soft doughy buns flavoured with beer and spices. Waving his fan, he disguised his voice as he enquired of the servant, 'My dear, I can't remember where Julie de Montausier's apartments are. You know, where the new favourite of the—'

'They're over there, Madame.'

'Ah, yes . . .'

He waited for her to leave then flung open the door. ''Tis I!'

Françoise, who had been sitting on a couch conversing with the old duchesse, leapt to her feet on seeing her husband in a dress. Now he swept it up before him, to show her that he was as hard as a rutting billy-goat.

'Françoise, I've found the solution for the two of us! I have spent a month in pursuit of shameful diseases and now I will take you and contaminate you as well. Thus, when the King hears of it, he'll want no more of you. Is this not a most excellent idea, my darling?'

He tore his whore's dress over his head and, naked, reached out and seized his wife by the shoulders, but she recoiled and made as if to run away. His fair lady's soft skin slipped through his fingers. It was like happiness departing, whilst he screamed, 'I'll abduct you and take you to Spain!'

But she was already nothing more than a blur by the French windows that opened onto the terrace and the grounds. As she scurried down the stairway with her round belly, she was like a wash painting, whilst he called, 'Françoise! Françoise, come back, or I'll bugger the old baggage! Well then, since that's the way it stands . . .'

He turned back to la Montausier, his cock in his hand. She became a frenzy of lace as goffered as her white hair, and regretted not having her slave there to clout this madman over the head with the parasol. He chased her round the furniture berating her. She would catch a lingering disease. He heaped abuse on her head apt to earn him eternal damnation. 'Old slut, you pimp of wives, I'm going to take you from behind. I promise, if I catch you, I'll bugger you. You'll get a fine dose of the clap.' He was not sparing in his next volley of insults. There was hardly an imprecation he did not vomit in her neck whilst she shrieked and wailed fit to shatter glass. It was a scene of absolute bedlam. She screamed for help and only owed her salvation to her valets, who were alerted by her cries. The marquis left in the nick of time, dashing stark naked through the French windows, disappearing like the villain in a play. Guards surrounded the duchesse, who was trembling with fear. 'What happened?' they asked.

'Monsieur de Montespan came in here like a fury and poured out his rage towards the King, and then said the most unspeakable things to me. And he wanted to ra— ra—'

She began to swoon and the blood drained from her face, whilst she stammered the most incoherent words. A sergeant came to the glass door and ordered, 'Find him.'

23.

There was a scratching noise at the door. Then it came again. That was the code.

'Who is it?'

'Lauzun.'

Montespan hesitated, then finally opened the door.

'How did you find me and how did you know the code?'

The captain of the royal guards came in and looked around.

'So 'tis here, in a servant's garret under the roof of a brothel behind Place de Grève that you've been hiding all these months.'

Louis-Henri, who had blown out his candle when he heard the scratching at the door, lit it again. The flickering flame wavered at the slightest breath in the miserable maid's room, illuminated otherwise only by a tiny *oeil-de-boeuf*.

'I did not have the time to thank you,' said the marquis, 'but when I was naked behind the huge oak in the garden, if you had not come to cover me with your coat and lead me out of the estate, I should have been lost.'

'You are lost,' replied Lauzun. 'You have caused an unprecedented scandal at Saint-Germain. They are writing songs about you in Paris.'

'I know. I hear them from the window.'

'For fear of being abducted, the favourite now has guards outside her door. And la Montausier never recovered from the outrage. Her reason vacillated so severely that one day, on leaving the King's mass, she thought she was encountering your ghost, dressed just as she was and calling her by name. She wasted away and died this morning. The sip of a glass of chicory was her undoing. She was close to His Majesty . . . 'Tis sufficient reason to be drawn and quartered, and have all one's bones smashed with a mallet.'

'Why did you help me?'

Again there was scratching at the door. ''Tis I, Monsieur!'

Madame Larivière, a basket of victuals in her hand, came in, complaining, 'Ah, I do not like this, coming every week into a brothel! And those bawdy wenches going down the stairs with their bundles – where are they off to? Don't look through any open doors to the bedrooms, Dorothée!' continued the cook, her back to Montespan.

On a little table she set down her heavy basket filled with sausages, cooked meals, fruit and wine, and only then did she realise that the marquis had a visitor.

Lauzun took his leave. 'Montespan, soon you will no longer be able to breathe the air in Paris . . .'

The Gascon asked, 'Would you lend me some money?'

The captain smiled – 'You'd only have to bend your knee to reap a fortune from the royal treasury' – but he left his well-stuffed pouch on the table and closed the door behind him.

Louis-Henri pouted. The cook was worried. 'What's wrong?'

'You've been followed, Madame Larivière.'

'Nay, we've not been followed! We are always very careful, and every time we take a different route to come to your hiding place.'

The marquis looked through the *oeil-de-boeuf*. Down below, on the banks of the Seine, the prostitutes who had been lodging him were embarking on a boat. The olive-skinned servant was also observing them. 'Where are they going?'

'They're being punished, sent in exile to Nouvelle-France, where there is a great dearth of women. In unexplored territory, they will provide a well-earned rest to the men who trap fur, above all beaver. They'll live on Indian corn and bear fat, and sleep in log cabins. Ladies of the evening, sorrowfully setting sail for the New World . . .'

Louis-Henri closed the window.

'Madame Larivière, you, too, will have to leave Paris, with the lass. People might be annoyed with you as well . . . As for me, I now know that I must resolve to leave my wife in her cage at court and I shall have to go back to Guyenne, but I shan't leave until . . .'

He bit his upper lip, hesitated, then forged ahead. 'Madame Larivière, you'll keep the money in the pouch for the two of you, but first of all I should like you to do an errand for me. You must go to a draper's, and find a painter, and—'

'A painter? Whatever for?'

24.

On 20 September 1668, Montespan returned to court at Saint-Germain-en-Laye; no one had thought he would have the audacity to reappear! And his carriage!

The marquis's bizarre vehicle drew up outside the gilded railings of the royal estate. Louis-Henri had painted his apple-green travelling berlin black, and had replaced the four feathers at each corner of the roof with gigantic stag's antlers. A large crêpe veil enveloped the entire carriage, giving it a funereal air, and the black horses were decked out with great pomp as if for a funeral. To his coat of arms on the doors on either side, the Gascon had added horns.

The guards, impressed, let the horned carriage through, and it came to a halt in the centre of the paved courtyard. The marquis, seated inside, climbed out, dressed in deep mourning. He had furtively hugged the walls on his previous visit, but this afternoon there was nothing discreet about his arrival. He was holding a hat out in front of him, upside down; only the inside was visible.

He climbed the steps that led to the chateau, walking past husbands who would gladly have thrust their wives into the monarch's arms if they had stood to benefit. How they did behave, that lot, such baseness . . . The fear of displeasing their master crushed their souls and degraded their consciences, while the Marquis de Saint-Maurice sniggered, 'I offered the services of my own wife to the King but, alas, he does not find her pleasing. So I persisted and said, "Not even, Sire, like a post horse you ride once and never see again?" "Do not insist," replied His Majesty, "I prefer Montespan's wife."'

Next to Saint-Maurice, a comtesse was carrying a little dog in her handmuff, and it showed its teeth and barked when the recalcitrant cuckold walked by. Louis-Henri held a finger out towards its nose and said, 'Down, Molière!'

The decor of the reception hall was sumptuous and the ceiling was so laden with garlands and voluptuous goddesses that visitors feared they might fall on their heads.

It was nearly five o'clock in the afternoon. Louis-Henri

was waiting for the King to leave his Council. The courtiers, alarmed by such sheer audacity, moved away. The marquis sat alone opposite the door where the King would come out. His face was inscrutable, his hand was on the hilt of his sword and, if he had had a glass of water on his head, not a drop would have been spilt, for he was sitting bolt upright.

The King came out. Montespan knew the King was short but was surprised by quite how short. He was tiny and tried to compensate for it by holding himself stiffly. He wore high-heeled shoes and had a thin moustache. Beyond that, Louis-Henri could not make out his features, for Louis XIV had stopped in front of a window with his back to the sun. After a short silence the radiant figure of the monarch, silhouetted against the light, with his ministers scurrying around him, enquired of the Gascon, 'Why are you all in black, Monsieur?'

While etiquette required one to remove one's hat in the presence of His Majesty, Louis-Henri now placed the grey hat on his head – a colour the King hated – and replied, 'Sire, I am in mourning for my love.'

'In mourning for your love?'

'Yes, Sire, my love has died. Killed by a rogue.'

At a time of universal and abject servility, anyone who dared to raise their heads above the fawning crowd had to be peculiarly hot-blooded and uncommonly determined.

The distinguished figures at the far end of the reception

hall were frozen with terror at the marquis's behaviour. The hot-headed Gascon had overstepped all bounds. Louis XIV would not tolerate this direct insult – a crime of *lèse-majesté*.

The marquis, having said his piece, bowed arrogantly and, in full view of the courtiers, broke his sword before the tyrant to show that he would no longer serve him, for he was a man who loved too much. Then he very casually turned his back on the King. The sound of his heels faded away across the waxed parquet floor and he returned to his carriage.

Such behaviour was unthinkable. No one had ever committed such an offence in His Majesty's presence. Everything – fire, water, night, day – was subject to the will of this living god, whose face was faintly pitted by smallpox. The King said nothing, and the silence spoke volubly of the crime committed. Then he spluttered with laughter. 'And so? I am fucking his wife! What more could I do for him?'

Everyone around him laughed; of course they had to agree. The horned carriage had not gone far before the King's henchmen caught up with it. Lauzun was at their head and he rode up alongside the marquis's door in a swirl of dust and shouted, at a gallop, 'Let your coachman go on and drive the berlin to Rue Taranne, but he will have to stop first to leave you outside Fort-l'Évêque.'

'The prison in the Vallée de la Misère?'

'I have a *lettre de cachet* which authorises the King to imprison whomsoever displeases him for an indeterminate period and without trial!'

25.

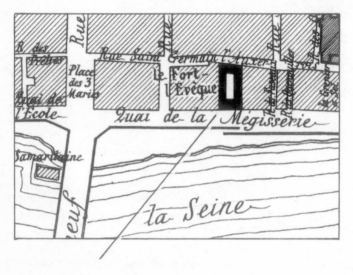

'The King did give me horns! Take heart, my soul
And admire thy bliss
Presently thou shalt go — be praised, oh wife —
To the highest point of honour!'

In the cramped, insalubrious prison on Quai de la
Mégisserie — nicknamed the Vallée de la Misère because of
the great number of animals that were put to death there —

Montespan, with blood on his nails, languished behind a door locked by the most secure of padlocks. Through a high basement window, a ray of light entered the dry well that served as a dungeon at Fort-l'Évêque, and left a little dusty patch of brightness on the earthen floor. The isolation could not appease his torment. While the animals being slaughtered outside screamed with pain, the marquis in fetters sang at the top of his voice the last couplets telling the good folk of their King's loves:

> *'To be a king's cuckold, 'tis untold honour,*
> *A plague on it, I know it well!*
> *Black sorrow is most blameworthy*
> *How dare I flee my own good fortune?'*

'Shut up in there! You're singing off-key! . . . I'd rather listen to the sound of those beasts having their throats cut! I have a musical ear, I do!'

Louis-Henri turned this way and that inside his pitch-dark cell.

'Is someone there?'

A voice replied in the obscurity, 'Aye, there is, someone they've thrown in this prison, but what for? I'm not a libertine writer, nor a shameless hussy, nor an indebted gamester. I'm not mad enough to have committed a crime of *lèse-majesté*. So what am I doing in Fort-l'Évêque, the prison for the King's arrests? And if now, in addition, a fellow inmate who is such a poor singer is inflicted upon me . . .'

Silence reigned in the dungeon, then Louis-Henri, in chains and on his knees, dragged himself across the mouldy straw to the faint ray of light. In the darkness he looked for his fellow prisoner. 'Where are you?'

The other voice continued, ''Tis true, indeed! I am naught but a maternity doctor, doing my job, so why have I landed here? It was the end of the afternoon. I was alone in my house on Rue Saint-Antoine. I was about to have supper when there came a knock at the door. I opened it. Hiding on either side were two soldiers (I could hear the clicking of their weapons against the buttons of their uniform) and they grabbed me by the arms. A third man arrived from behind and bound my eyes and ordered, "Not a sound or I'll cut your throat! Monsieur Clément, bring your instrument case." Forsooth! I thought, I have nothing to fear. Am I not used to these mysterious little expeditions to the homes of people of rank at a time when my young clients often come into the world as best they can? I was made to climb into a coach from court (I noted the delicate creaking of the oiled hubs as used at Versailles) and, after we had ridden for a while, I was left at the foot of a stairway, which I climbed, guided by a nurse (she had a millet-seed rattle bumping against her chest). And I went into a bedroom on the first floor of a discreet dwelling set back from Rue de l'Échelle.'

'How did you know the address if you were blindfolded?'

'My ears were not bound . . .'

Chains dragged along the floor and the face of Clément, the maternity doctor, appeared in the faint ray of light.

'Just nearby, I recognised the unbearable ring of the cracked bell at the Chapelle Sainte-Agonie. I had gone there one morning to assist a birth (miraculous, surely) and I had complained to the sisters, "You'll have to change that bell with that off-key knell to it, else I'll not come back to this hellish racket to bring any more little baby Jesuses into the world!" And I also knew it was set back from the street because downstairs I could hear the hammering of a wooden heel-maker. He uses wood that is too freshly cut. I bought some heels from him once and very soon they split. And I knew from the hammering that it was this wood that wasn't dry enough that he was hitting. You can tell things like that from the tonality . . .' he continued, clicking his fingers next to his ear and dislodging his dusty wig, which gave off a cloud of powder.

Louis-Henri coughed in the ray of light and withdrew his head. The doctor Clément left his head in the light: he was a sweaty red-faced man of fifty-odd years, with a drunkard's puffy nose. Montespan listened.

'As I went alone into the bedroom, still blindfolded, I exclaimed, "Ah, ah, it seems I am to fetch an infant from where it is by groping up the very same way that got it there." In her bed, undergoing her first labour pains, there was a particularly well-made young woman whom I could feel with my fingertips – a human statue of the sort you see only in the grounds of a chateau, a woman made for a lord from Mount Olympus. Standing next to her, nervous and worried, was a little man (his voice came, rather, from below). I asked him whether I was in a house of God, where one is not allowed to drink or eat; as for myself, I was famished, having left my home just as I was about to sup. The little man complied readily. He handed me a pot of jam and some bread. "Have as much as you like, there is more." "I believe you," said I, "but is the wine cellar less abundant? You have not given me any wine and I'm stifling." The little man became annoyed: "A bit of patience, I cannot be everywhere at once." "Ah, well done," I said, when I received a goblet filled to the brim. This gentleman was likely not a bourgeois – too many sounds of extravagant rings on his fingers clinking against the glass, and in the manner he handed the wine to me I understood that he was not at all in the habit of serving . . .'

The practitioner withdrew his head into the darkness. Louis-Henri, more and more interested in his cellmate's story, moved into the faint ray of light. 'Go on.'

Clément resumed his tale.

'When I had drunk, the man asked me, "Is that everything?" "Not yet," I replied. "A second glass to drink with you to the health of the good woman!" As the man said no, I told him with a smile that the woman would not give birth

156

so easily and, if he wished the child to be handsome and strong, he must drink to its health. And so, for the love of his progeny, he toasted with me. Just then a piercing cry signalled the infant's first attempt to enter the world. The child was in the breech position, but came out easily. I touched his little feet to make certain everything was all right, slid my hands up his little legs – 'twas a boy – and tied off the cord. I placed my palms on his chest, where his heart was beating very rapidly, and went on up to his frail neck, and it was then that the little man with lots of rings stopped my wrist and called out, "Lauzun!" The hinges on the door leading to the landing creaked. There came a squeaking of leather boots, no doubt this Lauzun fellow. I also heard the millet seeds bouncing in the nurse's rattle and the little man's voice ordered her, "You, only you, must stay secretly by this child who shall have no name." "As it pleases you," replied the maid. "I will not go out, save to pray at the neighbouring chapel at the eleven o'clock mass." Then, heavier by a pouch, I merrily set off to be taken back to my home, or so I thought, but I was brought here, to Fort-l'Évêque (which I recognised from the cries of the animals being slaughtered without). And since that moment I have been waiting – what for? Who for? You?'

Montespan withdrew into the darkness. He thought for a moment, then asked, 'When a married woman gives birth, is her husband always held to be the father?'

'Oh, yes,' replied the practitioner. 'And that is so whosoever the genitor might be. The husband remains legally the father according to the fundamental principle of Roman law *Is pater quem nuptiae demontrant!*'

'Thus, the husband may enjoy all rights to the child?'

'But of course.'

Silence fell again in the cell, then Montespan sang, lungs fit to burst,

> *'Bourbon so loved my wife,*
> *With child he left her, so*
> *To the fleur-de-lis long life!'*

26.

'Marquis, your turn has come to leave the dungeon! Yesterday, the doctor was set free. Today, you will be released. Mind the daylight! The sun will burn your eyes.'

The gaoler's torch, which was steeped in foul-smelling oil, smoked and flickered as he raised his arm towards the corridor, inviting the inconvenient husband to follow the light. Rats ran across the damp flagstones, their claws scraping against the stone, and the warder pushed Montespan out into the Vallée de la Misère.

Quai de la Mégisserie was dazzling in the sunlight and Louis-Henri, still in chains, raised his forearm to his eyes to protect them from the glare. While he was being unshackled, his pupils gradually adapted and through his sleeves he began to see the vivid colours of the *quai*, bustling with people and sedan chairs weaving among mountains of slain cattle. The marquis heard a drum roll. Soldiers moved apart and formed a circle around him. Nauseating steam rose from huge boilers. Sweating women plunged chickens into the swirling water to scald them before plucking them, and then, curious, they went over to the guard of honour the soldiers had formed. Burghers, yokels and a few noblemen clustered round. The drum stopped beating and a horseman of the watch moved into the circle facing Louis-Henri.

At nine o'clock in the morning on 7 October 1668, the horseman read the royal command, proclaiming in a thundering voice, "'By order of His Majesty the King!'"

Everyone fell silent. Even the mortally wounded beasts at the butchers' now died soundlessly on the shores of the river. Looking up at the sky, they watched as seagulls circled overhead, coming up the Seine from the sea. The web-footed scavengers swooped and seized bovine guts and hens' intestines from the water and carried them skyward like streamers of dancing red, green and blue; it gave a festive touch to the blue sky. As the gulls dipped towards the surface of the yellow river stippled with points of light, the Gascon followed the beating of their wings. The river Seine in the sunlight was like Françoise's blond hair; how he had loved to plunge his long fingers there, like the teeth of a comb. He sighed, whilst the horseman of the Paris watch again raised his voice: "'His Majesty, being most dissatisfied with the noble Marquis de Montespan . . ."'

'What? He is dissatisfied with me? Oh, the scurvy knave!'

The horseman pretended not to have heard, or to have heard another word, such as brave . . . grave . . . and continued, '". . . orders the horseman of the watch of the City of Paris forthwith, and by virtue of this order of His Majesty, that once said noble sir and marquis has been set free from the prison of Fort-l'Évêque where he was detained, he shall in the name of His Majesty be ordered to leave Paris within twenty-four hours and repair to his estate located in Guyenne, there to remain until further notice . . ."'

The husband gave a loud snort.

'So there it is. After stealing my wife, mocking me on the stage to unanimous amusement and imprisoning me, now he exiles me. As a cuckold all that remains is to get myself to my distant chateau of Bonnefont, where our daughter and my mother are waiting . . .'

'". . . His Majesty prohibits him from leaving his estate without his tacit consent, on pain of punishment!" Which means,' confirmed the horseman, 'that you will be beheaded or sent to the galleys.'

Then he concluded, '"His Majesty orders all his officers and subjects to come to his assistance."'

'And our son?' cried the marquis. 'I will not leave without him!'

'He has been brought back from court. You will find him at Rue Taranne.'

The circle of soldiers dispersed and the people around the Marquis de Montespan hurriedly moved away, averting their gaze. Walking amidst the chicken blood and feathers on the *quai*, Louis-Henri went home on foot, to the other side of the Seine, shouting all the way:

> *'One day o'er this earth*
> *We will scatter the bones*
> *Of the king of war:*
> *If the land will yield*
> *From one grain a hundred more*
> *Great God! Hail upon our harvest*
> *And take from us our crop!'*

27.

'In Saint-Denis as in Versailles
Lives a man sans heart and sans entrails
Waste not your prayers upon his soul
Such a monster doth not have one!'

'Stop singing your absolutely appallingly subversive ditties! They're like cuckoos' eggs in a nest of turtledoves!' Joseph Abraham was holding his head in both hands as clients fled his shop. Even those in the middle of being shaved had left at a run, with foam on their chins and towels still round their necks, when they saw the cuckold waltz in and heard his bawdy verse: 'He's a madman!'

The wigmaker was of a similar mind. 'They're right, or are you rolling drunk?'

Only Constance Abraham came to the marquis's defence,

slapping her husband with a cloth, as she asked him, 'Would you do all that to have me back? Would you risk your life?'

A child was walking across the tiles, striking poses. It was Louis-Antoine, in priceless silks and exorbitant satins. He was three years old, and now he examined his pater's black, muddy clothing with a disdainful air.

'Ah, good day, Father.'

He went on his way without paying his father further attention. He followed a line separating the floor tiles as if he were walking along a thread, learning to move as a courtier did, with his hands just so . . .

To the wigmakers, his landlords, Montespan explained, 'I will leave Paris before nightfall. Are the little maid and Madame Larivière no longer here?'

'They departed nigh on a month ago, but they left your clothes on the table in the salon. They also found, in a wardrobe, the wedding dress belonging to . . .'

'I shall tell the coachman to come and collect everything and stow it in the carriage. But first of all – what time is it? – I must go and fetch something. Madame Abraham, would you be so kind as to lend me a basket with some linen at the bottom?'

While Constance trotted off to the back of the shop, Joseph trained a professional eye on the marquis's scalp and offered to lend him an ash-blue periwig.

'Here, cover your head with this instead to go out on your errand, for your blond wig is still in such a state! The apprentices will remove the dust and put it right before you return.'

The apprentices? Louis-Henri looked up at them; they were slumped sadly over the workbench in the mezzanine.

'What's wrong with them?'

'For some time now, they have lost their zest for life. I have them eat horsemeat once a week, but there's nothing for it. They are listless, they sigh . . . When the shop door opens, they raise their heads as if they were waiting for someone, then they look down again with a moan. Give me your wig – that will keep them busy.'

28.

Near Place du Carrousel, an ash-blue periwig turned right on Rue de l'Échelle and continued towards a discreet grey house set back from the street. The bells in the adjoining chapel rang eleven o'clock. Montespan wondered how one could tell that the bell was cracked. The door of the grey house opened and a nurse came out and locked it behind her. She quickened her step towards the place of worship. The millet seeds bounced in the rattle on her chest and mingled with the sound of a wooden heel-maker's hammering. Louis-Henri strode ahead with his wicker basket. Just as the craftsman raised his arm and lowered it again to strike, the marquis smashed his elbow into the window on the ground floor of the grey house. The heel-maker looked at the ground all around him, astonished to have heard a sound of breaking glass.

'It must be true, then, that my wood is not dry enough!'

The Gascon was already in the kitchen, which led to a stairway. He went up to the first floor, found a door and opened it.

He went into a dark room with closed windows and shutters. There was a bad smell; it needed airing. He lit a candle on the mantelpiece, then lifted the candle with its long smoky yellow flame. He looked around and saw an infant tucked up in a cradle. With his basket under his arm, he drew closer.

'Here's your father come to take you to Guyenne . . .'

Out of caution, he shielded the flame with his hand as he drew near the baby. Through his fingers the infant's face was bathed in light.

'God's teeth!'

The child was a monster. A tiny body with a gigantic head, an enormous cowpat of a head palpitating like a calf's lung, something absolutely unnatural and unbearable to behold. In the middle of this immense flaccid heap that seemed to be full of burning liquid, the child's features were those of an ancient man expiring on his deathbed. His ugly, suffering mouth was open, struggling for air. The hydrocephalic bastard had been born (via his father!) of stock too long inbred. The genes were utterly confused. There was a defect in the race. Montespan abandoned the idea of abducting him.

'I should not like people to think he is my own.'

In any event, he could not be moved; the infant was not viable. He would never have been able to lift his head. He should not have existed at all, he was an error in the order of things. That was Montespan's diagnosis on seeing this pitiful child, whom no one had bothered to name. The Gascon trailed his finger in the soot of the fireplace then went over to give him a name. On the monstrous brow, the fruit of the love between the stage Jupiter and Alcmene-Françoise, the Amphitryon of the farce wrote: HERCULE.

29.

'Your blond periwig is ridiculous, Father.'

Montespan, sitting on the banquette in his carriage, turned to Louis-Antoine, who was staring at him.

'Monsieur Abraham's apprentices styled my wig like your mother's hairstyle. They cut it, stretched it up over the scalp, and made ringlets on either side . . . I don't know why they did that. The wigmaker shouted and scolded them, but never mind, it was time to leave.'

Wearing his *hurluberlu*, Louis-Henri looked through the small window in front at the trace horses' hindquarters, then out of the side window at the passing countryside with its shrubbery, and brambles that scratched the side of the horned carriage.

Draped in black crêpe, the mourning carriage with its stag's antlers was in use once again, and an astonished

France watched as the disgraced man made his way along the interminable road towards his native Pyrenees.

As everyone in Versailles and Paris knew of the marquis's misfortune, he in turn wanted the good folk in the provinces – the burghers of the towns they went through, the peasants in their fields, everyone down to the last beggar – to know of his cuckolding and how the King had abused him. He wanted the rumour of it to rouse the curious, and for word to spread. He saw the stupefaction in their eyes, the astonishment that caused jaws to drop, revealing toothless mouths. There were mocking gentlemen and priests and merchants who laughed at the cuckold as he rode through their towns. But other minds were fascinated and predicted that someday there would be those who would pore over dusty archives and offer the heady wine of praise . . . Next to the Gascon, and wrapped in a cloak of mauve serge, his three-year-old son had fallen asleep. All the way along the sandy highway the persistent dust of the road seeped into the carriage, getting into everything, including clothes and lace. Louis-Henri held Françoise's wedding gown spread across his lap. He could not help but continue to love her. His memory was filled with her presence, with her lively, witty speech.

As night fell after a first afternoon of travelling, they stopped at a semblance of an inn where Montespan ordered the horses to be unharnessed and the coachman to be fed, then he lifted his sleeping son in his arms. The little boy opened his eyes, saw the Gascon's blond curls and said, 'Maman . . . oh . . . Father, is it true I'm a marquis? Maman told me that—'

'You are indeed. Only one male in the family can hold the title, and as my brother was killed in a duel, you are now the Marquis d'Antin.'

The inn was an unimaginably poor and miserable dump: there was nothing there but old women spinning. Without getting undressed, they lay upon the fresh straw. The door's boards were loose and it banged and creaked; it had no lock. There were holes in the roof. The squire, stretched out on his bed of forage, gazed at the milky halo around the moon. Golden stars shifted like sand. Through the open door, the shadow of the trees along the fog-shrouded river spread like smoke, whilst in the sky . . .

Montespan dozed off.

30.

At first light the following day, the coachman hollered into the mist of the October morning and the carriage set off again along the rutted roads. As the horses whinnied, their breath showed in a volcano of steam. Their hooves made a fearful clatter and the carriage's iron-rimmed wheels sent out a shower of sparks, as from a smithy's forge, whenever they struck the stones on the road.

Although he was clinging to the leather strap hanging from the ceiling, Montespan's shoulder was dashed against the door several times and he feared that the berlin, swerving so violently, might topple over. Louis-Antoine frequently left his seat altogether. Oh, how cruelly the road buffeted them about. The carriage struggled to climb a hill despite the coachman's oaths and the cracking of his whip. Montespan got out to push the wheel, and looked at the sky.

'The weather has turned dreary. I expect it will rain.'

Roads that were dusty in fine weather became veritable quagmires when it rained. To continue along this muddy track, they would have had to lay down bulrushes covered with planks, so the horned black carriage made its way instead through a field, to the fury of the peasants. Then came a bridge that would have collapsed under the weight of the vehicle so they took a ferry to cross the river. Using the royal highways, they covered no more than twelve leagues a day. Montespan's coach overturned. It took many hours to repair. Then it became mired in the mud: oxen were sent for to pull them out of difficulty.

'This vexatious, wicked carriage. Once the healthiest and strongest of conveyances, it is now hastening to its tomb . . .' sighed the marquis when an axle broke.

It had to be replaced. That would take three hours or more. Fortunately, there was a coaching inn not far from there, with over a dozen spare horses and a blacksmith.

31.

The horned carriage had stopped in a large town in front of a platform where a nobleman was kneeling, about to be beheaded. The executioner raised his sword. He aimed for the neck. He had to make sure not to strike the shoulders, for then he would have to start all over again, nor the skull (everyone would have been splattered with bits of brain). The ideal target was between two vertebrae – *pop!* The head would fly off; it was child's play.

To reward his pupils for their good work, a schoolmaster had invited them to see the condemned man being sacrificed. The executioner still held his sword in the air. All that had been missing from this fatal marriage between executioner and victim was the drum roll: now came a first burst of the drumsticks against a stretched hide. A third man on the platform – a magistrate in his robes – began to speak, talking of the *lèse-majesté* that had besmirched the King's honour and, in a loud voice, he read out the authorities' proclamation. The executioner's shoulders twisted to the right to launch the movement of the blade. Louis-Henri lowered the leather curtain at the window of his carriage. In relative darkness, by his son's side, he heard the blade whistle through the air and *pop!* In the ensuing silence he could sense the crowd was about to applaud. The common folk always loved a firm hand that subjugated and a merciless whip. The man's torso would have remained tense and erect for a moment, and now it collapsed, making a sound like a falling cowpat. Montespan grimaced.

'There we are, that was a man. His family shall be banished from the realm, his lands confiscated, his home burnt down and his name shall never be borne by any of his children. He never existed.'

The square emptied. The horned carriage swayed as the coachman climbed back up on his perch – 'Gee up!' – and continued on its way. Louis-Henri raised the leather curtain whilst his son (visibly not terribly distraught over the event) declared, 'One must always be careful to obey the King and submit to his every desire; Maman said so.'

Montespan, who could well imagine the nature of the King's desires in regard to his wife, made a face.

In a tavern draped with spiders' webs, the serving wench – not the docile type with her coarse patois – brought some soup and poured mutton gravy onto dry mince. There was a foul smell in the insalubrious establishment.

Louis-Antoine, Marquis d'Antin, sitting straight-backed on his bench, found something lacking in everything he saw. There was too much drinking in these inns; it was vulgar to keep one's knife in one's hand the way these commoners did; he disapproved of their bawdy insults.

'One must avoid oaths! It is everyone's opinion that table manners are what distinguishes man from beast, and the well-educated nobleman from the ill-mannered ruffian,' the dainty child continued, his napkin over his shoulder, as was the custom at court.

He observed a labourer in clogs – his legs protected by gaiters, his breeches worn-out at the knee – slumped wearily over his soup, where bits of pork, beans and cabbage floated.

'To put one's elbows on the table, even just one, is inexcusable, except for people who are either old or unwell.'

Louis-Henri rolled his eyes as he poured his wine.

'Father, one must not drink before one has eaten: 'tis the very hallmark of a drunkard. Nor must one wolf down one's food as you are now doing, for that is how animals behave. To fill oneself to the gills then exhale in satisfaction, that is precisely how a horse behaves. Do refrain from swallowing pieces whole, for that is what storks do.'

Montespan scratched his blond *hurluberlu* wig.

'Father, I do not like poor people.'

'Louis-Antoine, you may speak most eloquently for your age, but I wonder if you are not also a truly revolting little individual.'

'Father, I should prefer you to address me henceforth according to my rank: I am a marquis, after all.'

'Is that so?'

32.

'Hello! Montespan! Is it you? Of course, it must be you – the horned carriage . . . Do you not recognise me? Charuel! We fought together at Gigeri. Have you come for a taste of the chains to which you are destined? Ha-ha-ha!'

The colourful captain, sitting at the rear of a carriage facing a convoy of captives, struck the coach with his fist to alert the person inside.

'Major Gadagne! Look who has stopped to let us pass in this gully! 'Tis Montespan!'

'The troublesome cuckold? Stop the convoy.'

The Duc de Gadagne stepped down from his vehicle and stretched. He was wearing a richly tasselled cravat and a short doublet open on a shirt that was full at the waist and in the sleeves. He had a sash in the shape of a flower tied round his middle, and he was wearing a fairly wide skirt, stockings held up with garters, buckled shoes, a long wig and a blue felt hat.

'The Marquis de Montespan! So, shall we take you with us? No, you don't fancy it?'

Louis-Henri gazed at the immense human ribbon: three hundred men condemned to the galleys, chained by the neck in twos, then joined together by a long chain passing through each pair.

'We come from Rennes,' said Gadagne. 'In one month we'll be in Marseilles. Well, you and I shall, no doubt,' he said with a smile to Charuel, 'but they . . . not all of them. One out of three will succumb between the prison and the port of embarkation.'

Louis-Henri pursed his lips at the sight of the men crushed by the weight of their chains. He thought of the frequent rain on their bodies which would only dry with time, not to mention the fleas and scabies. They were rogues, thieves, deserters, Protestants.

'His Majesty wishes to reinstate the fleet of convict-galleys and increase the number of galley-slaves by any means possible,' explained the commander of the gang of convicts. 'His intention is to condemn as many prisoners as possible to the galleys.'

'Any man who dares disobey – hand him an oar in the Mediterranean! Any woman who is wicked – deport her to the New World! The King knows how to maintain order in France,' said Charuel appreciatively, 'as do we with our chained men. The survivors arrive in a most deplorable state and then they row in perfectly Dantesque conditions. Would you like a chicken thigh?'

Gadagne and Charuel sat on a rock and made the most of this fortuitous encounter with the marquis to have a bite to eat.

'We also have some smoked sausages, *andouilles* or blackbird terrine if you prefer.'

The duc covered his shoulder with a napkin (a gesture much appreciated by Louis-Antoine, who had climbed down from the horned carriage). The child also admired the luxurious clothing worn by the commander of the chained men, who, with his captain, was eagerly describing life on the galleys to the marquis.

'You'll be sorry you turned down our cold meat when the day comes that you, too, will only be allowed one meal a day – crackers and a bowl of soup with a few beans – and a ration of plonk diluted with sea water. You'll shit in a wooden bucket and sleep head to toe on benches with the other churls, madmen and murderers.'

Louis-Henri nodded, whilst looking at the men condemned to such a fate.

'May I speak to them?'

'Pray do, Marquis, make their acquaintance! Who knows, you may soon journey by their side, for you are a gentleman all Paris suspects of having written a most insolent thing on the brow of the King's bastard son . . . Might you truly have dared such a thing? Whatever the case may be, the infant is dead.'

Montespan got to his feet and, with Louis-Antoine at his side, he walked past the column of men. He asked a few of them why they were there. One of them said he had been sentenced to the galleys for life for stealing honey bees. A boy wept – ten years of slavery for stealing a few leeks from his neighbour's garden.

The Marquis d'Antin said thoughtfully, 'I will always submit to the King's bidding.'

The Gascon looked at his son.

33.

The Garonne wound lazily through the hills, whilst on the horizon, growing ever higher, the blue chain of the Pyrenees loomed mighty and solemn. The landscape became rougher, more rugged. After six more changes of horses, the carriage rolled across the first snow, for, once past the banks of the river Baïse, the weather was freezing from November onwards. These were the lands of the marquisate of Montespan. In the distance a massive chateau seemed to crush the tiny village of Bonnefont huddled at its feet. The villagers could not believe their eyes when they saw what was coming towards them.

'Is that our master? Aye, 'tis our Monsieur le marquis.'

In the vehicle, Louis-Henri rubbed and examined his hands, still astonished not to find even the tiniest venereal pustule, and thought of the incurable pain of his existence.

The angelus was chiming at the parish church. Yokels were following the carriage, surrounding it and preceding it. Some had already gone to pound on the door of the chateau to give the alert.

It was Cartet – the erstwhile sergeant from Puigcerdá – who pushed open the gates with his strong arms. He still sported his dagger-hilt moustache, and his jaw did not drop at the sight of the carriage, which surprised Montespan, for as he alighted he saw that all the villagers were standing stock still to gaze at the stag's antlers dominating the black coach. With nudges and muttered patois they urged each other to ogle the marquis's new coat of arms on the doors. Louis-Henri, in his solemn mourning clothes, declared, 'I am a cuckold! Moreover,' he added, turning to Cartet, 'we shall have to raise the entrance by a *toise* so that when I enter the courtyard my horns shall have room to pass.'

The former sergeant, now the steward, was appreciative.

'There is a touch of the roughneck soldier in ye, Monsieur le marquis . . .'

Chrestienne de Zamet made her entrance into the courtyard.

'My son, such a wig! What a strange blond hairstyle – is it the new Paris fashion?'

'Alas, Mother, it is.'

Then it was Marie-Christine's turn to appear, this 15 November 1668. Her father knelt down and took her in his arms.

'Happy birthday, my sweet,' he said, although it was not her birthday. 'You are five years old today, we must celebrate. I've brought you a present.'

'Maman?'

'. . . a present I bought in Toulouse. Look, your little brother is giving it to you.'

The rather ugly little girl took the doll that Louis-Antoine handed to her, and she seemed disappointed.

'It's not Maman . . .'

Crouching down, the father removed his *hurluberlu* periwig and put it on the human figurine, which now disappeared almost entirely beneath the wig. This brought a smile to Marie-Christine's lips. She hugged the doll to her little chest and slipped her index finger into one of the ringlets, turning it round and round, whilst an adolescent girl came up shyly. Montespan looked up.

'Dorothée?!'

Behind her, Madame Larivière was drying her hands on her apron. Chrestienne de Zamet told her son, 'They arrived last week and that is how we learnt of your misfortune, my poor boy. We didn't have a cook, so I hired her. I suspected that you—'

'You did well, Mother. Good day, Madame Larivière,' he said, standing up.

The olive-skinned cook apologised.

'When I left Paris, I didn't know where to go with my daughter . . .'

'Dorothée is your daughter? Well, well, I'm often the last to be informed,' smiled the cuckold.

'You must be weary from the journey, and famished. I shall make the supper and lay the table. Come, Dorothée.'

'Let her stay,' interrupted Cartet. 'Look how happy they are playing with the doll. I will help you.'

The cook with her spindly legs and the rustic steward headed off together in the direction of the kitchen, whilst Chrestienne de Zamet whispered in her son's ear, while indicating with her hand, 'I think that the pair of them . . .'

'Cartet with Madame Larivière? Really? Better and better.'

Louis-Antoine stood in his luxuriant silks in the courtyard where grass grew amidst the loose stones, and he looked at the building – a dovecote and a square tower covered in ivy, surrounded by a stinking moat. He enquired innocently, 'Is this the steward's house, or the chateau?'

Behind him was a terrace overlooking a garden lying fallow, surrounded by two small groves leading to the river. With its blunt square shape, the chateau, in its rustic solidity and simplicity, was a model residence for a poor marquis. In the kitchen, Cartet lifted a heavy steaming cooking pot with one hand and held it out before him. Madame Larivière felt his biceps and shoulder admiringly.

'How muscular you are, Cartet! It's such an effort for me to hook it up on the trammel.'

'You need only ask. Ah, Captain . . . um . . . Monsieur le marquis, dinner is ready. I hunted some hare in your woods and Madame Larivière has made a divine stew the likes of which we did not see in Puigcerdá! We should have taken her with us.'

The olive-skinned cook flushed with embarrassment whilst Chrestienne de Zamet smiled at them knowingly and suggested, 'Let us eat together to celebrate being reunited, and for Marie-Christine's birthday!'

'Father, are we going to share the meal with the servants?' enquired a stunned Louis-Antoine.

The table would have been filled with happiness but for the absence of . . . The little Marquis d'Antin certainly entertained them with his comments. To the former sergeant he said, 'Dipping one's finger in the gravy is typical of village folk; lifting one's dirty greasy fingers to one's lips to lick them, or drying them on one's clothing is not appropriate. It would be more seemly to use the tablecloth or the napkin.'

The steward – who had the face of an assassin – looked at him, taken aback, then sliced into the hare as if it were an Angelet, whilst Dorothée held out her plate.

'If someone is cutting the meat, it is not seemly to extend either hand or plate before one has offered it to you,' scolded Louis-Antoine.

Marie-Christine did not want to eat. She held her spoon incorrectly, asked for too much to drink, and gesticulated, all of which displeased her brother.

Once the table was cleared, Chrestienne de Zamet, leaning against the dresser, lifted a candied cherry to her lips. Her grandson struck.

'Eating cherries on one's feet is eating like a lackey!'

'He speaks well for his age, does he not?' remarked the gentle grandmother.

'Aye,' sighed the father.

'And his skin is so remarkably like . . . so clear!'

The little boy, flattered, compared his hand to his sister's.

'My skin is whiter than yours.'

'It's only because your mother buried your umbilical cord beneath a rose bush!' blurted the father, who was beginning to find him difficult to tolerate.

'And what did Maman do for me?' asked Marie-Christine, with the *hurluberlu* doll in her arms.

'For you? Ah, yes, after cutting the cord, she lifted it up to your head to ensure long life . . .'

Now the little girl was sleeping sadly in her bed – it would have seemed, to look at her, that she was crying in her sleep, her eyes were so swollen and her breathing so laboured. Little girls have a sensitive heart. Oh, how sad her birthday had been! Pensively, whilst a tear fell silently from her big eyes, she murmured, 'When will Maman return?' Her father, the angel of cradles, dried her tears. In the child's heavy sleep he whispered a dream so joyful that

Marie-Christine's smiling half-closed lips seemed to murmur, 'Maman, there you are!' Louis-Henri left the child's room. He, too, could not banish Françoise's image: it filled all the space in his life. It was a terrible absence, as it was for his daughter. 'When is she coming back?' was the obsessive question. All along the gallery, its walls illuminated by the soft glow of his candle, the light was reflected in the mirrors and created a poetic still life. Louis-Henri put out the flame with a cone-shaped candle snuffer. In the huge fireplace in his room oak from his forests was burning. He tossed a log onto the embers and rekindled the fire. His bed consisted of a bedstead and three fustian mattresses. He slipped under the down-filled bolster. Outside, rats fleeing from owls scurried to the depths of the moat's green water in a rustling of leaves. The flames in the hearth reminded him of Françoise's thick curls. The marquis bit the lace on his pillow.

34.

The crowd entered the church in Bonnefont, anointing themselves with holy water. A little bell was ringing and the priests were kneeling at the altar.

'The Lord sayeth . . .'

Above an open coffin placed on trestles, the priest Destival, who was over eighty, had difficulty hearing or speaking because of his advanced age. The *Pater* and *Ave* were read in Latin, 'I believe in God' in French . . . Incredibly gentle, he drooled faith from his toothless mouth. In the name of the father, the son, and the holy ghost, he said that the person in the open coffin had died a good Christian and a good Catholic.

Louis-Antoine looked all round the church.

'Who died?'

Beneath his cap, the little Marquis d'Antin looked

somewhat haughty. He had a shock of curly locks. His mobile nostrils resembled his mother's. But who had died? It was not his grandmother – this tall, pious woman who was removing his cap. So who had died? wondered the little boy. Not his sister with her very thick eyebrows. He saw her, next to Dorothée, weeping, turning in her fingers a cap with two bells. Louis-Antoine did not understand why. When he asked her, she burst into tears. His father had not died – he was there, at the front, the country marquis who lived meagrely on his land and was proud of his pew at church. He wore full mourning and black silk stockings, and had replaced the decorative buckles on his shoes with simple iron buckles. Madame Larivière had not snuffed it, either: she was singing next to Cartet, who grumbled on observing Montespan's back: 'That whore will kill him yet.' Of whom was he speaking? Louis-Antoine's mother must still have been alive, else they would have told him and then, this morning, before the ceremony, everyone had been speaking of Françoise in the present tense, so it was not she. Who had passed away? A bumpkin from Aquitaine? No, there would not have been so many handsomely dressed people. With the whiff of incense came an overwhelming languor. Then there was the invocation beneath the cross. The old priest reached his lips towards Christ's nailed feet and once he had kissed them to see Paradise, he turned round, spreading his arms. Gentlemen in official livery, carrying a heavy candle engraved with the Montespan crest (with the horns added), went up to the coffin. One after the other they waved a holy-water sprinkler over the open box, a half-smile on their lips that Louis-Antoine did not miss. It must have been his father who had invited them. He remembered hearing him declare that they would have to send a notice regarding the burial to all the lords in the region.

Now Montespan motioned to his children to follow him down the central aisle. Marie-Christine went first, on tiptoe, and lifted the sprinkler above the coffin, then handed it to her brother, whom Louis-Henri was holding in his arms to help him. The little boy leant over the coffin.

'What? There is nothing in the box!'

There was nothing for him, nor for anyone else in the church, no doubt, but for Montespan there was everything. When the undertakers had placed the lid back on the box and were preparing to nail it down, the marquis's sighs and tears became cries mingled with kisses and embraces; Louis-Henri clung so desperately to the empty coffin that they could not close it. It took several persuasive lords to pull him away.

Outside, he took his two children by the hand and, with his hat under his arm, was followed by a bevy of stunned friends. People were walking in silence, disconcerted by the tragicomical spectacle of the marquis's sorrow as he followed the empty coffin behind his horned carriage. Even the black horses pulling the vehicle wore stag's horns.

This was a land of stone and blazing summer sun, where tempers easily became heated, and moustaches were twirled: the local people had come out in defence of their marquis and his extravagant behaviour – he was a marvellously exemplary Gascon! A cuckold who did not meekly bow his head. They praised his escapades, embellished them in their numerous lively retellings. The coffin, followed by the assembly from the parish, was taken with great pomp to the top of a hill for burial. Louis-Henri leant over the whirling void of an abyss.

'So what are we burying?' asked Louis-Antoine of his traumatised sister.

The bells of Notre-Dame-des-Neiges were ringing the death knell of the marquis's disastrous marriage.

'I have often been invited to funerals,' sighed the Seigneur de Gramont in the ear of the Seigneur de Biron, as they walked back to the village, 'but I have never before been invited to attend the funeral of a love.'

'Of what did it die? I have heard tell of abuse.'

'I fear it was also from a fit of undue vanity and ambition.'

To the sound of a little bell, the death crier announced that for one month mourning would be worn as far as the banks of the Baïse.

'He's a decent, polite sort, the best marquis on earth,' continued Biron. 'He has but one failing: a stubborn love.'

Montespan, alone on the hill, crouched down and planted

before the grave a simple wooden cross where two dates were carved: 1663–1667.

''Tis young to die at the age of four.'

He stood back up, facing into the tramontana blowing above the valley.

'May the wind carry you away from your terrace at Versailles, Françoise. If I thought it might bring you here upon a whirlwind, God knows I would keep all my windows open and welcome you!'

But the sky was growing darker. Night fell early in winter, darkness reigned for long hours. Nocturnal shadows were the domain of fear – ghosts, wolves, evil spells were the accomplices of the night.

Louis-Henri left his message on the wind and headed back down to the chateau, that isolated refuge for crows. In his bed, Louis-Antoine was crying, 'Oh, my God, where am I?' They ran to him. 'Oh, I do not know where I am.' His blankets had all fallen off; his father tucked him in again. Montespan's mother said, 'The little girl also woke with a fright, she woke several times . . . Her imagination is greatly overwrought by the ceremony. She complained to me of a headache and told me it was from weeping. Life is hard, and short. It quickly forces children to behave as adults, does it not?'

Louis-Henri did not reply, as if he had not heard.

35.

The day after the funeral of his love, Montespan found himself wishing he could believe in resurrection. After all, had Françoise not been born of a dead woman? When they had finished supper and he was still sitting with his elbows on the long oak table in the kitchen, he drummed his fingers against his glass and listened to the whistling of the water being boiled for the washing up. His short-necked steward, who was wearing a beaver cap adorned with feathers, observed him and said to the cook, who was scrubbing a cauldron, 'We must make him eat beef.'

Madame Larivière did not share his opinion.

'Beef may be solid food for the body, but it makes the blood thick and melancholic. Chicken is better; it revives even the weakest of natures.'

Cartet smoothed his moustache then took hold of a

varnished potbellied jug full of Muscat wine from Frontignan, and poured a plentiful glass for Louis-Henri.

'Come now! To keep your head above water, don't let despair get the better of you. A spot of wine can awaken and delight an entire soul. Let's make the best of things ...'

The marquis took up his glass and swallowed it down in one gulp. The steward refilled his glass with the nectar.

'And then, like the children and your mother, you must away to bed, Captain.'

'To bed . . . In wrinkled sheets, where my body lies heavy with painful dreams and my muscles ache. I have the vapours when night falls, my mouth hurts, my hands clench.'

The cook and the steward exchanged furtive glances; Cartet walked across the creaking floor to fetch an instrument and tried to string together a few true notes. 'It takes longer to tune a lute than to play it. It's tricky to play, unlike the guitar from Spain.'

The marquis was bored in the rustic solitude of Bonnefont. He was assailed by bitter thoughts. On his lips he still had the taste of Françoise's kisses. He reached for a wicker-covered bottle of rose-flavoured ratafia, grabbed it, pushed back his bench and left the room. Outside, snowflakes fluttered like feathers.

He was mired in the uselessness of his days and nights, and there was nothing left for him but to be patient and drink rhubarb tea in the evening for as long as his loving, faithful wife was caught up in the dizzy whirl of royal favour. All he wanted was for her to return to him – the memory of her voice tore his heart to shreds.

As he sat on the low wall by the moat, facing the chateau, remembered images paraded in front of him . . . Françoise's face haunted him, obsessed him, and he was wretched. Madame Larivière ordered Cartet to stop his dissonant scratching on the lute and to put it away in the old guardroom. Louis-Henri saw his love reappear before his eyes, but it was the steward inside the chateau walking past a window with a candlestick in his hand. The marquis took a long swallow of ratafia (there were not only roses in this potion) and would have liked to believe it was Françoise he could see. He rushed to the guardroom, flung open the door and cried, 'Cartet, go quickly and fetch my wife's wedding gown and put it on.'

'What?'

'Then you'll walk past the window with the candle, several times. During that time I'll sit on the wall and watch you. *Hic.*'

'But, Captain, I'm too fat, specially in my bearskin breeches; the gown won't fit me.'

'Then strip off your breeches and leave the gown unlaced at the back.'

'Oh, Monsieur le marquis!'

'Take off that hat, too, Cartet, that beaver thing with the feathers. I must believe you are Françoise.'

Sitting by the moat with his rose ratafia liqueur bottle to his lips, Montespan raised the bottom of the bottle and gazed at the windows. He prepared to enjoy the sight of Cartet imitating his wife. In the beginning he was disappointed, for Cartet galumphed round-shouldered in front of the windows, looking like an old-time brigand.

'Better than that!' shouted the marquis. 'You must strike a pose, affect an attitude, be plausible! Pretend you are powdering your face or something like that.'

The erstwhile sergeant did as he was asked. He walked along, swaying his hips; he twirled on the spot and gracefully lifted his paws to his face. In the snow and the dark, Madame Larivière observed him from the shadow of the horned carriage, near a tall wisteria. Montespan, *hic*, hugged the empty bottle to his chest and opened his eyes wide. His darkness lifted a little. He found himself pursued by illusions and ghosts. He got up, drifted for a moment, incredulous and wandering, then rushed towards the old guardroom. Madame Larivière followed him. On entering the room, the marquis cried out, 'The days have gone by so slowly; it seems like centuries since you left me, Françoise!'

'Hey, Captain, it's me,' said Cartet on finding himself entwined in the marquis's over-eager embrace, at the mercy of his groping hands. 'Monsieur de Montespan, I am your steward!'

'Ah, how soft your lips are, my sweet,' said the cuckold,

trying to kiss his former sergeant. 'How I love your ringlets . . .'

'That's my moustache!'

'Turn round. I see you have already undone your gown, you saucy wench . . .'

Madame Larivière came closer and stood in the doorway whilst Montespan tried desperately to make love to the steward, who resisted as best he could, tangled up in the wedding gown.

'Monsieur de Montespan, this is the second time you've confused me with somebody else! The first time was at Puigcerdá, when you were wounded . . .'

'The second time? I did not know, Cartet, that you indulged in the Italian vice!' exclaimed the cook, amidst the swirling snow.

The bare-bottomed steward in his pearl-embroidered red gown turned round. 'No, no, Madame Lariri, it's a terrible misunderstanding!'

'Indeed, so I see . . . Make the best of things then,' said she, leaving the room with great dignity.

In a wedding gown, and with his soldier's honour wounded, Cartet protested in the name of all the armies. 'I will not let you insinuate that . . .' But he collapsed among his pearls and tore off the incriminating gown.

'Madame Larivière, Madame Lariri!'

Naked and hairy, his fat thighs jiggling, he hurried after the cook in the falling snow to explain to her that . . .

36.

Dawn broke over the murky water in the chateau moat at Bonnefont. The fire in the hearth in the marquis's bedchamber was slowly dying. Weary, Montespan got up from his bed: he had a headache, and went over to a basin covered by a fine crust of ice. He pressed it with his fingers and the water seeped up from the frozen film, forming a mirror where the cuckold could gaze at his drawn features and the circles under his eyes. He pressed harder and the ice broke. The water was glacial. He pulled on a rope hanging along the wall to ring the bell in the kitchen.

Crystals of ice distorted the view from the window-panes of his second-floor chamber. A thin veil of mist was drifting over the whitened fields in the valley. Curls of smoke rose above the farms. In the distance lay the high chain of the Pyrenees. Madame Larivière scratched at the door then came in with a kettle of steaming water. Trails of vapour streamed from the kettle's spout and the cook's nostrils, as if she were fuming within.

'Is there something wrong, Madame Larivière?' asked the marquis.

'I slept poorly. An emissary from the King has just arrived and has asked to speak to you. He is waiting in the middle of the courtyard, observing the chateau.'

'Have him come up and wait in the reception hall while I perform my ablutions.'

'You would make him wait, would rather wash than scrub yourself with a dry towel, when 'tis known the doctors are wary of water? 'Tis a carrier of all manner of disease, it dilates the pores, and enters the body to corrupt and weaken it!'

In his long underbreeches, the marquis removed his shirt and felt the skin on his arms and torso.

'If I were to be contaminated, it would have happened already long ago . . .'

'As for the King, he has only washed once in his life. Every morning, the first valet places a few drops of spirits of wine on His Majesty's hands. His lord chamberlain brings the font: Louis makes the sign of the cross, he is cleansed. Next thing, you'll be bathing in the sea, a folly for madmen and maniacs!'

The cook slammed the door behind her. The marquis smiled.

Washed, and dressed in mourning, Montespan applied his perfume and went through another door that led to the reception hall where the emissary was waiting.

He was a proud cavalryman. He had long, curly hair and a thin moustache, and wore embroidery and lace under a heavy vermilion cloak. He smelt of his horse and of the urine and sweat of someone who had galloped for long hours. He looked the clean marquis up and down.

'The court is tired, Monsieur, of all this black you wear.'

And without being invited, the emissary went to sit in Louis-Henri's armchair and stretched out his red heels towards the edge of the hearth, where the cook had lit a fire.

'Marquis, your uncle, the Archbishop of Sens, is at great risk of incurring royal wrath for having taken your side. In his diocese, he has denounced His Majesty's adultery with a married woman, and has published the ancient canons branding it a violation of religious law. The King has threatened him with a *lettre de cachet* but the prelate responded with another threat: excommunication. He wants to force the Pope to issue a public reprimand to the King of France. It is becoming an affair of state.'

The emissary's tone was as icy as the season. He got up and walked from one side of the hall to the other.

'In the event that a man who has received the nine unctions of oil from the holy phial should be reduced to the sorry rank of the debauched, it will cause a most fearful uproar, one that will resound with horror throughout all nations. The King has sent me to obtain your consent to the *fait accompli*, and your agreement to cease this public commotion. How much do you want?'

When one is near a burning fire, but moves away from it, to go to the far end of the room, one is seized by the chill. The emissary came back to the fireplace, where Montespan, leaning on his elbows, opened a page at random in a book by Tacitus and found, 'In Rome, everything was running to servility.'

'Colbert,' said the emissary, 'who is supposed to find the time to worry about the state of your soul, whilst seeing to problems as trivial as the government and the economy of France, has suggested in the name of His Majesty that a hundred thousand *écus* might do. I did say *écus*, I did not say *louis*, it's thrice the amount.'

The man was haughty and full of scorn. While Louis-Henri examined the mantelpiece above the fire, the envoy from Versailles added, 'As well as assuming all your debts, naturally, and that does amount, after all, to—'

'How is my wife?'

'The King's favourite has begun her fairy-tale career; she is, indisputably, queen of France. She has driven La Vallière to the Carmelites and has demanded she be harangued wherever she goes. Her apartments consist of twenty rooms on the first floor immediately beyond the King's council chamber, whereas the Queen has only eleven rooms on the second floor. She graciously adorns every festivity at court. Her train is carried by a peer of France, whereas the Queen has only a page to carry hers. The King is proud of his conquest, and takes pleasure in having others admire her, the way foreign dignitaries passing through Versailles might admire the buildings and gardens. She is cheerful and gay, and makes pleasantries with the finest of wit. She seems to adopt anything amusing. She is at ease with everyone, and has a gift for putting everyone in their place. At court they are saying that there will not be a war because His Majesty cannot be parted from la Montespan . . . One of Athénaïs's chambermaids said of the King, "He desires her thrice a day, 'tis like a huge raging hunger. And so impatient is he, he won't hesitate to tumble her in plain sight of the servants. But this hardly bothers the marquise, she gladly overlooks the minor inconveniences such ardour might cause." The Sun King's libido, in your wife's presence, has turned out to be as exceptional as his patience with regard to you might prove limited. Two hundred thousand *écus*!'

Montespan could hear the crowing of the cockerels outside, along with a blacksmith's first hammering, and the creaking of cartwheels bringing barrels of wine, hay for the horses, and stone for construction. The marquis went over to a stained-glass window whilst the emissary continued, 'One day, your wife accompanied His Majesty to review his German mercenaries. When she went by, they shouted, *"Königs Hure! Hure!"* (The King's whore! The whore!) "What are they saying?" she asked. When, later on, the monarch wanted to know how she had found the review, she replied, "Perfectly lovely, although I do find the Germans rather too naïve, calling things by their name." Terribly amusing, don't you agree? You can well understand that Louis wants to keep la Montespan by his side, all the more so now that she has begun to wear her "innocent" gowns again.'

The cuckold turned round. 'I am to be a father yet again?'

'She is right to feel her power enhanced by a new pregnancy. But this time, exceptional safety precautions shall be taken. The bastard, along with its brothers and sisters, no doubt still to come, will be lodged, that much I can tell you, in a lovely house on Rue Vaugirard with a large garden surrounded by high walls where the children can play, shielded from external view and protected by guards. To raise her progeny, the favourite has seen fit to entrust her children to the ugly widow of a paralytic scribbler, who was much weakened by rheumatism, a virtual gnome by the name of Paul Scarron. Upon his death, the lecherous hunchbacked poet left a will: "I leave my property to my wife on condition she marry again. Thus one man at least shall regret my passing!" Your wife has introduced the royal bastards' governess to His Majesty.'

Montespan lifted his head to the ceiling, stared at it at length and scratched his neck. The stinking horseman went over to him, and ran a finger over the saltpetre in the wall.

'Your wife's children will be better lodged than you are. Your chateau is full of cracks, the stones are coming loose, it is falling into ruin. You need to repair a step that the frost has split. One might presume – at best – that this is the home of a priest! Your situation is far from easeful, all you own is debts. You have been ostracised from the lansquenet tables in Paris, and whilst they may have been your wicked stepmothers, they were also your wet nurses. What are you going to live off, since your income amounts to no more than four hundred *livres* a year? You also owe a small fortune to a labourer who is going to take part of your land from you. Your disgrace in exile is a social death sentence. You are at the bottom of the ladder of nobility and your wife's merit would serve more to elevate you than anything that you might be able to achieve. If you would agree to remain silent and bow to the royal will rather than coming to this province to languish in your bitterness, you would own an *hôtel particulier* in the centre of Paris with thirty servants, as well as hundreds of hectares of land, from which you would receive your seignorial dues, and forests, and hunting grounds!'

Montespan let the emissary continue to rattle on in this meaningless way and went to sit down on a folding chair of iron and canvas. He listened to the wind whistling through the foothills of the Pyrenees, like a Sardana dance, and heard the amount the emissary from Versailles was now offering.

'Three hundred thousand *écus*! That means nine hundred thousand *livres*, almost one million. It is yours for the asking. What do you reply?'

Louis-Henri looked at the icicles hanging from the roof, then at the emissary.

'I do not know what is keeping me from throwing you out of the window.'

37.

'I can't stand having to pay for everything with coins stamped with the head of my wife's lover! Particularly as he is hideous, the filthy dwarf! What on earth does she see in him?'

Louis-Henri picked up a silver *écu* and began to detail the defects of the engraved figure. 'His nose is hooked and over-long, he has a thick neck, his cheeks are flabby. His breastplate with that Roman draping is ridiculous. I don't like his wig at all! 'Tis said his charm is . . . *exotic*. Well, I can't see it myself.'

The marquis bit the coin and tossed it to the steward.

'Catch it, Cartet, and tell the carpenter to make a wooden crate.'

'Another coffin? What shall we bury this time, your hope?'

'No, it shall be for the painting. Don't forget to measure it.'

While the steward was on his way out, a voice with a Montlhéry accent could be heard.

'The pose, Monsieur de Montespan.'

The itinerant painter, who travelled the length and breadth of France, going from chateau to chateau to offer his talents as a portrait painter and decorator (friezes for walls and above doors, illustrated ceilings) to the petty nobility, adjusted his model's pose.

'Turn more to the right, with your head looking straight towards me; there, that's it. Now don't move.'

Louis-Henri was sitting at his desk in the study on the first floor of the chateau, a freshly cut crow's quill between his fingers, pretending to write on an immaculate sheet of paper. Bareheaded, wearing an off-white hemp shirt, he had not wanted to cover his scalp with a wig, or to wear any of the ribbons, feathers, lace or artificial flowers with which a marquis posing for posterity generally adorned himself. The cuckold had wanted something intimate, and he contemplated the artist as if he were looking lovingly at his wife.

The painter from Montlhéry sat on a stool with his legs apart and sometimes leant forward to examine his model, accentuating in silence the curve of an eyelid heavy with sadness, or enhancing the shadow of a faint smile on his lips.

'Your mouth and your eyes often contradict each other,' said the portrait painter. 'When your pupils sparkle with mischief, your mouth droops in sorrow, and when your lips are upturned and jesting, your eyes grow misty with tears.'

The marquis said nothing and began to write.

23 June 1669

Françoise,

The window was open. The cicadas were singing. There was a whooshing sound as the scythes sliced through the stalks of grain. Louis-Henri looked up at the painter for a moment, then dipped his nib into the inkwell, into the black liquid made of vitriol and oak-gall.

Here is my portrait painted by Jean Sabatel that you shall put in your bedchamber when the King is no longer there. Let it remind you of me, and of the excessive tenderness I feel for you, and how many ways I liked to demonstrate that, on every occasion. Place my portrait therefore in the light, and look now and again upon a husband who adores you: a poor spouse who, because his wife has been taken from him, no longer knows what he does. I have become as accepting of ruin as they tell me you are now accepting of the bad air of a palace built on quicksand and degradation; there are people for whom I no longer fear ruin – you!

The marquis's pen hurried over the page, scratching heavily on the paper.

My fair bird, my turtledove, with your neck adorned with pearls you are inside a gilded cage two hundred leagues from where I languish in forced exile. I could not like any place where you are not. Is it not possible, my goddess, for you to fly away and join me? Or might you not know the love that your beautiful eyes, my sunlight, have truly aroused in my heart? 'Tis more than rage that I feel in my soul, knowing that you have been stolen by another who does not love you as I do. If you do not blush, my lady, I blush for you. But I swear to you on your person, which is what I hold dearest on earth, that . . .

The door to the study opened. Montespan looked round. The painter lifted his brush from the canvas. It was

Dorothée, who had come to look for the doll with the *hurluberlu* that Marie-Christine, who was standing behind her, had left there. The child, who shared the marquis's sad fate, clung to the servant's skirts. Dorothée was her only playmate: she was sixteen now and she looked like a woman. As for Marie-Christine, her cheeks were hollow, making her nose appear large. She was withering like a flower deprived of water. Now she came up to Louis-Henri and asked, 'To whom are you writing, Father?' The marquis smiled, but his eyes were creased with sadness. Tall, big-boned, muscular, infinitely polite, he enquired of his daughter if she had slept well the previous night. The child replied that henceforth she would like to sleep with Dorothée.

'For I am filled with dreams, alone in my bed. I fear the spirits, since my maman died.'

Montespan did not know what to say. Dorothée, who was more sensitive than she might have appeared, broke the silence by offering breakfast to the child – she was so thin – but she refused.

'No, I am not hungry.'

'But you must eat – it's no laughing matter; you must look at the clock face on the church tower if you are hungry, and when it tells you that eight or nine hours have passed since last you ate, then eat a good soup, take the clock's word for it, and you will begin to feel better.'

The two girls left the room, closing the door behind

them. Louis-Henri took up his pose again and peered pensively at his letter.

Our little girl is so thin, and she is exceeding weak. I would like her to drink milk, as the most beneficial of remedies, but she is so greatly averse to it that I hardly dare suggest it. She often suffers from lethargy and weariness, and loses her voice. I believe you would have reason to complain of me if I were not to let you know that her illness is serious. All the more so, as it has been thus for years, and this length of time is much to be feared unless she can find your gentle presence beside her again, which would keep her from being devoured by sorrow.

And I no longer condemn your behaviour; each of us seeks his own salvation. But assuredly I shall not find bliss through the path you take. Cast off the ambition with which they have cloaked you there, and you may not be as unhappy as you might think, and I am certain, my lady, that when disappointment sends you running into my arms, your love shall return.

This most passionate of husbands continues to adore you.

Louis-Henri de Pardaillan
Marquis de Montespan
A separated albeit inseparable husband

The cuckold slipped his folded missive into an envelope and was about to seal it when the painter from Montlhéry advised him, 'If the letter is for your wife, and you send it together with my painting, it's pointless to close the envelope. At the palace, letters are inspected by the King's "black cabinet" and they will intercept your words.'

'Ah, you're right,' conceded Louis-Henri.

So the marquis, with an insolence and pride that were inversely proportional to his reduced fortune, wrote on the back of the envelope:

To all those bitches and bastards in His Majesty's entourage who find cause for amusement in my correspondence!

38.

That day in December 1669 was one to remember. Louis-Antoine, the little Marquis d'Antin, was riding an English mare for the first time – an old, calm mount that ambled slowly across the cobblestones in the courtyard. The father admired his son's bearing, the instinctive way he sat on the horse. Marie-Christine by contrast, was terrified of horses.

'I've never seen a child sit better in a saddle, his body straight and his legs positioned as if he'd had instruction. Look at that, Cartet. Doesn't he look the proper horseman?'

The steward, who was at the top of a ladder leaning against the chateau's red entrance gate, finished working loose some bricks that he dropped on the ground, then turned to watch the marquis's son. As he turned back to the gate, he cried, 'Upon my word, I can see a carriage approaching, Captain. You are to have a visitor. There are guards walking alongside. I think they are dragoons.'

'Dragoons?'

Montespan was pleased to have visitors; they distracted him from the boredom of his isolated marquisate, and sometimes brought him news of other provinces and even of court, but why should there be dragoons alongside that coach? He went up to the gate, whilst more bricks rained down. The carriage stopped outside the chateau and a gentleman stepped out, peering at the steward on his ladder.

'Are you doing repairs, Marquis?'

'We are raising the roof of the entrance. For my horns.'

'Ah, still at it with your Gascon tricks? Such poor taste . . .'

An anxious woman, taking weary little steps, came to join them. It was Louis-Henri's mother; the visitor greeted her. 'Good day, Madame. How are you?' Chrestienne de Zamet had aged greatly since her son's return to Bonnefont the previous year, and she had a bad cough, but she had not lost her wit.

'It is said one should not speak of one's troubles – nor of one's children!'

'Are you poorly? Are you taking care of yourself?'

'I am taking a goodly number of remedies, it would be easier to count the grains of sand on the beach. To what do we owe the honour of your visit, Monsieur, representing as you do His Majesty in Guyenne?'

The intendant was wearing robes, and gloves of Point d'Angleterre lace. He had a small, ugly face, and a great deal of hair, which spared him the need for a wig. From his breath it was obvious that he had ruined his stomach through an excessive fondness for vinegar. He said to Louis-Henri, 'Bring all your people together in one room. I must speak to you in their presence.'

'Indeed?'

Montespan gave a short whistle through his fingers. 'Cartet, come down!' Then he called, 'Madame Larivière! Dorothée!' The cook came out into the courtyard with a cloth in her hands, and Marie-Christine's playmate opened a window on the first floor. 'Coming!' They joined the marquis and Chrestienne de Zamet in the old guardroom. The intendant looked at Louis-Henri in astonishment. 'Is that all? Don't you have any other servants?'

'I am somewhat short of money, Monsieur Macqueron . . . And when my father passed away, this spring in Toulouse, the estate was so burdened with debts, because he lent me so much, that in the end I have had to renounce it.'

'You won't make me weep over the state of your fortune, Marquis. None other I know on earth could so easily become exceedingly rich.'

A clerk stood by prepared to take notes. Outside, the dragoons were posted around the chateau walls and in the grounds to prevent anyone from leaving, but the intendant seemed discomfited. He grimaced, then asked, 'Monsieur de Montespan, at the time of the War of Devolution, did you have a dalliance with a young brunette from these parts with shining eyes and hot blood, a lass you are reputed to have abducted and dressed as a soldier in order to introduce her into your company and have her under your thumb? The family of the abducted woman have filed a complaint against you.'

'What?'

'There is yet another charge against you. You are accused of threatening to attack a convent in order to abduct a pretty nun, a sort of amorous dragonnade, if you like . . .'

Montespan spluttered in protest.

'If these facts are shown to be true, you risk life imprisonment in the dungeon at Pignerol.'

'It's all false, utterly false! Oh, God's teeth!' exclaimed the marquis indignantly. 'I am not interested in that sort of trickery outside marriage. I have never been one of those charmers, those so-called "lovers of the eleven thousand virgins". Never! A well-blessed husband like myself?'

Louis-Henri's feverish mother immediately came to her child's defence.

'My boy is honest, Monsieur Macqueron, and civil, and is known for his high moral standards.'

'Madame, a major who was posted outside Puigcerdá, a

libertine duc who is delighted by this story, has accused your son.'

'Such a charitable instinct to wish wounds and gashes upon one's fellows is exceeding common in the army,' said Cartet.

The intendant of Guyenne did indeed have his doubts. In the marquis's frank gaze he detected real stupefaction, which he had expected. From his robes he took a letter sealed in yellow (for judicial matters). From the colour of the wax, Montespan suspected that the missive would also contain further barbs. Macqueron continued, 'Two months ago, a special envoy from Louvois brought me a letter which he asked me to read in his presence. I was much surprised, but as I feared some shady mischief, I sought to protect myself and used the pretext of going to fetch my spectacles from the adjacent office. There I ordered my clerk to stand right next to the door and to listen and write down what I was about to say out loud to the envoy. And this is what I read,' he concluded, handing a copy of his letter to the marquis, who unfolded it and read.

21 September 1669

To Macqueron, Intendant of Guyenne

Have the captain, the Marquis de Montespan, convicted of some offence in order to try, through whatever means

218

*available, to implicate him in a matter that will appear
to be of a legal nature.*

*If you can contrive to have him strongly accused so
that the Sovereign Council will have the wherewithal to
hand down a severe sentence, that would be a good thing
indeed. You may suspect the grounds thereof if you are
at all acquainted with what is happening in this place.*

*Pray omit nothing that might ensure a successful
conclusion to what I desire at this time, and give me news
of it every day by separate letter in your hand, returning
this one to me.*

Louvois

Montespan was stunned. He echoed the last words of the
letter.

'". . . returning this one to me . . ." He did not want his
perfidy to remain in the archives . . .'

'Whereas I,' said the intendant, 'insisted on having this
copy to absolve myself of responsibility, by leaving to
posterity proof of the minister and the King's
intervention.'

The enormous flue fireplace in the old guardroom drew
poorly and the room was smoky. The marquis didn't feel
well, his head was spinning. He was nauseous and opened
a window wide, despite the fact that it was winter. In the
courtyard by the horned carriage now covered in wisteria,
Louis-Antoine was doing exercises on a pommel horse.

The cuckold turned back to the room. Matters could not be clearer: from being quite well-disposed towards him and offering him plenty of gold, His Majesty's hand had turned to persecution. The marquis was to be accused of as many wrongs as possible, even if they had to be invented, and the Gascon's image of model spouse had to be sullied. The rebel had to be brought to ruin by means 'that will appear to be of a legal nature': so it was written in the letter.

'They are conspiring to find a way to get rid of me once and for all, falsifying the facts and accusing me of a crime punishable by life imprisonment . . .'

A long silence reigned in the hall until Macqueron resumed his story.

'To begin with, I obeyed Louvois's instructions most tamely, and ordered an investigation against you, and I demanded that a number of stories be constructed that would implicate you and seem plausible before a tribunal, even if they required false testimony. But now I have my scruples, this weighs upon my conscience . . .'

'It does not seem to bother them at Versailles, "if you are at all acquainted with what is happening in this place".'

'Before I look for a pretext to try and avoid the Sovereign Council, which would sentence you, I would like first of all to be absolutely certain of the veracity of your good behaviour. That is why I wish to question your people in your presence.'

'Pray do so,' replied Montespan, relieved.

The intendant of Guyenne addressed Dorothée first of all.

'Has the marquis always behaved well towards you?'

'Yes, sir.'

'Has he ever made any inappropriate gestures towards your person, or said anything of a somewhat . . .'

'Oh, no, sir!'

'Are you sure?'

'Of course I am.'

'If anything has happened, or you have seen anything that seemed a bit suspicious, you must tell me. You know it is a mortal sin to lie to a man of the law?'

'I am not lying, Monsieur.'

The intendant's gaze circled slowly around the group, passing like a veil over the steward with his dagger-hilt moustache and his air of a forest brigand, and came to rest upon the marquis's mother. 'Have you nothing to reveal to me, Madame?'

'From the moment my son met the woman who would become his wife, he has adored none but her. All other female forms are invisible to him. A mother knows such things.'

Macqueron's gaze narrowed upon Madame Larivière, who bowed her head before the man of law. This aroused his concern. 'Might Monsieur le marquis not be as virtuous as his mother claims? For example, with yourself, perhaps . . . ?'

'No, not with me, but with the steward – sometimes they have a romp together.'

'What?!'

Cartet's very moustache lost its curl. Montespan could not believe his ears. Chrestienne de Zamet staggered as if she had been struck in the head. Dorothée rushed to bring her over a chair. Arrogantly, the cook stood tall before her master.

'Begging your pardon, Monsieur, but I did see you one night wanting to have your way with Cartet. And, Marquis, I can't get it out of my head! When you know full well what ties there be binding me to him!'

The intendant was enthralled. 'Go on . . .'

'The steward was here in a wedding gown, open at the back, his buttocks to the four winds, and behind him was the marquis, his breeches round his knees, wanting to . . . you know, like the Chevalier de Lorraine with Monsieur, the King's brother . . .'

'The Italian vice . . .'

'Exactly!'

Macqueron turned to a crestfallen Montespan.

'Thus, you were giving lessons in conjugal fidelity to His Majesty . . . Pope Innocent XI was determined to defend your cause and not yield – the matter was leading to a schism. But if you were sodomising your steward, that changes everything.'

'And not just once!' said Madame Larivière, reiterating

her attack. 'As far as I can tell, it happened before, outside Puigcerdá, when Cartet was a sergeant, and that is why I reckon this business about an abducted girl and a nun, I don't know . . . but it would not surprise me in the least!'

The cuckold felt as if he were falling into an abyss. He had not expected such a thing! His mother was paler than ever, as if she had been bled of two pints of blood, and now she ordered him to explain. 'Is it true? Is it true, Louis-Henri?'

The marquis hardly knew what to reply, stammering, 'I . . . I was drunk, but otherwise, never, never . . .'

'Never what?' said the cook hotly. 'You lived for at least a month in a brothel behind Place de Grève! Were you drunk then, too?'

'Frequenting prostitutes!' said Macqueron, astonished.

Chrestienne de Zamet was about to swoon. Dorothée ran to the kitchen to fetch some drops of essence of urine and crayfish powder, and slapped white wine compresses on her brow. They concluded that perhaps no medicine could help her, nor would prayers be any better. Shattered, Cartet shook his large head this way and that as he faced Madame Larivière, who took offence.

'What is the matter with you, Steward? What has put you in such a pitiful state? Do I disgust you?'

'You should not have spoken of the past, Madame Lariri . . .'

'Stop calling me by that stupid name! There is no more

Madame Lariri, it's finished, *basta*! Madame Lariri doesn't exist any more!'

'And why should she not have spoken of the past?' enquired Macqueron.

'Madame Lariri, you have just given my captain a life sentence . . .'

'How? What? What are you saying? Oh, my God!'

The cook ran out, tearing her hair. Leaning against the bare stone wall, Montespan grazed his hands in vexation without realising it, whilst the intendant came over to him.

'Well, what say you, was it not time for a confession? *In extremis!* When I think I was prepared to take your side, that I thought, what a rare thing, this marquis's constant love, in a society where conjugal indifference is a sign of good manners! Which goes to show that there is some truth in proverbs: 'tis in preaching a lie that one discovers the truth. But I did not expect it. I did not even think to bring the stamp with the official seal in order to make the arrest in due form. I'll come back with it on the morrow. You have this afternoon and all night to put your affairs in order, for I am consigning you to residence in your chateau. The dragoons posted all round shall be your gaolers. Till tomorrow. Come, clerk!'

Macqueron departed, leaving Montespan dazed and distraught. Outside, Louis-Antoine was playing with toy soldiers and miniature rifles on Cartet's enormous thighs as the steward sat despondently on a little wall by the dragoons, who stared at him. Louis-Henri understood what was at risk if he submitted to the decision of justice. If he was taken, he would never again be able to plead his cause; he would be imprisoned in Pignerol, near Fouquet. He sighed and said, 'I am lost.' He gazed at his chateau as if for the last time – the rampart walk, the drawbridge, the large, wide-bottomed moat with its sloping crenellated wall and its entrances to underground passages and . . . escape?

Madame Larivière, her face crushed with shame and remorse, went up to him. 'What am I to do? Shall I throw myself into the mud of the moat, prepare my things and go?'

'No, because Marie-Christine needs Dorothée, and I am in a good position to know that when one is vexed in love, one is sometimes driven to say or do certain things . . .'

'. . . that I regret, Monsieur.'

'I do not! Go back and patch things up with that unhappy Cartet who loves you so, Madame Larivière. Ask him, too, to go to the dovecote and fetch the pigeon belonging to the Seigneur de Teulé.'

'That wretched nobleman – a ruffian and a counterfeiter, to whom all the marquis in the region send a small pension so that he will not fall too low among the riffraff?'

'The very same.'

Teulé,

*Before nightfall, pray tie a mount to a tree near the large
rock at the place where the two lanes cross in my forest.*

Montespan

Louis-Henri attached the message to the carrier pigeon's leg. The bird took flight on its short wings and, carried on the wind, headed directly south.

After dark, the marquis tiptoed into his daughter's chamber where she slept with Dorothée. He then went into Louis-Antoine's room, took him in his arms and said, 'Come, we are going for a ride.'

Carrying his son and some old clothes, but with no candle, Montespan went out into the courtyard through a door hidden from view, but his mother, who had heard the floor creaking a little while before, now saw him from her window.

'My poor boy, if you escape now, you risk being sentenced *in absentia* and all your property will be confiscated and you'll lose all your titles of nobility. You will only fulfil Louvois's deepest desires, and look well and truly like a criminal . . .'

She dried her tears and said many a prayer on seeing her son and grandson disappearing beneath the slab at the entrance to a tunnel. They vanished from sight. She was not sure if she would ever see them again.

Stooping, Montespan groped his way along the narrow underground passage, which had surely not been used for over a century, clambering over glowing tree roots, hearing animals squeaking as they fled – large field rats, no doubt. Spider's webs and scurrying insects caught in his hair.

They reached the end of the tunnel. Louis-Henri came up against the rungs of a rusty ladder fixed to a vertical clay wall and he climbed up. At the top, he struggled to open the grate that blocked the entrance to the underground passage. Holding his child in one arm, the marquis shoved several times with his shoulder and bent head, and finally the grate lifted with a tearing of grass, pushing aside clumps of icy soil.

They emerged from the ground near a large rock. Next to it, a horse stood tethered to a tree trunk. Louis-Henri wanted to leave on the sly, passing through the sleeping villages without making a sound. He wrapped the horse's hooves with what he had thought were rags, snatched up at random in the gloom of the chateau, but he had been mistaken: it was Françoise's wedding gown. Never mind. His son yawned and shivered with cold. The father lifted the boy onto the back of the horse and mounted pillion behind him. Below them, in the valley, the Château de Bonnefont seemed to be snoring, inside a circle of light made by the glowing pipes of the watching dragoons.

'Where are we going, Papa?'

'To Madrid.'

The child was somewhat frightened by the enormity of the journey, but his father gave him courage and wrapped him in a heavy buffalo cloak. Montespan, in his felt riding-cloak, put an arm around his son's waist and held him close to keep him warm.

'Gee up!'

The horse made its way along a path glazed with black ice. Louis-Antoine, one cheek against his father's biceps, gazed ahead at the Pyrenees, blue and white in the clear night. The swaying motion of the horse's gait lulled the child and he slept. Beneath the horse's trotting hooves, the pearls on Françoise's red dress shattered like little stars.

39.

'Monsieur de Montespan, how is Louis XIV?'

At the court of Spain, Louis-Henri wondered if the ten-year-old dauphin – the future Charles II – had a sense of humour and was mocking him outrageously, or if he was a complete and utter idiot.

'I enquire,' continued the Habsburg heir to the throne, 'because as for myself, I am not very well . . .'

The frail child, a virtual invalid, had to hold on to the mantelpiece to keep from falling.

His adult features were already discernible, those of a degenerate not destined to live long.

'Does the King of France suffer from toothache, Monsieur de Montespan?'

'I really don't know,' replied the marquis.

'And nightmares, does he have nightmares?'

'I have no idea. In any event, I often have nightmares because of him.'

'The other night,' said the dauphin, 'I dreamt that I had become an oyster, and Indians were opening me to steal the pearl I had inside me. Then they left me to close up again all by myself and departed with my treasure. I awoke to find myself curiously . . . dry.'

'Really?'

'There are times, too, when I dream that I have no arms, only hands attached directly to my shoulders, wiggling like fins.'

'Well then, tell me . . .'

'Monsieur de Montespan, do you believe that I am a marine animal?'

'Of course not, Your Highness.'

'*Ha-ha-ha! El hechizado! El hechizado!* . . .' (There's a spell on him!) In the gloomy official salon of the Spanish palace, the dauphin's half-sisters, a bevy of sickly, dwarfed infantas, giggled and ran off to the hall of mirrors to see their reflection multiplied a thousandfold. Dressed in skirts that looked like enormous lampshades, they circled round and round and squeaked like wooden dolls on wheels. Louis-Henri told himself that it was not only in the court of France that there was something rotten.

'Would you like some fruit?' The future monarch's words emerged from his mouth in fits and starts, as if he had had to search for each one individually.

A voice explained to the French marquis: 'The heir to the throne did not walk or begin to talk until he was five years old.' The voice, with an Austrian accent, was that of Cardinal Nidhart – an inquisitor who during the regency had been entrusted with the post of prime minister by the queen mother; he was her confessor. Dressed in red robes with a thin white collar, he wore a little beard and moustache, and his eyes were immensely sad. On his head, dominating his scalp, was something that looked like the little boats that children make by folding a sheet of paper. Montespan politely chose an apricot from the porcelain bowl the sickly prince was holding out to him. The fruit was so ripe and spoilt around the stone that it tasted like cheese.

'Another apricot!'

'No, thank you.'

'I would like very much to see you again, Monsieur de Montespan!'

'It's just that . . .' said Louis-Henri, 'in fact I'd come to take my leave and thank Spain for the asylum granted me this year and more. As soon as I crossed over the

Pyrenees, the populace came to their windows and blessed my journey all the way to Madrid. Wherever I went, I was greeted with manifestations of joy. My son and I have been lodged by the palace, with liveried footmen at our disposition. One of your coaches was always at my door to serve me . . . with four mules and a royal coachman. I have been greatly touched to receive such treatment and hospitality normally reserved for extraordinary ambassadors, but now that I am able to return to my home . . .'

'You have been here for nigh on a year? And why did no one inform me?' asked the little prince angrily, addressing Cardinal Nidhart, who replied, 'Because you were asleep, Don Carlos.'

'Ah, 'tis true, I sleep a great deal! Sometimes for months. They call me "the sleeping corpse". Have I already told you my dreams, Monsieur de Montespan?'

'Yes, Your Highness.'

'Would you like an apricot?'

'No, thank you.'

There was an air of awkwardness in the salon that Louis-Henri was eager to leave behind. He was about to make a deep bow when the unsteady heir asked him, 'Why could you not go home before?'

The cuckold tried to explain his situation as a husband betrayed by the King of France. 'I suspected that if I came for protection to the very devout kingdom of Spain, I might be making an excellent move, that Louis XIV would not risk damaging his reputation by going too far. Your obvious decline, Don Carlos – for you will most probably die without an heir – opens the succession of your throne to claimants from all over Europe. Marie-Thérèse's French husband is duty-bound to explore all diplomatic measures, therefore he must handle me with tact. He has yielded, with a letter of remission!' Louis-Henri waved a sheet of paper, and read: '"We hereby pardon said Marquis de Montespan, to this end annulling all direct summonses and other judicial proceedings that have been made." I have won! I am free, and glad to return to Bonnefont!'

'The King of France wrote to you?' exclaimed the young dauphin delightedly. 'May I see his letter? I am very fond of Louis XIV and of France . . . although I'm not very sure where it is.'

'Don Carlos,' interrupted Nidhart, trying not to become annoyed, 'we are *at war* with France, and Louis XIV is our *enemy* . . .'

'Indeed? How so?'

There was a sense of hesitancy in the air.

'When will he be king?' murmured Montespan in the cardinal's ear.

'In four years,' sighed Nidhart.

Louis-Henri nodded, thinking, well, that bodes well for Spain; what sport they will have, the Madrileños . . .

'As for myself,' said the Prime Minister, 'the moment he becomes monarch, I will return to Austria.'

The frail invalid looked at Montespan.

'Will you find your wife at home?'

'I should like to . . .'

'It must be very pleasant to be married, no?'

'That depends . . .'

'And Louis XIV, is he married?'

'Yes, and to a Spanish woman, moreover.'

'Really? But I thought he was the King of France!'

A certain weariness had become apparent on the faces of both Nidhart and the French marquis, whom the dauphin now asked, 'How are children made, Monsieur de Montespan?'

'Well now, Your Highness . . . Look, I do not really have the time to—'

'Would you like an apricot?'

'No!'

The Gascon would end up stuffing those rotten apricots in his face, the Spanish dunderhead! The latter was now trembling, his legs quaking. The confessor scarcely had time to catch him in his arms.

'It is because you shouted, Monsieur de Montespan. When people shout, it puts him to sleep. There we are, he is off again for another eight months in bed.'

The marquis turned round and took his leave, whilst the dauphin, yawning, his head drooping on his shoulder, had just enough time to utter, 'Embrace Louis XIV for me . . .'

The Gascon had formed his opinion. The future Charles II had no sense of humour and was not mocking him. He was a complete and utter idiot.

40.

Montespan drove his white steed through the blue landscape of the Pyrenees. Louis-Antoine, sitting between his father's legs, clung to the horse's mane. It was the return of the hero. Outside the brick gate to the chateau, peasants who had come to bake their bread cried out, 'Here he is! Here they are!'

Cartet and Dorothée came running. The cook called out, 'Madame Chrestienne de Zamet! Madame Chrestienne de Zamet, it's your son with the little Marquis d'Antin!'

Louis-Henri dismounted and embraced his mother.

'Oh, dear Lord! How is everyone here?'

'Well, just consider this: the horses are thin, my tooth is loose, the tutor has scrofula, but I am exceeding happy to see you again before I die!'

The Gascon's mother had become all skin and bone

since he had left, and Louis-Henri was worried. Her back was twisted owing to a cruel attack of rheumatism and her knuckles were swollen.

'She is pitifully thin because of the dryness of her lungs, which are beginning to waste away,' whispered the cook, 'and your daughter, too, was very ill. I made her drink vipers' broth, which revives the soul. People might think that when you tear the vipers' hearts out, it's all over with them. Not a bit. They are still alive, and in a broth they provide strength. They've invigorated the little girl.'

Montespan crouched down next to his daughter.

'Marie-Christine, from the depths of my heart I rejoice in your recovery. But why do you pine so, and fill your father with such terrible fear?'

'I believe it is because I am waiting for Mam—'

'And I believe in chicory!' interrupted the cook. 'With fricassee of nightingales' hearts and, every three months, a pilgrimage to the basilica of Notre-Dame-de-la-Daurade in Toulouse!'

'Madame Larivière takes me there, too, in Père Destival's cart,' smiled the marquis's mother. 'She purges me, and overlooks nothing, so I go to mass with an honest pallor.'

'What shall we do?' the cook asked the old lady. 'Shall we have a banquet this evening to mark the marquis's return to the chateau, a feast to celebrate the loyalty of his friends?'

'Then we must invite the villagers,' suggested Cartet,

'for last summer, when the surrounding wall on the chateau side threatened to fall down, they came to shore it up and, aware of the state of your finances, Captain, they asked for no wages.'

'Well then, go to!' decided the marquis.

The energetic Madame Larivière clapped her hands.

'Ring the bell at the gate so the farmers' wives come quickly to help me! Cartet! Go and draw water from the cistern, and take down the game hanging to cure in the shed. The yokels are not allowed to hunt, so they never eat any! I will prepare some haunches of venison and a roast from the wild boar that you caught with the spear, and *croustades* with a *sauce Robert* of mustard and onion. That should make enough for a revel! Will you also have a bite to eat this evening, Madame de Zamet?'

'A bit of boiled chicken, perhaps half a wing . . . Louis-Henri, your wife has sent you eight outfits, but without any accompanying letter.'

The cook raised her eyes to heaven and walked away, exclaiming, 'That woman! If she thinks that by doing a little bit of good and a great deal of wickedness . . . The best one can say is that if you average the two, she was a decent woman.'

After ringing the bell Cartet took hold of the long dagger he always kept in his boot, and with the tip of the blade he traced a cross on top of a loaf of bread. He sliced into the loaf and put a large piece in his mouth.

'Don't throw yourself upon the food, you'll have huge pouches in your cheeks like a monkey!' scolded Louis-Antoine, then he turned to his father. 'Are we going to sup with commoners again? Is that the custom here? From what I can see, 'tis the servants who run the house!'

The six-year-old headed furiously to his bedchamber upstairs in the chateau. Looking out, he saw a flight of wild geese. The devoted inhabitants of Bonnefont were starting to arrive bearing bouquets. The high prairie grasses gave off a pleasant scent and the river sang over polished pebbles. Musicians brought a harp and a few violas da gamba. In the courtyard of the chateau they were now dancing a few Bohemian steps with a delicacy and precision that were charming. Some exhausted, malnourished men also arrived. They had come down from the mountain, goading the oxen carrying the wood for the royal navy. The villagers were busy inside the chateau walls. Women sliced vegetables that they tossed into pots of boiling water. The men blew on the embers, preparing a huge fire to grill the pieces of game. Sitting on a chair in the middle of the courtyard, Chrestienne de Zamet was overwhelmed by the joyous activity, which was producing lots of steam and smoke. She asked, 'Where is my son?' and someone replied, 'There above you, on the hill.'

Marie-Christine crossed the drawbridge to join her father. Dorothée was about to go after her but Madame Larivière held her back. 'Stay.'

'Come and help me put some planks on trestles instead,' Cartet suggested kindly.

The marquis's mother watched as Marie-Christine climbed the hill, and sighed sadly.

'Who will look after that poor little girl after I die?'

'I will, gladly,' said the cook's daughter, as she set out plates on the tables arranged in a U shape.

As for the . . . 'Marquis d'Antin', he stood at the open window of his chamber with his arms crossed, looking haughtily at the people busy below him, and said, 'In any case, I refuse to help! I am not a servant. I was received at the court of Spaahn!'

At the top of the hill facing the chateau, Montespan placed flowers on the grave of his love: a few roses lying on a clump of earth surrounded by lavender bushes. The cuckold sat with his back to the tomb and gazed out at the landscape. Outside the chateau, the villagers were dancing some country jigs, bold figures that made their bodies quiver all over. Their heads followed their feet, then their shoulders and all the other parts of their body. They danced towards each other, met, moved apart, then came together again in a way that so affronted the priest of Bonnefont that he promised to excommunicate those who persisted in dancing this diabolical dance.

'So, Père Destival,' exclaimed an iron craftsman, 'eighty-eight and still with us?'

'The Good Lord hath forgotten me,' apologised the

priest, whilst everyone danced more furiously than ever.

Louis-Henri saw his daughter climbing up the path. She sat between her father's knees. Behind them was a wooden cross with two dates. The marquis's arms encircled Marie-Christine. The child picked a sprig of lavender, pulled off the tiny buds one by one. She scattered them over the slope.

'The mountain will be all blue now . . .' said Montespan, smiling into the child's neck and hair.

Marie-Christine said nothing and continued to blow the seeds from her hand.

41.

On the morning of 2 April 1674, despite heavy spring rain, Montespan and Cartet took the little Marquis d'Antin hunting in the mountains. The former captain of the light cavalry and his sergeant enjoyed going into these dense forests which were plentiful with wild boar, or climbing up to the passes to chase bears or the izards that sprang from rock to rock.

Louis-Henri would have liked to teach his son how to kill hares, partridges and game. He wanted to train him for this rough sport that the young boy seemed unwilling to try.

Louis-Antoine preferred to follow his tutor, who took him out into the garden on long walks conducive to lessons of Latin, philosophy and French.

'Father, may I not go to see Abbé Anselme instead and

catch up on my instruction? I've fallen behind, you see, because of our stay in Spain . . .'

'No, you may not! Here, hold this spear, today no doubt you'll kill your first young wild boar.'

In the torrential rain, d'Antin, who had not worn children's clothing since the age of seven, was dressed in a doublet and hose. His muddy feet and wet legs could not get warm, and the black brambles scratched at him and terrified him: he was a marquis better destined to hunt for social promotion in the alcoves of gilded salons.

The father observed his son's incredible cowardice; at the same time, the boy could be barbarically cruel to the poor village children. When they played hide and seek, he cheated, peering out from under the blindfold. He hit the children, using his noble title as a pretext, for he knew that the little urchins, under orders from their parents, would not dare answer back, and this greatly saddened Louis-Henri. Louis-Antoine displayed a natural inclination to obsequiousness and seemed already to have a talent for cunning. Montespan had a foreboding that his own son, in sharp contrast to himself, would become a model courtier for the very same Louis XIV who persecuted his father and who, from the boy's earliest childhood, had deprived him of the caresses of a mother . . . a mother who, it must be said, was anything but sensitive to this wrenching separation.

As they approached the hills swathed with thick forest,

Cartet and Montespan could smell the hunt: they breathed it in, heard the sounds, experienced the violence, the necessary cruelty, and Louis-Antoine, trembling, held his little spear in both hands. Suddenly the steward motioned them to be silent and whispered, 'There's a female up ahead with her young ... I'll go off to the right to send one of the young ones in your direction ...'

This news was greeted by the chattering of Louis-Antoine's teeth; his father explained to him in a hushed voice, 'You hold your spear like this ... One hand in front, palm turned up, and the other hand behind, palm facing down. When the little wild boar heads straight for you, and is only about two *toises* away, you take a step forward, bending your knees, and you aim below the head, to strike right at the animal's chest. You have to make an upward thrust, as if you were tossing hay onto a cart with a pitchfork. You always strike from the bottom up, never the other way round, otherwise you might hurt yourself. And hold your spear firmly so that the beast doesn't run away with it.'

D'Antin's knees quivered and knocked together like castanets. When the child heard something rushing towards him amidst the sound of crushed foliage and the cracking of flying twigs, he thought longingly of his history, geography and mathematics lessons with Abbé Anselme.

But now a little fawn wild boar with a black stripe down

its back was heading for Louis-Antoine. The animal was about four *toises* away, and the Gascon's son took a step back, closed his eyes, and stabbed his spear from top to bottom at random. He felt a violent shock in his shoulders that knocked him over, and when he opened his eyes, he saw that the animal was dragging him along on his stomach whilst he clung desperately to the spear he had rammed through the beast's cheeks, shouting all the while. There seemed to be an echo in the valley. Louis-Antoine was sliding and crashing about through grasses and brambles and splashing rain, and he screamed at the beast in his little imp's voice, 'Stop! Stop!' His shouts only excited the young wild boar, making it go faster than ever, which in turn made the boy shout even louder. Cartet came running on his bear-like legs, laughing. Astonishingly quick and agile despite weighing nearly a quintal, he soon caught up with the boar and pulled his dagger from his boot. As he was cutting the little boar's throat, he heard a voice calling.

It was the cook from the chateau wearing only a lace cap in the torrential rain. As she held up her skirt, revealing her ugly stork legs, her entire body steamed with sweat from her mad dash up the steep path, and now she called out, 'Monsieur de Montespan! Monsieur de Montespan! It's your mother, Chrestienne de Zamet. She is! She is . . .'

42.

A year later, almost to the day, on 5 April 1675, Louis-Henri was weeping at the foot of Marie-Christine's bed in the convent of Charonne in Paris. His dying daughter looked at him and said, 'Your clothes do not fit you, Papa.'

'When the news of your poor health reached me in the Pyrenees, I quickly shoved a change of clothes into my saddlebags, the ones your mother sent me. She had them made too small. I don't know who she was thinking about . . .'

Montespan went up to the head of the bed: his silk breeches were indeed too short, and his pink hose not long enough, so his knees were exposed. As he sat down, his doublet, which was several sizes too small, pulled at his shoulders, and his sleeves reached no further than the middle of his forearms.

'Would you like to play hide and seek? The kind where you have to guess the object hidden in someone's clothes?'

'Papa, your shirt is so tight that I can see it. It's a book.'

'Yes, but not just any book,' said her father, unbuttoning his shirt to pull out the book. 'It's a tale for young girls entitled, *The Sigh of a Flea Kept in a Currant Seed*. It's the story of the sigh of a flea . . . kept in . . . a currant seed . . .'

Montespan burst into tears. 'Forgive me,' he said, trying to pull himself together. 'Marie-Christine, for days I have been trembling from head to toe, I am losing my reason, I cannot sleep; and if I sleep, I awake with a start that is worse than not sleeping at all. You must live, my child!'

It was the end of the day, and the candles on the bedside table illuminated the stained-glass windows of the convent room where Marie-Christine's regular breathing gently lifted her nightgown with its collar of Valenciennes lace.

It was like seeing the Virgin Mary herself, on the straw of a stable among the animals, waiting to give birth. As if the ass and the ox were breathing gently on her nightgown.

'But what's the matter with her?' her father asked a doctor standing on the other side of the bed.

'I describe the pain in her head as a rheumatism of the membranes. Since she came here, she has not complained, or cried, but she has been getting thinner, and is gently leaving the world, despite the life-giving syrup, the holy water, the healthful herbal teas and the clysters to refresh her stomach with water and milk. Of late she has been stunned, afflicted, vomiting; these are all signs.'

In the dormitories of Charonne people moaned, half dead, and sought help in the boiling heat of this Christian stronghold.

'Last year, my mother passed away, and she had been very concerned about her granddaughter,' said Montespan. 'Her will is proof of her unquiet solicitude over the fate of the child. Despite five hundred thousand *livres* of debt which meant that I was obliged to renounce her legacy, she was careful to ensure Marie-Christine's happiness, or at least her peace and security, and she ordered that she be brought to the convent with Dorothée as her companion.'

Madame Larivière's daughter, standing to the right of the doctor, looked down at the floor.

'". . . And this for many considerations that I cannot express,"' quoted Louis-Henri. 'She arranged every detail of my daughter's existence: a private room, firewood, access to the infirmary; and granted her the sum necessary for a future marriage or taking the veil; but all of that was idle fancy. I sent a letter to my wife to alert her. Has she come to see her?'

'We have informed both of the girl's parents,' said a nun on the doctor's left. 'But whilst *you* have been appalled by her fever and decline, and judged it meet to come immediately in your terror at the thought of losing your child, we have not seen the marquise . . .'

'Last month,' sighed Marie-Christine, 'when she was returning from taking the waters at Bourbon-l'Archambault, in a painted golden boat bedecked in red, with a thousand streamers, she stopped at Moulins to visit Louis-Antoine for a few minutes at his Jesuit boarding school.'

'She did?' exclaimed her father. 'But how do you know that?'

'My brother wrote to me. "It is the first time I have had this honour. She was very amiable to me but reasons of court prevent her from seeing me more often, for which I am extremely mortified."'

'Perhaps she is very busy,' said Louis-Henri, trying to find an excuse.

'"Very busy . . ."' echoed the doctor with a sigh as he walked around the bed to whisper in the marquis's ear, 'Come and find me tomorrow, at four o'clock in the afternoon, outside the construction site at the chateau of Versailles. I shall lend you my spyglass and then you shall see what this exemplary mother is busy at whilst her daughter . . .' The physician departed, followed by the nun, who took Dorothée by the arm. 'Let us leave the two of them alone now.'

In the convent's spartan bedroom with its red hexagonal floor tiles, there wafted a smell of incense mingled with wax. Marie-Christine was twelve years old and now, with her eyes closed, she was dying as a consequence of her mother's absence. She had stopped speaking and did not seem to hear. Her father watched as gradually the spirits of life withdrew from her. But like all the dying who feel their soul departing, images of her life played before her eyes and she opened them once again.

'Father . . . do what Maman used to do . . .'

'What did she used to do?'

'Grrr . . . grrr . . .'

'Ah, yes.' Louis-Henri recalled the happiness of former times, a family with its laughter. 'Frrr . . . oh, oh, oh!' he murmured gently, like a distant echo. 'Frrr . . . oh, oh, oh . . . grrr, grrr!' he continued, raising his voice slightly. 'Watch out, for I am a demon!' Sitting on the edge of the bed now, he rolled his eyes and made faces at his daughter. 'Frrr . . . oh, oh, oh! Grrr . . . grrr! Watch out, I'm the devil!' he shouted in the convent. He slipped his tongue into his lower lip and pushed it forward, imitating a toothless old tramp, then placed his thumbs against his temples and wiggled his fingers in the air. 'Frrr . . . oh, oh, oh!' He stuck out his tongue at Marie-Christine, thumbed his nose at her with both hands, this time waggling his fingers as if playing the trumpet, and imitated the sound of diabolical farts, vibrating his lips. 'Brrr!' He spoke in a squeaky voice, comically imitating Françoise: 'Frrr . . . oh, oh, oh!' and launched into an amusing charade that knew no bounds, puffing out his cheeks like a blowfish, then abruptly emptying them, sucking them in exaggeratedly and crossing his eyes, his pupils trained on the tip of his nose. 'Watch out, 'tis I, your mother Beelzebub. If I catch your heart, you—'

Marie-Christine, smiling, turned her head on her pillow and did not raise it again. Her nightdress stopped moving.

43.

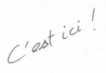

'Where, Doctor?'

'There, to the left of the terrace, in the King's wing. No, not there, Monsieur de Montespan! You have your spyglass trained on the Queen's wing . . . On the other side, first floor, seventh window from the left.'

'The one that is open?'

'Aye, that's it. Are you there?'

'It's not possible, I cannot believe it!'

'Then you are there . . .' smiled the physician, standing by the flabbergasted marquis, who had his right eye pressed against the optical tube.

Louis-Henri adjusted the sharpness of the image in the telescopic lens. 'Françoise, what are they making you do!'

'"Making her do, making her do . . ."' said the physician, putting things in perspective.

In an antechamber boasting bronze statues and Chinese vases, Montespan's spouse could be seen on her knees, sucking the royal member. Somewhere a clock chimed four o'clock in the afternoon.

'His Majesty is always on time,' said the physician appreciatively, looking at his watch. 'From east to west, the way in which the rooms of the palace are laid out corresponds to the rhythm of a typical day in the life of the Sun King. At four o'clock, like a mechanical puppet, he stops in the antechamber where his mistress awaits him on her knees, with her mouth open.'

The monarch stood with one hand out to the side, majestically holding the knob of his walking stick, and looked straight ahead with his chin raised whilst the marquise sucked him. Although Louis-Henri was hopping mad, he pulled out the seven sections of the spyglass to have a better view.

'Go to,' the physician said encouragingly. 'It enlarges up to fifty-four times. I am referring to the telescope, obviously,' he added maliciously.

'A man who has bathed only once in his entire life . . . It would be hard not to be disgusted.'

'I do not believe your wife is.'

Beside himself, the cuckold had blurred the view through the eyepiece; now he focused again. Françoise was wearing a low-cut gown with six layers of fine lace on her sleeves, and in her blond hair were woven ribbons and rubies. Louis-Henri recognised her well-formed, attractive mouth, which he knew to be voracious, then he noticed something white and sparkling dangling above his wife's lips.

'What is that? A pearl necklace? Does he wear a pearl necklace around his—'

'Precisely! Now watch what happens. You'll see how the King, who hates to be asked for jewels, will offer them to your wife.'

The mother of the deceased Marie-Christine released the streaming genitalia – what a wash! (but her kisses, henceforth, must have a different taste). A magnificent pearl necklace encircled the King's arrogant little penis at its base and tapped against his balls. Françoise gave a few flicks of her tongue then took in the whole length.

'And off they go again,' said the cuckold sorrowfully.

'Ah, she makes a good whore, does Madame Quatorze!' The marquise's head, facing the King's crotch, moved rhythmically backwards and forwards until His Majesty stiffened and his fingers opened convulsively on the knob of his walking stick. A few seconds of immobility, then Françoise swallowed. Her husband's knees were shaking above his too-short pink hose. The mother of his children now placed her upturned palms beneath the Bourbon member as it went soft and drooped. The pearl necklace slid downhill and fell into Françoise's outstretched hands; she straightened up and fastened the pearls around her neck whilst the King, doing up his breeches, walked away and opened a door.

'He is leaving the antechamber,' announced Montespan.

'... to go into the council chamber where his ministers are waiting for a brief interview,' surmised the doctor from the Charonne convent. 'Someone must be opening a window.'

'Indeed,' confirmed the Gascon, adjusting the telescope's field of vision to the left, along the façade of the King's wing.

'His Majesty cannot bear to be in an enclosed space. Summer and winter alike, the moment he enters a room a window must be opened, and too bad for anyone who feels chilly or unwell.'

Louis XIV sat in an armchair, striking a theatrical pose, playing with the knob of his walking stick, whilst three ministers came up behind him waving their arms, certainly with some important events to relate. The monarch heard them out without interrupting, then turned his bewigged head to each one of the three, undoubtedly giving orders, and then he got up.

'Look! He's on his feet again,' said Louis-Henri.

'And now, still heading west, the window in the next room must have been opened in turn . . .'

'So it has,' said the marquis, 'and . . . oh! There is a golden four-poster bed with floating curtains, and a woman is on all fours on the edge of the bed. She has just pulled her skirts up over her back and her head. Such a big bottom!'

''Tis yet again your wife.'

'Really? But how did she get there?'

'Through a secret passage. The palace is full of them.'

'She has gained weight,' said Montespan.

'Nine times with child and an excessive fondness for victuals have got the better of her figure, which had a natural tendency to plumpness to begin with,' diagnosed the physician.

'It suits her rather well . . . Nine times with child? Since our marriage my wife has had nine children? That I did not know,' said the cuckold, astounded, whilst the King entered Athénaïs's many-mirrored chamber.

Louis XIV continued on his solar trajectory, again opening his breeches embroidered with scenes of battles he had won. Hard once more, he headed straight for Françoise's vast bare bottom. Montespan slapped his left palm over the end of the spyglass. He had seen enough.

44.

On the rocky hill with its cross overlooking the chateau of Bonnefont, the lavender that Marie-Christine had sown had taken root. It had spread along the slope, but it looked as if fate had dealt a blow upon the marquis's lands, bruising the landscape. Louis-Henri, stretched out on the wall of the moat, closed his eyes and dozed off or, rather, pretended to.

When in the early hours of a baking summer afternoon the cicadas had paused in their song, because they had heard the sound of approaching hooves, Montespan had felt the cool shadow of a horse gliding over him, but he had not even deigned to sit up.

Madame Larivière had come out of her kitchen and crossed the courtyard, waving her arms and stirring the air. 'Sshh, he's asleep . . .'

The horseman dismounted and asked in a hushed voice

and an English accent, 'Is . . . Is this Monsieur de Montespan, this bare-headed man?'

'Now what do they want from him?' whispered the cook. 'What disaster this time?'

'I bring good news.'

'Ah, then if it's good news . . . He's in great need of it. For months, since he brought his daughter's body home to be buried next to his mother, he has been . . . as if stricken. And not long after that came the news of the death of his uncle, the Archbishop of Sens. It was also as if he saw something he ought not to have seen during his journey to Paris . . .'

'He dared to come out of exile without the King's permission,' asked the visitor, surprised, 'despite the risk of beheading or being sentenced to the galleys?'

'What?' asked the cook, annoyed. 'Of course not, you'd make me say anything!'

'What did he see?'

'That I don't know, but it was the final straw for him. Nothing interests him any more. The steward of the chateau even has to keep the books and do the rounds to collect the rents . . . which grow fewer and fewer, moreover, since he renounced both his parents' inheritance. Now you're very smartly attired, have you come from the court, is that it?' she asked suspiciously. 'I hope you've not come to harass him?'

'No, indeed, 'tis to offer . . .'

'If it's *écus* you're offering, you may leave again with

them. He has already said that his wife was not for sale.'

'That is not my business.'

'Ah?'

And so reluctantly Madame Larivière gently nudged the cuckold's shoulder.

'Monsieur le cuck— Monsieur le marquis . . .'

Louis-Henri was breathing deeply and regularly, his eyelids closed. Flies buzzed all around him, and finally he opened his eyes and sat up on the edge of the wall. He yawned and stretched whilst the visitor introduced himself.

'Chancellor Hyde, originally from the court of England, now in the service of the King of France . . .'

'A chancellor now?' said Montespan, dumbstruck, rubbing his hair, which was completely dishevelled. 'It would seem I'm entitled to increasingly prestigious emissaries. Does Louis XIV plan to come in person? Tell him I am ready to challenge him to a duel, there, on the planks of my drawbridge and beneath the horns of stone I have added to my coat of arms on the gate.'

'Here we go,' said the cook, annoyed with the chancellor. 'You haven't come to harass him, but you make him spout such gibberish. Ah, if the steward were here, he'd already have taken you by the scruff of your neck with one hand and shoved you back on your horse, and gee up! With one hand. That's how he is, Cartet, he's strong, he—'

'That's enough, Madame Larivière,' interrupted Montespan.

'Oh, you're right! And I'd rather go back to my kitchen than hear . . . And what are you doing here?' she shouted at Dorothée (now twenty-one), as she bumped into her. 'Are there no rooms to be cleaned? Why have you got hay in your hair? And why is your skirt inside out? Where have you been? You think we don't have enough to do already in this house without a certain "slut"?'

The Englishman with the blond eyebrows was calm and elegant. He gently pressed a lace handkerchief to his forehead, throat and neck; his white skin was sensitive to the sun. Without animosity, Montespan suggested they go and sit somewhat further along, in the shadow of the gate. Dorothée came out with a jug of cool water from the well, and two glasses each containing a slice of Spanish lemon. She served them, then left again, removing a few more blades of straw from her poorly refastened bodice. The chancellor took short, refreshing sips of cool water whilst Louis-Henri held his glass in both hands, gazing dreamily at the thin slice of lemon floating in the water.

'Is my wife happy?'

The visitor sat with his back to the lotus flowers rotting in the stagnant waters of the moat, and surveyed the tumbledown courtyard of this wretched, crumbling chateau. There, to the right, was the famous horned carriage, abandoned against the wall, next to an enormous wisteria. All dusty, with traces of bird droppings everywhere, the door hanging off its hinges, windows broken, the coach had become a hen house, and the fowl laid their eggs on the cracked leather seats. An arrogant little cockerel, perched on the stag's antlers above the black vehicle, crowed in the dazzling summer heat.

'In any event, she is very demanding,' said the Englishman. 'Some courtiers have begun to call her "Quanto", because of the Italian card game, *quantova*, which means "how much". Athénaïs wanted her own chateau in Clagny. She had the inhabitants expelled, the church demolished, the village razed and the cemetery moved, but when the King showed her his plans for the palace, she was so brazen as to remark scornfully that it was a residence fit for "an opera girl". So now it is Mansart who is building her a little fairy-tale chateau. It will cost a quarter of the budget for the navy. At the court of Versailles, known as the "Gambling Den", the King systematically pays all the debts that your spouse incurs. She burdens the treasury of the realm with tremendous expenses. Every evening she gets drunk, gambles, loses enormous amounts and throws her pearl necklaces onto the green baize, as many as seven in a week.'

The Gascon watched as a bee rose drunkenly in the air in the path of an awkward, fluttering butterfly.

'So she's not happy, it would seem.'

'Marquis,' said the chancellor, a note of finality in his voice, 'His Majesty has ordered me to come to Guyenne to give you an excellent piece of news: "Inform Monsieur de

Montespan that his marquisate shall be raised to a duchy-peerage, and that I will add the appropriate number of privileges, not wishing to depart from what is customary."'

Louis-Henri, who was wearing a vast white shirt, loosened over a bare shoulder, was still staring at the glass between his long legs, spread wide in his worn boots. The Englishman, seeing that the squire had failed to react, feared he had not made himself understood and explained, 'The King is not asking for anything in return for offering to make you a duke. The duchy of Bellegarde has just reverted to the crown.'

'Is she ever known to sigh, as if she were regretting a past happiness . . . or perhaps even weep in private?'

'Ah yes, she weeps exceedingly . . . since the widow Scarron was made Marquise de Maintenon. Your wife has been demanding to be made a duchesse, in order to be higher in rank than the governess of her royal children. You may appreciate how her pride is suffering; she is outraged by the fact that in public she must remain standing in the King's presence, although she is the most important person at court. To have the right to a stool, one must be a duchesse, but Athénaïs cannot be a duchesse unless her husband is made a duc, whence the purpose of my visit . . .'

Montespan remained silent and put down his glass, then got up and went to sit again on the sunny part of the wall. Hyde walked along the moat to the marquis, who raised his head and declared, 'I am sensitive, my lord, as is my duty, to the great honour you bestow upon me by your visit; however, allow me to find it strange that a man of your importance would agree to become embroiled in a negotiation of this nature. The King of France did not consult me when he wanted to make my wife his mistress; it is quite extraordinary that a prince of his rank should defer to my intervention to reward a behaviour that I condemned, and still condemn, and will condemn until my last mortal sigh. His Majesty has given eight or ten children to my spouse without a word to me; he may equally present her with a duchy without calling upon me for help. Let him make her a princess or even a highness if he so desires. He is all-powerful. I am but a reed; he is an oak. Madame de Montespan may still have ambitions but my own ambition was satisfied forty years ago. I was born a marquis, and I shall die a marquis, barring some unforeseen disaster . . .'

And Louis-Henri lay down on the little wall once again. His forearm over his eyes, he fell asleep. He did not even hear the hooves of the chancellor's mount ringing on the cobbles as he rode away. The song of the cicadas resumed.

45.

'"What? How can that be!" she is said to have lost her temper when she saw Hyde. "He would deprive me of being a duchesse? Well, I will complete his ruin, I will strip him to the bone – that gooseherd, that vulgar little good-for-nothing arse-wipe!"'

'But who was she talking about?'

'About you, of course, Marquis.'

'About me?'

Louis-Henri, climbing the stairway at Rue Taranne, could not believe what he had heard. That was what the love of his life said about him? Standing next to the Gascon, Monsieur and Madame Abraham winced, embarrassed and puzzled.

'How that young woman has changed,' sighed Constance.

'The poor thing has completely lost all sense of reality at the Gambling Den,' said the cuckold, trying to excuse her. 'She warned me, "Versailles is a dreadful place; there is not a single person whose head is not turned by it. The court changes even the best of souls." I must get her out of that hell,' he continued.

As he said this, a guard on the first-floor landing was listening and a bailiff was drawing up an inventory of the salon. Next to the bailiff a secretary wrote down, 'One Rouen tapestry representing the story of Moses, eight folding chairs, two cabled chairs with horsehair stuffing, one Venetian mirror . . . thirty inches high, one little table . . .'

Once the man of law had added each piece of furniture to the list, the guards took it down to the street and loaded it onto a police cart. The bailiff recognised the marquis and introduced himself. 'François Rhurin. And the kitchen is upstairs? May I?' He went past Montespan and on the second floor began to dictate, 'Iron spits and frying pans, stewpans and casseroles in tinned copper . . .'

Joseph Abraham, the wigmaker, looked truly sorrowful and turned to his tenant.

'When they placed the seals and informed us of the day of the seizure, we wrote to you immediately. Oh, if only you had accepted the title His Majesty offered you . . .'

'I want nothing to do with a ducal crown for the purposes of my wife.'

'. . . Larding-needles, rolling pins, a marble mortar with its pestle.'

The bailiff made his tally and climbed up to the room on

the third floor. He was followed by the ageing Abraham couple, to whom Montespan – making no effort to conceal his gibes from spiteful ears – explained, 'The King's lawmen are attacking me in my weak spot: money. In Françoise's name, they demand I reimburse her dowry, something I have never touched! I received only the interest. But by striking me so low, they leave themselves open to my scathing reply. The moment I arrived in Paris this morning, I went to see my father-in-law and, at the risk of provoking the total collapse of the house of Mortemart, I demanded immediate payment of the sixty thousand *écus* his daughter's lawyers require. In the light of this attack, I hope the plaintiffs will curtail their fees and temper their unreasonable claims!'

'One walnut bed, one blanket . . . Monsieur le marquis, I estimate the entirety of your property at a total of nine hundred and fifty *livres*, which shall be paid to your wife.'

'Nine hundred and fifty *livres*,' echoed Louis-Henri. 'She has my furniture seized for nine hundred and fifty *livres*, when the King is building her a palace in Chinese mosaics for three million *écus*.'

He burst out laughing. 'She has lost touch with reality.'

The bailiff informed him that Parliament would no doubt decide to do the same with the marquis's remaining property in Guyenne, unless he paid the dowry forthwith, along with four thousand *livres*, annually, of alimony which the favourite demanded, by virtue of their physical separation.

'How could I possibly do that? I haven't a pistole to my

name and I don't even know where I shall sleep tonight.'

And if the squire found himself tossed out onto the cobblestones of Paris, in danger of losing even the last clod of earth on his Gascon estate, this did not seem to be Rhurin's problem.

Montespan felt as if the Pyrenees had fallen on his wig. He reminded the bailiff, to no avail, that according to the law in force, whatsoever her reasons might be, a woman could not leave the conjugal home, on pain of being deprived of her rights and, if caught *in flagrante delicto* in an act of adultery, she could be sentenced to the iron collar, the pillory or banishment, forfeiting her dowry to her husband – provided he had not already murdered her, for there was no punishment prescribed in that case.

'D-do you intend to kill the King's mistress?' stammered François Rhurin.

'No, far from it . . .'

That very afternoon, at four thirty, surrounded by numerous mirrors, Louis XIV buttoned up his richly coloured brocade breeches again then wrote a letter.

Monsieur Colbert,

As I went through the council chamber of late I forgot to tell you that word has come to me again that Monsieur de

Montespan is in Paris and has dared to make indiscreet assertions. It would be most opportune to observe his behaviour. He is a madman, capable of the most extravagant acts; it shall be your pleasure to keep me closely informed. In order that his pretexts for being in Paris should be short-lived, consult with Novion so that Parliament acts quickly. I know that Montespan has threatened to come and abduct his wife. As he is perfectly capable of it, once again I rely on you to ensure he does not appear in the environs of the palace, and that he leave Paris at the earliest opportunity.

46.

Montespan moved through the grounds of the chateau of Versailles like a wolf through the forest in Bonnefont. He prowled amongst the lawns and flower beds; head down, he followed the pools of water – like mirrors that made the sky part of a *jardin à la française*. He hid side on behind the statues. He crouched in the thick clumps of narcissi, hyacinths, irises and fluffy anemones, and with long easy strides made his way towards the palace . . .

Versailles was a permanent construction site. Thirty-six thousand men were working there: stonecutters, masons, carpenters, roofers, earthmovers and labourers. They lodged at the edge of the immense royal estate in barracks known as 'hôtels de Limoges', as the majority of the stone workers were from Limousin and Creuse. In summer the work continued by torchlight. There were tents that served as infirmaries, and servants of the royal pantry sold the leftovers from court in stalls alongside the chateau. Montespan had, in broad daylight, taken advantage of the teeming activity to hide under the tarpaulin of a cart transporting the pineapples and green peas that the King was mad about, along with barrels of fruit ice cream. Once the cart had gone through a service gate in the outside wall, Louis-Henri had left the cart and hidden in the bushes.

Five thousand idle courtiers, hiding their smallpox beneath layers of rouge, met on the paths where they greeted or ignored one another loftily, and the Gascon scurried, head bent, towards the rear of the palace. He wanted to abduct Françoise – 'I have to get her out of here' – but it was impossible. He saw her in the distance, ten times more protected than the Queen. Forty bodyguards, for her alone, were by her side – officers who stared hawk-eyed into the distance whilst she walked up the steps of the royal residence; the cuckold followed.

A young sergeant was in charge of screening people at the entrance and asked the identity of those he did not recognise. 'Who are you?' Ahead of Louis-Henri, vexed ducs and princes offered all sorts of replies: 'Julius Caesar!' 'The Pope!' The guard was annoyed at having to deal with such jesting – not refined enough for his taste – but he forced himself to smile deferentially as he let them go through. When the Gascon introduced himself as 'Monsieur de Montespan', the sergeant burst out laughing.

'Ha-ha! That's a good one! Pray, come in, Monsieur de . . . Montespan! Ha-ha-ha!'

Inside the palace there was noise all day long. Workers knocked down walls, servants ran down halls, supplicants walked back and forth along the galleries. Louis-Henri was quickly wearied by the whirl of activity.

Upstairs, the cuckold realised he would not be able to get any closer to his wife. A veritable little army stood posted outside her apartments. So be it . . . then he came to a halt before a painting hanging on the wall, a canvas by Mignard no doubt. It was Françoise! The Gascon's heart began to pound as he looked at the likeness of the woman whose voice and face he could not forget. How beautiful she was, languishing on an oriental carpet, leaning on her elbow in a leafy setting. Around her neck she wore a pearl necklace . . . Grr! She was surrounded by four children. Were these some of the bastards she had had with the King? A copper plate plaque indicated that they were, from left to right, Mademoiselle de Nantes, the Comte de Toulouse, Mademoiselle de Blois and the Duc du Maine. They're beautiful, thought Montespan.

*

No, they were absolutely hideous! Louis-Henri came upon them in the garden, seated more or less as they had been in the painting, without Françoise, alas. In the shade of a thick grove, he happened upon them – quite by chance – sitting on a rug, staring at him. The one standing on the right, the eldest, introduced himself.

'The Duc du Maine . . .'

Montespan understood why the painter had portrayed him with a long vizir's coat trailing on the ground. The adolescent had an atrophied leg that was much shorter than the other, and he limped in a most pathetic fashion, despite a huge wooden sole. He sat on the rug with a smile.

'They have nicknamed me "Frisky"; but that's exactly

what I'm not. When I was three years old, and I was teething, I had such terrible convulsions that one of my legs ended up much shorter than the other. They tried to lengthen it, but ever since, it has only dragged all the more.'

Mademoiselle de Blois sat down in front of du Maine and laughed. With one shoulder higher than the other, this daughter of the King resembled a cockroach. She sang salacious songs and seemed to have an unbridled sexuality, totally abnormal for her young age.

'She sleeps with her father, the King,' said Mademoiselle de Nantes, who was horribly cross-eyed and very hairy. She squatted down like a female monkey and began to style and plait the long hairs on her knee. The Comte de Toulouse was a hunchback. His Majesty's legitimate offspring were not graced with extraordinary health; now the adulterine fruit of the Sun King's loins, conceived in full view of an open window, seemed to have been cursed as well. Ah, they were not at all like their painting, these bastards of Louis XIV! The painter had lied, misrepresented reality, and yet what a painting it would have made.

Montespan asked, 'Do you have no other brothers and sisters?'

'Oh yes, but they . . . they went off to commit buggery with the angels,' sniggered the freakish Mademoiselle de Blois, lifting up her skirt and showing her shitty bottom to the Gascon.

'Last June,' sighed the low-limping duc, 'our brother,

the Comte de Vexin, left us. He lived eleven years only to show, through his infirmities, how eager he was to die. He could no longer bear the daylight. Would you like to play cards with us, Monsieur?'

'Of course, children . . . Let me deal.'

The card dealer was only too aware of the comedy of his own situation, there on the rug in the grass. The Marquis de Montespan was at Versailles playing cards with his wife's children . . . He played very respectfully, dealing a card to his wife's daughter as if she were his own, kissing her hairy hand, which left long hairs between his teeth. 'There you are, my little lass.'

From time to time he turned to one side and laughed to himself. The hunchback asked the cuckold, 'What should we call you, Monsieur?'

'Papa.'

An interested passer-by, some distance away, had noticed the five of them, and was approaching the rug. Montespan got to his feet.

'Now I shall have to abandon the game. Amuse yourselves, children, and be good.'

The Gascon walked away quickly and turned a corner of the palace before the passer-by had reached the bastards to ask, 'Who was that man?'

'Monsieur Pâhpâh.'

*

At night, after the open-air festivities and torch-lit concerts, the crowd of courtiers returned to their apartments or to the gaming tables in some princely suite inside the palace. Montespan, who was still in the grounds, was lurking among the trees when he suddenly noticed six heads in a row popping up from behind a hedge. They wore short blond wigs in the *hurluberlu* style, and although their faces had aged, the Gascon recognised them – above all from their grey smocks – as the six apprentices to the wigmaker Abraham.

'What are you doing here?'

The six heads vanished behind the hedge again and then he heard six voices, one after the other.

'Thanks to an accomplice we have here, we are able to infiltrate the estate, and we come on Sundays and holidays to try and see her . . .'

'At dusk we climb the trees to look at her through the windows when she bathes naked in the water room, but tonight it's impossible . . .'

'The night watch has left the rest of the chateau to gather around her part of the building and prevent anyone coming near, for the King, aware that you have come out of exile, fears an abduction . . .'

'But in the afternoon, at four o'clock, in front of the palace building site . . .'

'We gaze at her with a telescope . . .'

'And there, what we behold . . .'

'Enough!' said the marquis, vexed, as he stood up. 'Come and help me instead.'

The six heads reappeared all together.

'To abduct her?'

'Nay, of course not, since it is impossible.'

Together the small group walked across the Parterre du Midi whilst the royal security were at the opposite end, and they arrived outside the Queen's apartments. Montespan located her room one floor up where the light had just been blown out. A former captain, he waited for a few minutes then ordered, 'Let's do it!'

The tall thin apprentices galloped up to the façade then, with three at the bottom, two standing on their shoulders, and yet another on top, they quickly made a human pyramid that Montespan hurried to climb as if he were going up the stairs – a foot on a shoulder, then a head, then a hand – until he was just below the windowsill. With all the strength in his arms he pulled himself up and entered the bedchamber with its open window – since His Majesty would join the Queen presently.

'The King fucks my wife, so I will fuck his.'

He heard the pyramid of apprentices quickly dismantling their human scaffolding along the façade and hurrying off to hide in silence, and then the 'daring madman', as the other fellow would have called him, stole like a wolf to sit at the bedside of Marie-Thérèse, whom he had never seen. She slept buried among her pillows in a faded decor overflowing with gold all the way to the astral ceiling, and Louis-Henri spoke to her in a hushed, barely audible voice.

'Your husband, at this moment, is making love to my wife. Let us do the same so that he, too, shall know the weight of horns.'

Very delicately, inch by inch, the way one removes a bandage from a wounded man's burning sore, Montespan lifted up the magnificent bedspread: it was embroidered with a stag hunting scene depicting in silver threads the hounds being called to the quarry. He pulled back the blanket and satin sheet together. The queen's nightdress had corkscrewed around her legs. 'You are rather short,' said the marquis regretfully, slipping a palm beneath her garment and up the back of her thigh. He did not like her skin; he found it . . . unpleasant. As for Françoise, though, her skin was spiritual and her arse was spirited, whereas Marie-Thérèse's, noted the Gascon, lifting up the nightdress – oh, woe! A square thing with nothing in the way of hips, which gave her a figure like that of a young wild boar.

'You would not earn one pistole in the brothels behind Place de Grève.'

At Versailles, Montespan stared at the Queen's bare bottom. A cough, the slightest movement, the slightest intervention of fate could have revealed the foolhardy intruder, and then what would have become of him?

'It is said that you say a special mass whenever the King

climbs upon you. With me, the priest would not see you very often.'

He parted her lace bodice to look at her breasts: ugly. With the flat of his palm, Louis-Henri slowly crushed the down in one of the pillows to reveal her profile, and discovered ruined teeth and a waxy complexion aggravated by brown spots scattered around a gigantic nose. Montespan sprang to his feet in terror and recoiled, observing the horridly dumpy Queen with her bottom exposed.

'Goodness, how can this be! Like a lump of Auvergne sausage! I understand why your husband prefers my wife . . . It's the first time I've actually understood the King. How can one have one's way with you?'

Louis-Henri was at a loss to find any motivation. He searched all around him and concluded that unless he drank himself senseless from the carafe of alcohol set on the little desk, he'd never manage. He slumped into an armchair and put his feet up on the desk, his crossed red heels muddy from the gardens, then he poured himself a golden liqueur from Alicante and drank it straight down. He refilled his glass. He was tempted by an open box of chocolates. He gobbled up a few, then all of them, then knocked the box over with a chuckle. The cuckold was beginning to feel splendidly drunk. He took a pipe from his doublet, lit it and belched rings of smoke towards Le Brun's painted ceiling. The embers in the little stove crackled and glowed red in the darkness of the bedchamber. Outside, through the open window, one could see, over the surrounding wall, the forges in action with showers of sparks from the metals that shrieked like a madman. Louis-Henri removed his periwig, which he set down next to his pipe, and got up. He drank the rest of the liqueur from the carafe, wiped his lips, and pulled down his pink silk breeches, then went up to the monumental four-poster bed but . . . nothing.

In her sleep the Queen had rolled over onto her back and, with her slack mouth wide open, she was snoring. Louis-Henri, standing with his cock in full view, wandered around the huge royal chamber and muttered, 'I was so happy with Françoise . . . I loved her laughter, and everything she said to me. I am a solitary man, 'tis my inclination, but I was happier with her than alone. The moment she was there, I could breathe better, felt calmer. Above all I loved her intelligence. I miss her, if you only knew . . . I cannot become accustomed to her absence. The moment she opened the door to the room I was in, a smile lit up my lips: "Good day, my darling, my beloved!" Often, as I fell asleep beside her, I would join my palms together. Waking up by her side was a dream that would last the entire day and I would bite my lips with happiness. Some mornings my lips were covered in blood, and she would kiss my wounds: "You love me so." "Too well?" I asked, and she laughed. If one night she panicked, filled with anxiety, I would console her, reassure her: "Do not be afraid, all will be well . . ."'

Marie-Thérèse was talking in her sleep.

'That vitch shall ve the death of me!'

The dull, austere Queen born in Madrid had never managed to learn French properly, and the subtlety of the courtiers' witty phrases cast her into an abyss of bewilderment. She could not distinguish a 'v' from a 'b'.

'Hey! What did you say?'

Montespan frowned and squinted, ready to smash one of those large Chinese vases in her ugly face, but he controlled himself and turned his back on the stupid woman (she was a fervent adept of games, and her participation was particularly valued because she never understood any of the rules).

'In any case, what would be the point of waking you? You would want no part of me. The mere thought of lowering your gaze upon a man who has not been consecrated by God is inconceivable to you. He must be dressed as a Roman emperor, in a tunic of gold and diamonds, wearing a helmet with a plume! Whereas Françoise now, I know she is sweet and gentle, with simple tastes, and her sex was pink and gleamed like mother of pearl, faith, like the inside of this mollusc shell, this little font hanging from your wall. Oh aye, hers was as delicate as a shell . . .'

If Marie-Thérèse had awoken and sat up, she would have seen, from behind, the marquis's right arm shaking frenetically up and down. Tears of milk suddenly spurted into the holy water, eddying in long filaments. A few more drops fell and burst like pearls, then there was the sound of doors opening and footsteps on the parquet in the corridor. Montespan, already at the window, leapt into the void. Fortunately the apprentices had immediately run over and rebuilt their human pyramid up the façade. The last boy, climbing on the two below him, felt the marquis land on his shoulders, and they quickly tumbled down together.

On the gravel, the six boys with their *hurluberlu* wigs shot off like stars in a silent bomb blast. They waved their hands, fingers spread, to bid farewell to the Gascon. Louis-Henri saw a covered cart filled with orange trees in huge crates: with the arrival of autumn, they were to be transported to the shelter of the royal greenhouses outside the palace walls.

It was not known whether the King, on entering the Queen's bedchamber, had wished to anoint himself with holy water and been surprised by what he found on his brow and lips, or whether it was because he had seen, on Marie-Thérèse's desk, the man's pipe still smoking next to an abandoned periwig, along with the glass, the empty carafe, the upturned chocolate box and the traces left by muddy heels on the precious wood, or his wife's bare bottom turned towards the astral ceiling: but for whatever, or all these reasons, the Jupiterian voice had roared, booming in the Versailles night like thunder, 'Lauzun!'

47.

'I don't think I like my son. He is a harpy. His ferocious ambition should make him the most perfect and refined of courtiers, despite the fact we live in a century where among many the art of vileness seems impossible to surpass. On my return journey from Paris, I stopped to visit him at his Jesuit boarding school in Moulins. I was not at all pleased with Louis-Antoine.'

'Is it because we've gone hunting, Captain, that you're thinking about him? It puts you in mind of the time when we tried to teach him—'

'He told me that I must no longer come to visit him, for it would harm his access to the court.'

'And . . . the favourite, does he see her?'

'She has granted him a pension of six thousand *écus* and often has him brought to Versailles. He is very lucky at games of chance, and is suspected of contributing to her fortune. This year Françoise promised him a lieutenant's commission in the first infantry of the King's regiment when he turns eighteen.'

'Eighteen years old already? How time flies . . .' Cartet shook his head in disbelief as they arrived at the huge rock where the two paths crossed in the marquis's forest.

Down in the valley, bent old women gnawed at cabbage stalks by the side of the fields and scavenged for walnut shells to make bread. The second crop of hay would bring the beasts a bit more forage for the winter, which the old folk predicted would be worse than any other within living memory.

'Versailles ignores the poverty of the country . . .' lamented Montespan, turning back to his former sergeant, who had dropped his hunting net amongst the leaves; they would stretch it between two trees to catch wild game.

The Gascon stood at one end of the woven mesh and took hold of a rope that he began to tie around a tree trunk.

'Leave that,' said Cartet. 'I'll do it.'

The marquis went on tying his sailor's knot.

'Louis-Antoine confessed to me, "I have succumbed to the love of grandeur. 'Tis the sweetest of thoughts to me." D'Antin has his absurd notions. Not many men so completely dishonour themselves as my boy does,' said the father regretfully, testing the resistance of the stretched net with his hand as he lowered it to the ground. 'I don't know where this comes from. I—'

Cartet put his hand over the cuckold's mouth. 'Sssh!'

'What? What's happening?' murmured Louis-Henri through the steward's stubby fingers before he pulled his hand away.

'I can hear some noise approaching.'

'Animals?'

'No.'

'Poachers?'

'No. They would have taken greater care with regard to the wind, and now I can smell them,' said Cartet, sniffing; his moustache, like an insect's antennae, seemed to stand to attention. 'Hunters of men, there are four of them, not brigands, either. I scent their putrid smell of the tannery and the military wash house. It's a squad of dragoons coming for you, in response to your escapade in Versailles, Captain . . . Methinks 'tis the King's shadow drawing closer. They'll enter the clearing from the left.'

'Hide behind that thick oak tree, Cartet, I shall wait for them at the crossroads.'

What vigilance the marquis required to stay alive! The ambushed dragoons finally emerged from behind a thicket, with a flash of unsheathed swords.

One of them, who had a thin moustache like a line of charcoal beneath his nose, seemed to be the leader of these killers and declared in a terrible voice, 'To the death, cuckold, I will skewer you, and your wife is a whore!'

Louis-Henri acted the part of a man whose fear of

weapons rendered him impervious to insults. As they advanced, he withdrew, calling to the leader, 'One against four, brave sir, let us meet elsewhere, where our swords will not all be on one side.'

Then, turning towards the thick oak tree, he fled at a run, beginning to feel the effects of age in his legs. The King's young official assassins, who were more lively, set off after him, swords drawn and held straight ahead. Just as they reached the thick oak tree, Cartet raised the net and they were caught in the mesh, whilst the leader's drawn pistol fell and slid on the ground. The steward took his long dagger from his boot and stabbed one of the men. Then he fought another, who was very strong, with his bare hands. They grappled, becoming entangled in the net. Montespan had reappeared and he picked up the pistol and rammed the barrel against the leader's teeth.

'I don't like wicked things to be said to my face about my wife. You'll be excommunicated like a werewolf.'

He fired the pistol into the charcoal-streak moustache, which vanished.

'This is how one deals with those who dare misspeak their mind.'

Next to him, the former sergeant, spattered with brains, was stunned. 'Did you not tell me, Marquis, that before meeting your wife you were of a very peace-loving nature?' Then he went on to snap the neck of another dragoon with the crook of his arm, whilst the last one escaped. The pistol was empty, so Montespan hurled his hunting knife deep into the fugitive's shoulder. As they tried to decide whether to pursue the still running youth, Cartet reassured the Gascon.

'Stay here, Captain, he's done for, and if he goes in that direction he is not about to find any help in the immense tangle of forest that goes as far as the Bielsa pass. The wolves will get him. Whoever finds his body will be a clever sort. What should we do with the dead?'

The marquis was standing by the huge rock and he raised the grate of the underground escape route.

'Let's drop them in here. In any event, this tunnel no longer serves, since the intendant had the entrance in the courtyard demolished.'

After folding up the net to sling it across his back, Cartet headed along the path towards the chateau's smoking chimneys and complained of pain in his joints.

'I think I'm getting too old to run about with young bloods. Faith, 'tis no longer my age to sport with such rowdy knaves – or else it's a sign of a deep freeze . . .'

Montespan, on his right, sighed.

'My son is ashamed of his father . . . When I tell him I love him in spite of everything, he sniggers and cackles malevolently. I do not know where he gets it from . . .'

The steward, his bearskin boots scraping against the loose stones, said nothing.

48.

In the ruined chateau of Bonnefont, with its collapsing roof, the cold was almost worse than in the peasants' cottages. The huge residence could not be heated, with its crumbling rooms, its draughty corridors and its closets. Water would have frozen in the jug and wine in the bottle had they not been placed by the hearth, where the fire hissed with a continuous sound like a spinning wheel twisting the hemp.

At the end of the long table in the kitchen, Dorothée was standing with a wide brush in her hand and was covering all the clothes and shoes with *cirure*, a mixture of wax and tallow used for waterproofing. She raised her green eyes to the frozen window and saw the flickering of a torch flame in the distance, coming nearer.

'Hello, there's someone coming!'

The marquis was in his armchair at the other end of the table, his back to the window, and he turned round. Cartet was sitting on a bench to his right, and had been in the middle of advising him to chop down those trees whose wood had rotted, for otherwise they would be utterly worthless; and they should inspect the woodpigeons' roosts. Madame Larivière was finishing washing up the supper dishes and putting them away. The door opened.

The fine veil of mist in the courtyard was suddenly lit up, swirled above the cobblestones and rose in the black night. A man came in.

'Brrr! I wanted to pull the chain of your bell next to the gate but it is frozen.'

'Lauzun?' Montespan was dumbfounded. 'You here – but to what do I owe the honour? And how have you been all these years?'

'I was briefly condemned to life imprisonment at the fort of Pignerol,' said the visitor, who wore a heavy fur coat, as he went to warm his hands above the flames in the fireplace. 'I escaped, was recaptured and then everything was forgiven. Here I am again buried in the King's trifling paperwork. You should follow my example . . .' smiled Lauzun, spinning on his heels and opening his coat to display a marvellous suit of brocade decorated with pink and gold ribbons. 'His Majesty has given me a commission as colonel of the dragoons.'

'Dragoons?' echoed the marquis. 'Are you thirsty, or

hungry? I think there's still some soup in the pot, with some crusts of bread made from ferns in it.'

'Just a bit of hot wine, if you please, Madame,' the colonel asked the cook. 'Good even, Mademoiselle,' he said to Dorothée, who could not take her eyes off him.

He greeted the steward as he sat down by him on the bench. He was a small, erect man whose dirty-blond wig was spattered with snow and dripped beneath the wide-brimmed felt hat he wore; he looked reluctant. By his side was a large satchel, which he now opened.

'On the subject of dragoons, just before the winter I sent four of 'em from Versailles for a walk in your woods. This is all I have found of 'em!' he continued, removing from his satchel a human vertebra that he set down on the table.

''Tisn't a great deal,' Montespan was forced to concede, unruffled.

'Where exactly did you find it?' asked Cartet, intrigued.

'Well beyond the marquis's woods, in the immense forest between here and the Bielsa pass.'

The former sergeant, amazed, turned to face the visitor full on and watched him.

'Next to it I also found this,' said Lauzun, placing on the table a shoulder blade run through with a white weapon.

'Do you intend to show us many more of these disgusting objects?' complained Madame Larivière. 'What is the point of cleaning the house if you—'

'No. That is all. There was nothing else.'

'Oh, look, Cartet, it's my hunting knife! I thought I had lost it. Yes, it's definitely mine. See, it has been carved with my coat of arms, with the horns added. The wind and the storm must have carried it and flung it into the bone.'

'It's true we've had some frightful weather,' said the steward. 'Part of the chateau roof blew away. First there was a frost that lasted nearly two months during which the rivers froze, and the seashores were able to bear the weight of horsecarts. A false thaw melted the snow that had covered the land, then was followed by a sudden return of the frost, which was even more severe than before and lasted another three weeks. That second frost was so harsh that all was lost. The fruit trees were ruined. There are no more walnut trees, or olive trees, or vines. The animals died in the stables and the game in the woods. The gardens perished, and all the seeds in the ground. There is devastation everywhere. Everyone is hoarding their old grain: the price of bread is increasing in proportion to the despair over the coming harvest.'

'I know,' said Lauzun. ''Tis the same all over France. In Auvergne, the famine is so great that women devour their dead children. During my journey, at the post houses I saw people arrive so exhausted and weakened by hunger that when they were given a crust of bread they could not even unclench their teeth to eat. There are dark years ahead of us . . . The renewed persecution of the Protestants, the deterioration of the climate, with direct repercussions on the harvest, the common folk crushed by taxes and poverty, and ruinous wars blazing on every border.'

'Really?' said Madame Larivière, astonished, her hands on her hips. 'The King is starting conflicts?'

'At Versailles,' replied Lauzun, without turning to look at her, 'the work has just been completed, and Europe is greatly concerned because this means that the money will go to finance new wars. It is as if the King were beginning to weary of something . . .' continued the colonel, staring at Montespan.

Louis-Henri was contemplating the objects on the table: the mustard pot – a little earthenware barrel – next to the vertebra; the salt in a small shell-shaped bowl next to the hunting knife rammed in the shoulder blade, and he asked the cook to bring the bottle of ratafia and some glasses.

'So, you have not seen my dragoons?' Lauzun persisted, blowing on his wine to cool it.

'Nay,' replied Cartet. 'If there were four of them, we'd certainly have seen them.'

'And if that were the case, you would tell me.'

'Oh, yes. Anyway the last time we went to the woods, that was . . . well now, it must have been the day before the first big frost: the day before Saint Thomas's Day.'

'I believe that was the day they were in the forest also.'

'They must have got lost, and the wolves ate them,' concluded the steward, pouring out the drink.

Madame Larivière prodded about with the fire tongs, and the flames rose high and lively in the chateau in the Pyrenees. The alcohol oiled their speech and loosened their tongues. Dorothée admired the noble sparkle of the rings on the visitor's fingers and, by the table legs, his magnificent shoes encrusted with pearls and diamonds. The cook was anxious, for she thought there was too much drinking around the table.

As the evening passed, the bottle emptied. Eventually, by dint of all they had swallowed, the colonel and the marquis were inebriated. Lauzun merely grew all the more serious, whilst Montespan was so dazed and heavy that he leant on the table and said, 'So now my wife's lover wants to send me to kingdom come! Quickly, Madame Larivière, thaw the inkwell so that I might write my last will and testament. I would like to have everything in order, should an "accident" befall me – if I were to collide with a sceptre, for example . . .'

'And in this will, do you plan to invoke His Majesty?' asked the colonel of the dragoons.

'Why, of course I do! *In vino veritas.*'

'If you plan to write it now, Marquis, allow me then to follow the maid, that she might show me the room where I may sleep, and tomorrow I will return to Paris to have it published by the minstrels on the Pont-Neuf.'

'Done, as good as a contract!' said the Gascon. 'Madame Larivière, where is that ink?'

'Of all your foolish tricks, this is the greatest one that you could commit, Monsieur,' scolded the cook.

'Come now, Madame "Cartet"!'

'What! Marry that steward drinking the way he does – do you take me for a fool? I'd rather be buried under a hundred thousand feet of shit!'

The former sergeant, after one too many, his eyes creased up with laughter, said, 'That's not very nice . . .' The cuckold's pen raced over the paper.

Last Will and Testament

As I cannot be glad of a wife who, entertaining herself as much as possible, had me spend my youth and my life in celibacy, I shall limit myself to bequeathing to her my great portrait painted by Sabatel, and I shall beg her to hang it in her bedchamber when the King no longer enters. Although the Marquis d'Antin bears an amazing resemblance to his mother, I no longer hesitate to call him my son. In that capacity, as the eldest, to him I bequeath and leave my property. To their Highnesses Monsieur the Duc du Maine, Monseigneur the Comte de Toulouse, Mademoiselle de Nantes, and Mademoiselle de Blois (born during my marriage to their mother and consequently presumed to be my sons and daughters) I leave that to which they are legitimately entitled on condition they call themselves by the name of Pardaillan.

*To the King I bequeath and give my chateau at
Bonnefont, and beg him to institute there a community for
penitent ladies, on condition he place my spouse at the
head of this convent and appoint her the first abbess.*

Louis-Henri de Pardaillan
Marquis de Montespan
Separated albeit inseparable spouse

49.

'Feathers, ribbons, lockets! Braids, laces, artificial flowers! Handkerchiefs, buttons, odds 'n' ends!'

A wild-haired pedlar, shouting as he went, approached the cuckold's chateau and entered the courtyard where the entire village had gathered that spring day.

'Almanacs, tales and legends, stories of incidents, each one more incredible than the last! Cookery books: *The Royal Pâtissier*, *The School of Stews*! Holy images, last will and testament of Montespan . . .'

Louis-Henri turned round. 'You're selling my will?'

'Are you the Marquis de Montespan? Ah, of course, I am in Bonnefont.'

Thick smoke permeated the chateau courtyard. On grills above the embers sizzled pieces of offal – ears, brains, eyes . . . Pigs' trotters, boiled, grilled and minced, had been prepared by the cook. The marquis called to her, 'Madame Lari— Cartet! Come and see!'

Dorothée's mother came over, her head covered with a wedding veil; the church bells were still ringing.

'I should have liked to offer you a more lavish nuptial banquet,' apologised Montespan, 'but since everything has become so costly, and the forests are empty of game . . . Alas! This wandering merchant, I hear, sells artificial flowers. Choose one for yourself and fasten it to your brow. It is late April yet we have not seen a single flower in the garden or along the paths.'

The cook chose a daisy made of white satin petals, with a pistil of yellow velvet, and pinned it to her veil. 'I thank you, Monsieur . . .' Filled with emotion, she tried to speak of something else. 'Have you seen my daughter? I'll ask Cartet,' she said, going off to find her . . . husband, in his clean clothes, with espadrilles on his feet.

The steward, after shaking his head, moved among the guests, drinking toasts and offering food from a heavy tray. The grilled guts of chicken, turkey and rabbit were tasty morsels for these peasants whose diet consisted primarily of bread made from millet – it turned folk yellow, and so weak that most of them found it hard to work or even to stay on their feet.

'How much do I owe you for the flower?' Louis-Henri asked the pedlar.

'Nothing!' he exclaimed. 'Thanks to you, I have some

business. In these times of famine, 'tis hardly my cookbooks that sell like hot cakes . . . nor my holy images. What everyone wants to read is your last will and testament!'

'Upon my word . . .'

The Gascon walked along the moat towards the half-open barn door, to the left of the courtyard. The merchant unbuckled the trunk he had been carrying on his back and put it down. It was his turn to be surprised.

'Did you not know, Marquis? Your will has been the cause of immense merriment in Paris. The minstrels on the Pont-Neuf sell masses of copies, as do I in all the towns of all the provinces I visit. The text is copied out, handed round, read in the salons, and everyone laughs at the provisions and praises the wicked joke! At Versailles, too, they're snapping up your monumental slap in the face to the King. It's being passed round clandestinely, to the great fury of Athénaïs and the extreme displeasure of His Majesty, who now wants to have you locked up as a madman in the Petites-Maisons . . .'

Louis-Henri heard the cook on the drawbridge calling, 'Dorothée! Dorothée!' then he turned to the pedlar.

'So, the provisions of my will . . . did not amuse my wife?'

'Oh, your wife, I do not know what might amuse her now. There is talk that Louis XIV is beginning to weary of his mistress's haughty capriciousness. They also say he has tired of the exhausting physical relations which he used to indulge in with such heady delight. This year, the favourite was even omitted from the list of guests for the springtime fêtes at court. The King is publicly renouncing her. It is scarce believable, so far has Madame de Montespan fallen. His Majesty hardly looks at her any more, and you may well imagine that the courtiers follow his example.'

'People are cruel . . .' said Montespan sorrowfully, whilst the pedlar helped himself to cockscombs, then, nibbling all the while, continued, 'In January, she had a fit of pique: "If that is the way it is to be, if the sovereign has no more consideration for the mother of his children, then I will leave my bedchamber!" The King agreed and announced that he would give the marquise's apartments at Versailles to his son the Duc du Maine, and the duc's apartments would go to young Mademoiselle de Blois. Athénaïs was snared in her own trap.'

'Poor woman . . .' sighed the cuckold, drinking a glass of water. 'Then where does she sleep?'

'Your wife must make do with the bathroom on the ground floor, far less favoured. This is the first significant step in her fall from grace, the end of "Quanto".'

Thud! Behind him, the marquis heard something falling like a big sack of sand. He turned round and went through the half-open door to the barn. Dorothée was lying on her stomach on the ground, at the foot of a ladder. She got to her feet unsteadily and tried to climb the ladder again in order to throw herself into the void. Montespan stopped her, grabbing hold of her by the waist.

'What's going on?' The cook in her bridal veil, with the pedlar hot on her heels, rushed up to her daughter in the barn.

'What has happened to you?'

Cartet appeared in turn, a drink in his hand. The wedding guests had not heard anything, and continued to feast on birds' guts, whilst the local orchestra tuned their hurdy-gurdies.

'Maman, I'm with child!' Dorothée confessed, sobbing in the marquis's arms.

'What! Is it you, Monsieur, who . . .' The new bride frowned suddenly at the man with his arms around her daughter.

'Enough, Madame Larivière!' said Montespan, annoyed.

'Cartet! Madame Cartet, if you please!'

'Well, Cartet, if you insist, but you nearly had me locked up in Pignerol once before.'

'Then who is it, Dorothée?' The cook's artificial daisy trembled on her veil. 'Who has got you with child? Give me the name of that village swine! My husband shall rip his head off!'

'Whose head, who, who?' stammered the big steward, his eyes shining from all the toasts he had drunk with the bumpkins.

Enveloped in the fragrance of liquorice and orange-flower water that wafted from the marquis's silky clothing, Dorothée explained. 'I threw myself on my belly to force a miscarriage. Maman! He said to me, "Such extreme grace! Such an exquisite demeanour! Where can one find a goddess equally endowed?"'

'But who?'

'He had me glide over the parquet floor in the steps of a minuet, with a grace fit to stir a heart beneath a gown . . .'

'But who?'

'The gentleman with the magnificent shoes encrusted with pearls and diamonds.'

'Lauzun?'

Montespan was flabbergasted at that.

'Maman!' pleaded the young pregnant woman, her skin damp in her chaste dress. 'I would need to take a bath in a decoction of ergot of rye, root of rue, and juniper leaves to dislodge the child . . . But we haven't any! Take a knitting needle and rid me of it yourself!'

'Are you mad?' said the Gascon indignantly. 'Only to bleed to death? We can bring the baby up all the same! Why get rid of it?'

'Because a girl must remain like a sealed vase until her marriage!' said the cook sententiously.

'And you're the one saying this, Madame . . . Cartet?' said the marquis, astonished.

'That's a point – do we know who the father of our daughter is?' the steward suddenly asked his wife in a daze.

The pedlar, watching the scene, tried to reassure them that it was not only in this barn that one encountered mysteries full of suspense and sudden twists of plot. 'At Versailles, for example, there is a parody of "Our Father" doing the rounds, something unthinkable only a few months ago, and it ends, "Deliver us from la Montespan." Those who praised her to the skies only yesterday treat her as the lowest of the low today. Even Racine, who owes everything to her, has publicly scoffed at her in his play *Esther* – a comedy that tells of the fall of la Montespan and the rise of la Maintenon. Another fine example of ingratitude! But people are saying that the King, since the operation on his anal fistula, is now in greater need of a nurse than a whore. She's as deaf and perfidious as an underground current, la Maintenon; they call her "Madame de Maintenant". The widow Scarron has risen in favour whilst your wife, Monsieur le marquis, has fallen from grace before our eyes. One morning, la Maintenon met la Montespan in the stairway: "How now, Madame, you are coming down, whereas I am going up." One evening His Majesty, heading for la Maintenon's chambers, left his dog Malice in your wife's rooms: "Here, Madame, some company for you, it should suffice."'

Louis-Henri clenched his fists. 'I will tear out the eyes of anyone who dares treat Françoise so cruelly!'

50.

'Ah, could you but have heard me, Master Jean Sabatel, a year and a half ago, the morning after the wedding of my steward with my cook, when I shouted out, "Françoise has fallen from grace. She shall return! Let us undertake some repair work to welcome her home!" Is that not true, Madame Cartet?'

The cook, carrying a heavy basin of laundry, walked past Montespan. 'I will not say a word, Monsieur, about these accounts and calculations of yours, and all the horrible payments, the untold expense: a hundred and twenty thousand *livres*; there are no limits!'

Madame Cartet, her face lined, crossed the drawbridge and left the chateau walls, still shouting at Louis-Henri. 'You are drowning in debt and your house only survives by a miracle; your fine façade may have been restored, but it is being eaten away from within by a mountain of debt and depleted credit which might cause it to collapse like a house of cards at any moment . . . and it may even lead to you being stripped of your nobility, and from gentleman you shall become a commoner, subject to tallage and unworthy of any office! Ah, such a—'

'Such a what?' asked the marquis whilst, outside the chateau, the shrew hung her sheets on a line to flap in the sunlight. 'One must learn how to make peace, Madame Cartet, and prepare a worthy reception for a woman who was led astray! But don't leave that sheet there, foolish woman. If Françoise were to return today, I should not like her to be greeted by drying sheets, after all!'

'I don't know,' sighed the steward's wife, putting the still wet laundry back in the basket, and returning to the drawbridge, 'this is becoming ridiculous. And now to cap it all, Monsieur is hiring an itinerant painter . . .'

'She still has her temper,' recalled the artist from Montlhéry, the very same who had visited so long before to paint the marquis's portrait. 'The decor, on the other hand, has changed considerably!'

'You've noticed? The new gate at the entrance, which I ordered from the ironworks in Auch, is an imitation, though not as glorious, of the one at Versailles. And I've repaved the courtyard. Have you seen how it is now? Before, there were nettles growing everywhere, and brambles that would have torn her gown. The courtyard was muddy and carriage wheels used to get mired up to their axles on rainy days. She would have stained her little boots. I also had that step replaced, where the frost had cracked it, so that she will not twist her pretty ankles. The chateau has been given a new roof: I did not want it to rain on her lovely face when she sleeps again by my side in our chamber. You may say, "'Tis not the work of a Mansart", but all the same! And the grounds, at the back, come and see the grounds.'

Moving stiffly and pressing his hand to his lower back, the marquis led the artist into the garden and sang its praises.

'Look, all the undergrowth has been cleared. Everything has been trimmed, scraped and cleaned, ready to receive her, so that her graceful figure can stroll on the grass. 'Tis not the work of a Le Nôtre, but . . . it does have six orange trees in crates! It will remind her of where she used to live. She shall not suffer too greatly from homesickness. And have you seen, in the middle of the lawn, the little circular basin with its fountain? It doesn't rise very high; it cannot be compared to the great fountains of the Bassin d'Apollon. But in spite of that, it's a fine fountain, is it not? With one, yes, only one statue . . . but it is a statue of Venus, with Françoise's features, and I had it made in Toulouse. 'Tis not a sculpture by Girardon . . . but from her open mouth there spurts a jet of water, where she will come to seek refreshment. It's very pure water that flows from a spring six leagues hence, carried here by means of underground connecting pottery pipes. The water emerges from the lips of Venus-Françoise and goes on to feed the moat. The stagnant pools have been purified,' continued Montespan, stretching as he led the painter back to the chateau. 'And so there are no more mosquitoes, so terrible for her delicate skin, nor any stagnant smells rising to the windows to offend her sensitive nostrils on days of great heat, which would have made her sick. The flowers are blooming again. We will place bouquets in every room. I believe she will be happy . . .'

From the middle of the courtyard they could hear raised voices exclaiming from behind the old guardroom door, which the marquis now opened, wiping his brow and explaining to the painter, 'I also want her to have her theatre. She is so fond of it. Alas, it's not the Comédie-Française – there are only eight chairs in white wood that I have had painted in gold – but she will be able to applaud the performances of passing thespians who will perform for two hundred and fifty *livres*.'

Louis-Henri put his index finger to his lips and whispered, 'They are rehearsing . . . to be sure, 'tis not a play by Corneille, but . . . Pray come in, and note the walls that I should like you to decorate with flowers, foliage, acanthus. I imagined shades of nasturtium red and a bluish grey. Would that be possible?'

'Naturally, although . . .' warned the modest painter with a smile, 'do not expect the likes of Le Brun, obviously!'

'That doesn't matter. And in our bedchamber I would like a ceiling with plaster figures depicting symbols of love: quivers and arrows, and cupids. But let us sit, for I am weary, and listen to this comedy. A little marquis, a courtier at Versailles, is preparing to marry the youngest daughter of a moneylender who has provided a sack of pistoles as a dowry. And he is educating the girl in advance, and she is greatly surprised by what she hears.'

Walking over planks placed on trestles, a young actress came from the back of the stage towards an actor all in ribbons, and she placed her hands on her hips.

'Her hair is not in the *hurluberlu* style,' Montespan sighed regretfully in the painter's ear, 'but . . .'

'That is the La Fontanges style,' replied the decorator.

'Who?'

The actress, whose long hair flowed onto her shoulders, was absorbed by her role; she was expressing her astonishment.

MONEYLENDER'S DAUGHTER: *Is there harm in loving my husband?*
MARQUIS: *At the least, there is ridicule. At court a man marries to have heirs, and a woman to have a name; and that is all that she has in common with her husband.*
DAUGHTER: *To take one another without love! When*

306

love is the means to having a good life together!

MARQUIS: *One has the best of lives together, as friends. One is smitten neither by tenderness, nor by the jealousy, which demeans a man of refinement. A husband, for example, might encounter his wife's lover: 'Hello, good day, my dear chevalier. Where the devil have you been hiding? I've been looking for you for so long. By the way, how is my wife? Do you still delight in one another? Is she amiable, at least? Upon my honour, if I were not her husband I feel that I should love her. Why are you not with her? Ah, I see, I see . . . I'll wager that you have quarrelled. Come, come, I will send for her, to ask her to sup with us this evening: you shall come and I will set things right again betwixt you.'*

DAUGHTER: *I confess that everything you have said seems most extraordinary.*

MARQUIS: *I well believe it. The court is a new world for those who have only seen it from afar. But we are at ease here, for we are the natural inhabitants of this country.*

Montespan applauded, seeking the painter's approbation. 'It's not bad, is it?' The door to the old guardroom – the theatre – opened and the cook came in, carrying an infant in her arms. She was looking for Cartet or Dorothée to give the swaddled child to whilst she did the ironing.

'I'll take her,' offered the Gascon. 'Come, Marie-Christine . . .'

Louis-Henri smiled and cooed at the infant in the crook of his arm. The tiny girl had Lauzun's pointed nose.

'Françoise will love her too. With the eight or ten she gave the King, she has a great love of infants.'

'Your wife is a monster.'

'What did you say? Take that back!' growled the fierce Gascon, suddenly looking at his decorator as if he were a Turk at Gigeri, but the artist would not back down.

'There is something rotten in the state of France; something your wife found in the wretched neighbourhoods of Paris has infiltrated Versailles . . .'

'Why do you say that?'

'The court is drowning in a sea of hysteria and witchcraft; it is teeming with poison and tales of murders. The Princesse de Tingry, the Duchesse de Bouillon, the Comtesse de Soissons, the Marquis de Cessac, the Vicomtesse de Polignac, the Marquise d'Alluye, the Duchesse d'Angoulême, the Comte de Gassily, the Duc de Vendôme: all have been charged. At their trials the spectators bombard them with miaowing cats.'

Louis-Henri got abruptly to his feet, holding the new Marie-Christine in his arms.

'My wife has nothing to do with those madmen!'

'Outside my lodgings on Rue Saint-Antoine, a drunken poisoner boasted between swigs of wine: "What a fine trade! And such a clientele! I see none but duchesses and marquises and princes and lords coming through my door!

Three more poisonings and I shall retire having made my fortune!' The Poison Affair is turning into a political nightmare. At court, be it in soup or wine or perfume, everyone is administering enough powder to everyone else to make them sneeze one last time. We have reached the dregs of the century. It is said that Racine poisoned his mistress, the actress Madame Duparc.'

'That scarce surprises me, coming from him! 'Tis what he deserves for writing tragedies! But Françoise!'

'La Reynie has laid his hand on a veritable hornet's nest. He is able to destroy the worker bees but is fearful of attacking the queen: Athénaïs de Montespan.'

'Have you lost your senses? Françoise . . .'

'. . . poisoned the stupid long-haired Mademoiselle de Fontanges — whom she had shoved into the King's arms without thinking, to try to lure him away from the widow Scarron.'

'You're insane!'

'She offered her a nightdress impregnated with cyanide. During the night, the poison mingled with La Fontanges's sweat and permeated her skin, and she died on 28 June last, spitting a most horrid pus.'

'This is calumny! Françoise had nothing to do with it!'

'The young woman had just enough time to deliver a diatribe against your wife: "You are the one who has poisoned me! But they are waiting for you, tigress, in Tartary, where the poisoners go, a terrible place where the wretches scream and grind their teeth. There you shall join the ranks of La Brinvilliers and the others who have taken the lives of innocent creatures!"'

'Proof! What proof do you have?' shouted the marquis.

Frightened, Marie-Christine began to cry. The cook came running into the theatre. 'Oh, dear me! What are you doing to this poor infant to make her cry so? Give her back to me!' She left again, whilst the painter continued his assault.

'The King has ordered that no autopsy be performed, which shows that he, too, has his doubts: "If you can avoid opening up the body, I think that would be wisest." But he has ordered an investigation. We'll never know the exact contents of the documents that were delivered to Louis regarding the involvement of the mother of his children in the Poison Affair – after reading them he burnt them with his own hands.'

'What of it? That proves nothing! It's not true!'

'She doesn't just eliminate the women who are in her way. Not far from where I live in Montlhéry, in the chapel of Villebousin, she does far worse.'

'I don't believe you!'

'Would you care to come and see?'

51.

Wearing a cassock and leaning on a table, Montespan gazed out of the window of a deserted inn between Paris and Orléans and looked first at the quiet waterlogged countryside. A windmill overlooked the fields. The disguised marquis then turned to look at the isolated chateau of Villebousin, whilst the painter Sabatel, who was seated next to him, said, 'You haven't forgotten the purse with the pistoles?'

'No,' replied Louis-Henri, putting his hand in his pocket to pass it to him.

'It's not for me,' said Sabatel, refusing it. 'At the last minute, you must give it to the monk I've managed to bribe, and whom you shall replace.'

'Who will be there?'

'Abbé Guibourg will preside over the ceremony, and

will go in first. You can't miss him: he has a ghastly face, the stuff of nightmares. He'll be followed by Lesage and Abbé Mariette, then by four cowled monks in single file with the shortest first and the tallest last. You'll replace the last one. When you have taken your place, you'll wait for Athénaïs de Montespan to arrive.'

Louis-Henri's heart began to pound as if for a lovers' tryst.

'Keep your cowl well over your face,' the painter insisted. 'Whatever happens, don't try to interfere. You have promised me. My life is at stake should you be discovered. Look, there's the first carriage. Go on.'

The marquis went out in his habit, crossed a path and entered the courtyard of the chateau that had been deserted for the afternoon, heading for the chapel. A fifteenth-century tower backing onto a wall marked the entrance. Louis-Henri lowered his head to go through the little door. He hid in a dark recess in the doorway. To his right a corridor led to the place of worship. This feudal demesne belonged to a relative of Mademoiselle des Oeillets, Athénaïs's maid of honour.

Iron-rimmed wheels rang on the cobbles in the courtyard. Soon the first figure entered the chapel, dressed in a white chasuble decorated with black pine cones. He was indeed extraordinarily ugly – his complexion and features were like those of a gargoyle, with long pointed ears – and he seemed to be the very incarnation of evil. An abbé wearing surplice and stole followed him, with another man holding a basket. Then came the monks in single file. When the fourth one lowered his head to go through the door, Montespan stepped out of his hiding place, handed the purse to him with a jangle of coins, and they changed places. The third monk, on hearing the clinking sound, turned round, but he was reassured when he saw he was still being followed by a tall ecclesiastic with clasped hands and bowed head.

A rectangular stone tomb dominated the centre of the little chapel. Abbé Guibourg, a crucifix and pocket knife in his hand, watched as Lesage covered the tomb with a sheet. Abbé Mariette sprinkled holy water as he murmured the Gospel of the Kings. All the monks were facing in the same direction, standing in the four corners of the gothic room. The Gascon, as he had come in last, was now near the door, his back to the tomb where the ceremony would take place. High, narrow stained-glass windows cast their heavenly light onto the flagstones. Montespan looked at the mural friezes and recognised Sabatel's style. His vast brown hood, pulled down low, almost hid his entire head, and he lowered it still further when he heard the jolt of a carriage arriving.

Louis-Henri blushed every colour of the rainbow beneath his hood. One rainbow hue after the other.

Pink! The cuckold was pink with emotion: he recognised the rhythm of her small heels clicking. Athénaïs came into the chapel. Without raising his head, her husband shifted his gaze towards her: she was wearing a pleated gown in Point d'Angleterre with a jewelled fastener beneath a gauze cloak. She had put on weight and, like him, she had aged (they were both forty-nine). She brushed past him. For years he had not been this close to her.

Red! The marquis blushed red when he heard his wife removing her clothing behind him. He heard the rustling as all her garments slipped from her skin and onto the floor! He could just see that she was lying flat on her back on the tomb, and it was the belly of Athénaïs's naked body that would serve as an altar.

'Astaroth, Asmodeus, princes of Friendship and Love . . .' – Louis-Henri recognised Françoise's beautiful voice – 'I beg you to accept the sacrifice that I shall offer you for the things I request.' What sacrifice? And why had she begun by invoking the names of two demons? What was this mass celebrated the wrong way round? 'I want the King to continue to show me his love, I want the princes and princesses of the court to honour me, and I want His Majesty to refuse me nothing I ask for.' Then Montespan heard the creaking of a wicker basket being opened, and the cries of an infant that had been awoken, and then the sound of a knife, slicing . . . There were no more cries, only the dripping of liquid into a chalice. Then the sounds of someone drinking. Oh, the sound of that swallowing! Louis-Henri was green.

White . . . The Gascon turned deathly pale whilst his wife got dressed again, as if he was the one who had just been drained of his blood. His captain's legs were about to crumble beneath him, and he struggled to stay on his feet. Once again there was the clicking of little heels over the flagstones, slowing down as they drew level with the Gascon, then stopping. Françoise sniffed the air. She seemed to pick up a scent and ask herself if . . . She looked at the monk's hood, then left the chapel.

As for the husband, he was completely undone. He would never get over it.

52.

'Is it serious, Doctor?'

'Very.'

The red-headed, potbellied, bearded doctor, in a red velvet robe with lace at his wrists, was taking Montespan's pulse. With the other hand he picked up a glass phial containing the marquis's urine and examined it.

'When did this start?'

'On the way back from a journey between Paris and Orléans; all this summer and autumn I've been unable to recover. I am prey to haemorrhaging. I am in pain. At night, my eyes stay wide open and I sweat with fever. I feel the end is near.'

'It is.'

The dark surgery in the town of Toulouse smelt stuffy; only a single candle burnt as the man of science gazed at the contents of the phial. Through the fine glass, the candle flame projected upon every wall the fluttering glow of the Gascon's urine as the physician analysed it.

'Potent vapours from the spleen and the melancholy humour, most visibly marked by the sorrow they display. These vapours move through the arteries to the heart and lungs, where they cause palpitations, disquiet and considerable fits of breathlessness. From there they rise to the brain and converse, agitating the spirit.'

'Which means?'

'You are done for.'

Through the thick curtain masking the window came the street sounds of Toulouse, the voices of a carnival hullabaloo crying, 'Death to all cuckolds!'

Beneath his neatly groomed wig with twin protuberances, the marquis, dressed in a grey doublet and pink hose, listened as the physician explained the hubbub from the street.

'There are nearly eighty days of merry-making, where the city forbids all work . . . The carousing and mockery aimed at conjugal misfortune have been going on since early February.'

'Doctor, how long might I hope—'

'You will not see out the year 1691, Monsieur de Montespan. What are you doing this evening?'

*

The next afternoon, after alighting from the coach at the post house three leagues from his home, Montespan continued his journey to the chateau on horseback, clinging to the saddle. His head was spinning. He felt sick and thought that his bones must be swelling and crumbling. In the courtyard he slipped from his mount, bathed in sweat, with Cartet's help.

'There is a letter for you, Captain.'

'Oh? A letter from whom?'

'I do not know. It is from the abbey at Fontevrault.'

Collapsing into his armchair at the end of the kitchen table, his back to the window, the cuckold unsealed the missive.

15 March 1691

Louis-Henri,

I have just awoken from a nightmare. I had a bad dream, where my name was Athénaïs ...

Stupefied, the marquis read the rest. When he had finished, the letter fell from his hands.

'Françoise has been driven from Versailles and has gone into a convent. She is offering to return to me.'

'What!'

'She asks forgiveness from her husband and permission to return to his side if he will condescend to see her again ...'

The cook was dumbfounded. The steward's moustaches drooped. Dorothée opened her eyes wide whilst Marie-Christine, on her lap, asked, 'What is happening, Maman? Is a lady going to come and live with us? When? Is she kind to children?'

The little girl's grandmother set a glass of water down in front of Montespan – a shimmering liquid mirror where the cuckold could see his features stretch, collapse, expand and undulate, greatly changing his appearance.

'I do not want her to come back.'

'What?' exclaimed the cook. 'But Monsieur, if you recall, ever since Rue Taranne . . . You've been waiting twenty-four years for this day to—'

'To what?' replied the marquis curtly, with a horrible chuckle. 'Offer her my aching knee and my slippers? I do not want her to witness what will become of me in the months ahead. I do not want her to see me wasting away. I do not want her to keep such an image of her husband. I did not long for her so deeply, for so many years, only to offer her now the sight of a poor broken husband, an invalid on a pisspot. Bring me some paper and ink.'

Madame,

I wish neither to receive you nor to hear speak of you for the rest of my life.

That evening, sitting by the moat in the moonlight, the steward put his arm round the cook as she leant against his shoulder. They turned to look at the light in the window upstairs in the chateau and listen to the marquis crying and weeping, which he was to do all night long.

53.

On 1 December 1691, at the age of fifty-one, Louis-Henri de Pardaillan, Marquis de Montespan, was fading away in his bedchamber in the chateau. Sheets covered the chairs in his theatre; the fountain had been turned off in the garden; a green moss was beginning to grow once again on the waters of the moat.

The enormous wisteria had invaded the horned carriage, abandoned for over a quarter of a century against a wall in the courtyard. Branches had made their way through the windows, forcing the doors off their hinges and dislodging the roof with its tall antlers. The plant had thrust with phenomenal strength around the wheels, lifting them from the ground or breaking them in its tight embrace, twisting the vehicle into a grotesque position. One could imagine the poor coach's lament, oppressed by the reptilian movement of the branches crushing its black veneer in a shattering of wood. Nature was chewing it up. The marquis was in the same state . . .

His parents were dead, his daughter had died of sorrow, he would never see his wife again and his son disgusted him.

His offspring, at the age of twenty-six, had become a fat monolith; now he was leaning on the mantelpiece of the bedchamber in front of a wall with a sky by Sabatel, and he stared scornfully at his bedridden father.

A notary – Maître Faulquier – was reading out loud the cuckold's new last will and testament. The marquis had ordered that after his soul departed from his body, the latter was to be shrouded and buried without ceremony at the foot of the cross in the parish cemetery of Bonnefont.

The dying man's son, listening to what followed, told himself that this was one grave that he would not often be visiting with flowers . . . For whilst his father might designate him the sole heir and legatee, he was asking him to keep on the employees, to whom he had granted handsome sums – three thousand *livres* to the Cartet couple and one thousand five hundred to Dorothée. Louis-Antoine, in an ermine-lined cape, thought it a waste of money. He sulked even more when he heard that his father had offered new clothes to all the inhabitants of Bonnefont, in recompense for true and loyal service, and had exempted them from a full year of seignorial dues.

'That's the end, he must be finished off. He's raving . . .' remarked the fat courtier of a son.

D'Antin was very attentive, not to say downright scrupulous, where inheritance was concerned, and now he grumbled, sneered and swore that he would not be so well-mannered when it came time to execute his father's will.

'Ah, but it is not up to you to decide,' said Maître Faulquier to the indignant son. 'Your father has called upon his wife to execute his will.'

And the notary read the following to an enraged d'Antin to illustrate his point.

'... The aforementioned testator has also said and declared that he has always placed his entire trust in the charity of Madame la Marquise de Montespan, his wife, and particularly at the present time when the aforementioned marquis needs it most greatly, finding himself to be infirm and afflicted by disease, which causes him to fear for the future. Therefore he begs her to pray to God after his death for the relief of his soul, which he hopes to find, and implores her to consent to being his testamentary executor, in light of the very sincere friendship and tenderness that he has retained for her. And the aforementioned testator affirms, in gratitude, that he shall die a happy man and very satisfied to have known her.

> *Louis-Henri de Pardaillan*
> *Marquis de Montespan*
> *Separated albeit inseparable spouse'*

The pathos of such an ardent confession, couched in legal jargon, aroused no emotion whatsoever in the son, who walked out without even a last look at his father.

The Cartets, along with Dorothée and her daughter, who had been standing to one side, now went up to the bed. The cook patted her hands all over her clothing and felt in her pockets.

'If it is your rosary you are looking for,' said her husband softly, 'it is there, wrapped around your wrist, Madame Larivière . . .'

'All right, never mind, I've got it, thank you!' scolded the cook, in a state of confusion.

Montespan looked up at the cook in surprise.

'You call your spouse Madame Larivière?'

'It's a question of habit, Captain.'

Marie-Christine went up to the head of the bed. She had Lauzun's pointed nose.

'Maman says you're going away. Where?'

Montespan whispered into the child's ear, 'I'm going to go and hide behind a cloud to wait for Louis XIV with a bludgeon . . .'

The cook lost her temper with the dying man (it was about time). 'Will this never end! Even up there! For all the good it's brought you here on earth . . . Nothing! Nothing! Nothing! What have you gained?'

Louis-Henri murmured, 'I can claim only the glory of having loved her . . .'

Then he lowered his eyelids, as if to rise up to heaven. The former sergeant removed his plumed beaver cap and held it to his chest. Madame Cartet hurriedly touched her fingers to her forehead, her belly and each shoulder. Seeking to unwind the rosary from her wrist, she tore it off, breaking the thread, and the beads bounced and rolled on the tiles. 'Aaargh!' she shouted, whilst Dorothée clasped her hands and bowed her head.

54.

'What day is it today?'

'Thursday, 26 May 1707, Madame de Montespan.'

'1707...' said she, a widow these sixteen years. 'Torches! Torches! Night is falling.'

'They are bringing them and lighting them. Look, Marquise, I shall even leave this candle for you on your bedside table,' said the maid soothingly.

'The shadow is coming alive. Its claws are reaching out to me, catching the sheets! A light! A light!'

Massive candelabras now filled the room with light. Through the window, its curtains drawn, the dusk behind the three towers of this half-feudal, half-thermal town was red with flames and destruction. Athénaïs panicked. The bedridden marquise had foresworn her legendary gowns, gold and pearls for a 'conjugal shift' pierced with a hole . . .

a shirt made of rough, stiff canvas. Her once-perfect body had grown very thin. Her lovely blond hair was white. She suffered from a disgust of self, and wore bracelets, garters and a belt with metal spikes that left sores upon her skin. Françoise never took her eyes from the portrait of her husband that she had had hung on the wall.

> *... my great portrait painted by Sabatel, and I shall beg her to hang it in her bedchamber when the King no longer enters ...*

From the corridor there was a sound of brisk footsteps approaching. The door to the room was flung open. In came d'Antin, followed by the Maréchale de Coeuvres, who was telling him, 'On the night of 22 May, your mother had fainting spells. We brought her vinegar and cold water. As we feared a fit of apoplexy, we administered an emetic, but I believe she was made to absorb too much. She vomited sixty-three times. The physicians have declared that she is lost. A priest came to administer the last rites. At that time we sent you a message regarding the "great attack of vapours" suffered by the marquise whilst taking the waters at Bourbon-l'Archambault.'

'I was in Livry and curtailed my hunting expedition with the Grand Dauphin to come as quickly as possible by post horse.'

'Monsieur d'Antin, you shall be the sad witness to the death of a sincere penitent.'

The sad witness . . . Louis-Antoine went up to the bed. He listened to the dying woman complaining of her weakness, that she was neither so strong nor so healthy as she once had been.

'I have no appetite, I cannot sleep, I am suffering from indigestion.'

'It is because you are getting old.'

'But how can I escape this decline?'

'The quickest means, Mother, is to die.'

The affectionate son then distinguished himself by an exploit that revealed the beauty of his soul: he pulled a key from around his mother's neck and opened a drawer in the secretaire.

'I was taken for a fool once, it shan't happen a second time.'

He took possession of the dying woman's will.

'Given the fact that you own a great deal of property, and I am fearful of being dispossessed in favour of bastard half-brothers and -sisters or even servants, it occurs to me that if you were to die intestate – and your last wishes in writing were not found – I would be the sole heir in the eyes of the law.'

The marquise, with her garters adorned with metal spikes, sighed.

'I should have so liked you to take after your father . . . And now what are you doing?'

'I am removing this portrait of your husband, and I will

burn it. Thus no one shall ever know what he looked like. I had a sledgehammer taken to the stone horns on the gate and on his coat of arms. I have burnt all his letters. The King, on hearing of it, has promised me a street in Paris. Just imagine, Mother . . . the Chaussée d'Antin!'

Without another word, the fat courtier took his leave, without waiting for his mother to be placed in her coffin, or even for her death. He strode away, his red heels tapping on the parquet. He mounted his horse in the courtyard of the *hôtel particulier*.

'Gee up!'

The marquise turned her head towards the door, left wide open, and in the next room she could see the nuns gathered around a painting.

'What are they doing?' asked a cook. 'And why do they have paintbrushes in their hands?'

The maid, sitting at the table shelling crayfish, told her, 'Before she left Versailles, the former favourite wanted to have her portrait painted as a repentant Mary Magdalene with a book open in her left hand, since she is left-handed. But the nuns in the convent of La Flèche to whom she gave the painting say that this Mary Magdalene is revealing too much bosom, so they are doing a "modesty repainting". The good sisters are adding a blue tulle cloth to la Montespan's bosom whilst she's dying. Would anyone else like a crayfish?'

Seven or eight girls were eating and drinking in the

room, conversing freely as if the marquise were no longer there. And yet she was still breathing. From time to time she drifted off, then emerged from her torpor in a sweat, screaming. At around three o'clock in the morning someone said, 'Look, she has stopped breathing.'

The physician from Bourbon-l'Archambault certified the death.

'Are you sure?' insisted the maid. 'Because in her lineage there has already been one woman resuscitated!'

The physician confirmed that no condensation had formed on the mirror he held to the marquise's lips – 'She is dead' – and went out.

The maid asked, 'Now where did the Maréchale de Coeuvres go?'

55.

'Who shall pay my fees for the funeral?' asked the curé of Bourbon-l'Archambault beneath the vaulted ceiling of his church.

'Of that we have no idea, Père Pétillon. D'Antin cannot be reached and the marquises and maréchales of the region who were wont to visit her in the event she might someday be restored to royal favour, and who honoured her like a queen at the beginning of her stay, now reply that it is no longer their business. Courtiers are eminently practical people.'

'Well, that's as may be, but you can't leave her here like this! It has been three weeks! She stinks!'

'What are we to do . . .' apologised the maid, surrounded by the dead woman's servants. 'The Duc du Maine had some difficulty hiding the joy he felt on learning of his mother's death. And when we spoke to him of burial fees, he burst out laughing. As for the Comte de Toulouse, when he heard that she was on her deathbed, he set out at once for Bourbon, but when he got to Montargis and learnt of her death, and that we were waiting for him to organise and pay for the funeral, he turned round and fled at a gallop. And went to hide his sorrow on his commode.'

'On the other hand, we did wonder . . .' interrupted a valet, 'since before dying she endowed all the Capuchins of the town, and the parish clergy, whether you mightn't, all the same, perhaps . . .'

'No, no, no,' said the curé. 'For the biggest harlot in all of France? You jest! Go rather to her erstwhile lover.'

''Tis said that the King, on hearing of the marquise's imminent demise, remained expressionless, and went stag hunting as planned before the news arrived, and then he walked alone in his gardens until nightfall, but he has contributed nothing to bury her.'

'Then you shall pay!' decided the curé. 'You are the ones who brought her here, so you shall pay.'

'What?' protested the maid. 'This powerful lady has come to naught, her dreadful eyes but recently closed, now everyone flees and her corpse is left to rot, and her servants are to be responsible?'

'The servants shall share the cost of the funeral. What a stench!' lamented the priest, standing near the coffin, which had been set down on the flagstones of the church.

'It is because her body, once so fair, was subjected to the indignity of an ignorant scalpel. Before we brought it to you, her corpse was entrusted to an amateur physician, and he opened her up without really knowing how to go about it. The marquise left precise instructions regarding the way she wished her body to be treated after her demise – she wanted to bequeath her heart and her viscera to the priory at Saint-Menoux.'

'Her heart? Did she even have one?' smiled the curé. 'And there, what is in that urn?'

'Precisely, her heart and her . . .'

'Ah, that explains the stink! Look there, the urn is poorly sealed. Remove it from this place! Mesnier!' Père Pétillon called, addressing a local resident who was kneeling on a prie-dieu, wearing a shepherd's cape and cheap coloured stockings. 'Take that urn to the priory at Saint-Menoux. Go! 'Tis only three leagues from here. The hag's servants will give you a coin.'

The man in the shepherd's cape picked up the urn and sniffed it with a grimace, then went out, whilst the curé said to the servants, 'Until you are able to find d'Antin and he takes a decision, I shall keep the remains here and leave you a copy of the death certificate that I drew up on the day she arrived.'

On this day, 28 May 1707, I the undersigned curé do hereby declare that the body of Françoise de Montespan,

who died in this town on Friday 27th after receiving the
last rites, was brought to me in this church, where she lies
until other dispositions are made.

On the dusty highway leading to Saint-Menoux, on a hot late afternoon in June, the man to whom the urn had been given held it as far out in front of him as possible. The whiffs coming from the poorly sealed receptacle disgusted him and made him so nauseous that he wanted to retch, and after he had gone half a league, the man felt too repulsed by the odour emanating from the urn to continue the journey.

'What the devil is inside there?'

He opened the flask with its rounded sides and what he saw disgusted him so much that he tipped the contents out into a ditch. Pigs and dogs rushed over to the entrails. While the pigs devoured the stomach and liver in the grass, the dogs dashed off with the marquise's intestines, heart and lungs.

The man with the coloured stockings watched as the scrawny yellow hounds loped away down the dusty road, dragging behind them the entrails of the King's former favourite. And she who had had the devil's own beauty seemed born again.

Her long intestines trailed behind the curs and seemed to rise in the air, spinning and swaying from side to side, the way the skirt of her gown took flight when she danced, twirling in one of Benserade's ballets. The green, blue and pink colours of the small intestine accentuated the effect. The dogs' hind legs became entangled in the large intestine and tore it, and their claws left narrow parallel tracks of shit, not unlike the gaps in the parquet floorboards at Versailles.

There was a brilliant dazzle of sunlight, and the silhouettes of the poplar trees glowed bronze like monumental statues by Girardon. The mastiffs' long legs were consumed by light, flowing, floating, and there was a sound of jaws grinding. Two of the dogs were running shoulder to shoulder, fighting over the marquise's lungs. The lungs stretched out, compressed and were stretched again. And now she was breathing! At the head of the pack a Cerberus, his chops drawn back over his fangs, chewed up Athénaïs's heart, spattering blood on every side. It beat again – she lived once more, in a mirage.

At the foot of the cross in the cemetery at Bonnefont the wild grasses and flowers danced and swayed beside a grave, and a whisper rose, like a word. Some would say it was the wind blowing through the leaves, but it was in fact the voice of Louis-Henri, who had begun to hope again and was calling out 'Françoise . . .'

An interview with Jean Teulé

Jean, can you tell us what your novel The Hurlyburly's Husband *is about?*

The novel tells the story of a husband turned cuckold by Louis XIV who, contrary to the other married nobles at the time who practically pushed their wives into the king's bed so they would receive compensation in the form of money and suchlike, never accepted his fate.

What inspired you to write about such a subject?

I fell upon the story of this Monsieur de Montespan whose world had caved in and who had then been forgotten. I felt it was important to bring him back to life in a book because, frankly, he wasn't just some ordinary guy.

How did you go about the enormous amount of historical research you must have done for the book?

I spent about eight months in a library reading all I could on the seventeenth century. I wanted to be able to describe exactly the way people dressed and washed at the time.

The seventeenth century was one of the dirtiest times in France's history. For example, we know now that Louis XIV went his whole life without taking a single bath. And at the Château de Versailles, for 5,000 people, there were only two toilets! People did their business everywhere. It was a veritable cesspit.

Monsieur de Montespan seems like an extraordinary character: a desperate and infatuated man. Would it be right to call him the hero of your novel?

Oh yes, he's the hero! To love your wife would seem the normal thing to do but in Monsieur de Montespan's case it becomes something heroic.

And Madame de Montespan? Is she the anti-hero of the novel?

I didn't want to treat her like a whore because that isn't the case. She was a normal woman who didn't have a choice because, at that time, women didn't have the right to refuse the king's advances. A wife who said no to Louis XIV would find herself either in prison for the rest of her life or banished, along with her husband and the rest of her extended family, to the French colonies.

Having said that, Madame de Montespan did eventually take a fancy to Louis XIV. To the point even where she turned insane and made animal sacrifices in her desperation to retain his affections. She is a very interesting character but, naturally, it's her husband I admire.

If you had to classify this book, what would it be? A comedy, a tragedy, a love story or a little bit of all three?

First of all it is a love story about a husband whose whole world is his wife. He never gives up on her. He messed up his life by trying to win her back. But he was also funny, with a real cheek. Nobody else in France in the seventeenth century would have dared, as he did, to provoke and make fun of Louis XIV.

He was the first man during that era of servility and subservience to dare to say to the king, 'No, I won't let it happen. A monarch can't just do what he wants. No one can tell me he has the right to grab any taken woman he wants.'

For me, the Marquis de Montespan is the seed of what, one hundred years later, we call the French Revolution. I love this man. I would have loved to have met him and been his friend.

Reading Group Questions

1) To what extent is this novel about Monsieur de Montespan's revenge? What does he achieve?

2) Monsieur de Montespan's campaign of revenge gets increasingly desperate and sordid as the book progresses. Is he justified? Does the act of revenge have limits?

3) What is your view of the relationship between Monsieur and Madame de Montespan?

4) Which character do you find most sympathetic, and whom do you like least? Do your sympathies change in the course of the story?

5) The book is based on a true story. Does Jean Teulé succeed in bringing that particular chapter of French history to life?

6) One critic described *The Hurlyburly's Husband* as a 'bawdy romp'. Do you agree?